THE CODE
OF THE K-9 CORPS . . .

"Before eating, we recite the Law," rumbled Beowulf, the leader.

The other eight formed a rough circle around him.

"What is the Law?" intoned Beowulf.

"To place duty above self, honor above life."

"What is the Law?"

"To allow harm to come to no Man, to protect Man and his possessions."

"What is the Law?"

"To stand by Man's side—as dogs will always stand. Together, Man and dog."

K-9 CORPS

KENNETH VON GUNDEN

ACE BOOKS, NEW YORK

This book is an Ace original edition,
and has never been previously published.

K-9 CORPS

An Ace Book / published by arrangement with
the author

PRINTING HISTORY
Ace edition / February 1991

ISBN: 0-441-09128-8

Ace Books are published by The Berkley Publishing Group,
200 Madison Avenue, New York, New York 10016.
The name "ACE" and the "A" logo
are trademarks belonging to Charter Communications, Inc.

PRINTED IN THE UNITED STATES OF AMERICA

10 9 8 7 6 5 4 3 2 1

PART ONE
Ray

1

Ray Larkin hefted his energy rifle impatiently as Beowulf sniffed the air again and walked forward a few steps. Larkin watched the scout dog amble over to Littlejohn's point and then to Anson's. When brief, gravel-voiced conversations with each assured him the area was clean, the scout dog trotted back to Larkin and growled, "Safe, Ray."

To a human ear untuned to a scout dog's harsh and grating voice, the slurred and flat speech might have been unintelligible, but to Ray Larkin it was perfectly understandable. The three huge dogs and the man moved out, a well-coordinated unit ready for almost anything.

One of the other scout dogs had reported a large herd of antelope in the area, so Ray felt that a little expedition was in order. The antelopelike creatures always attracted predators—hide cats and Centaurs. The danger both posed could not be ignored.

Larkin's eyes never stopped moving, darting from small hill to small hill, questioning the slightest quiver of the low bushes. His caution was superfluous, he knew, for the dogs were well able to sense any danger long before it became apparent to his inferior human sensory organs. He was careful not to allow his caution to edge toward paranoia, however—it wouldn't do to blast every small animal that was flushed from its home by their advance, not even those repulsively slimy, snakelike

3

things that darted out of their holes to seize and swallow
unsuspecting rodents.

As he walked, Larkin inspected the small plants and wild
grasses that would no longer exist after the voracious cholos
passed this way, devouring everything in their path. The cholos
had been at work terraforming the surface of this continent for
over two months now, but Larkin, who'd never worked with
cholos before his current assignment, still found the giant slugs
a source of wonder. Right now they ought to be about two to
three kilometers behind him, being guided by Mary and Taylor
and the six remaining scout dogs of his team. Their proximity
was the reason he and the dogs were making sure the area
ahead of the rest of the team would allow safe passage.

He suddenly snapped out of his brief reverie, aware that the
dogs had stopped and were testing the air. He watched their
noses wrinkle and twitch in that funny way peculiar to dogs.
"What is it?" he called to Beowulf.

"Hide cats. 'Bout seven of 'em heading this way."

"Think they know we're here?"

Beowulf nodded his shaggy head at the rippling grass and
answered, "Yes, Ray, bad wind."

Larkin agreed. Beowulf was right; the erratic wind, changing direction every few seconds, was surely carrying their scent
to the cats.

It was the dogs who'd named them "hide cats." The
powerful feline creatures preyed mainly on the antelopelike
animals that grazed on the many wild grasses of the prairie.
The cats were big, about one and a half meters tall at the
shoulder. For all their size, though, they were lean and sleek,
the biggest one not going over one hundred and twenty
kilos—obviously their design was for explosive bursts of speed
for short periods of time over limited distances. In the open,
however, if the chase endured for more than twenty seconds,
not even the fastest of the cats could have caught the slowest of
the amazingly fleet antelope, given their intended prey's comic
but effective leaping gait.

But nature had given the hide cats an extra advantage to
compensate for their lack of endurance. Each hide cat bore
markings on its sides which enabled it to lie down on one side
and melt into the grass so perfectly that a careless antelope
could stumble over the camouflaged cat before becoming

aware of its presence. The hide cats, Larkin recalled, were not six-limbed like the antelope, but carried tiny vestigial grasping limbs on both sides of their throats.

Hide cats were fascinating, but to Larkin they represented yet another hazard—there seemed to be so many!—on this endless plain of winds that he would have cheerfully forgone. The hide cats were remarkably unintelligent for predators. This, combined with an intense ferocity, made them fearless in the face of a danger such as that represented by Larkin and the dogs.

Larkin slipped the safety on his energy rifle to its off position and warned the dogs to be ready. "Those dumb bastards will rush us the second they see us," he cautioned Littlejohn and the other two.

A trickle of sweat rolled down Larkin's back in spite of the chill edge to the wind. He wasn't the only one feeling the pounding tension that builds before action: The hair on the dogs' necks was rising in ragged clumps in anticipation of the fight. He wanted to crack a joke for the benefit of the dogs but couldn't. And, though humans had pretty much lost the ability, he felt his testicles trying to ascend into his abdomen for protection. "I know how you feel, boys," he said, gripping his rifle.

Larkin and the dogs topped a small rise and suddenly they were face to face with the hide cats. For one excruciatingly long second nothing moved but the tops of the grasses. Then, like characters in a holodrama which unexpectedly shifts from slow to speeded-up motion, both groups exploded into action.

Larkin was aware of a streak of yellow hurtling through the grass at him and he brought the rifle up to his shoulder in one quick motion, squeezing the firing stud more by reflex than conscious thought. The energy bolt was far faster than the hide cat's charge and blew the animal's head off. The momentum of the cat's attack carried its headless torso to Larkin's booted feet, spraying them with blood.

Beowulf, one hundred and fifty kilograms of snapping, barking fury, bowled over two cats larger than himself with an audacious charge. Confused and surprised by this aggressive maneuver by their opponent, the two cats slashed out at each other as they tumbled over and over together. Beowulf took advantage of the situation and ripped out the throat of the nearest one while it fought with its companion.

Anson and Littlejohn, screaming canine obscenities, darted among three of the cats and slashed open their bellies. The enraged animals could only claw and bite futilely at the long hair of the two dogs which protected them as efficiently as armor as long as the cats were unable to find a secure hold.

While Beowulf bit through the spinal cord of his remaining opponent, Larkin killed the surviving hide cat with a hurried shoulder shot.

Anson, his muzzle stained a deep red, looked down at a pile of steaming entrails on the grass, then turned to Littlejohn. "Fun, hah? Kill plenty hide cats this time. We teach them cats to fool with dogs." Then, remembering Ray's part in the confrontation, Anson added, "And a Man, too."

"Yeah," croaked Larkin, wiping hide cat blood from his cheek. "Lots of fun."

Beowulf led his small party back to the temporary camp Ray had devised for the scout dogs. His lips curled back in pleasure as first the females greeted him and then the males.

"How it went?" asked the pregnant Mama-san.

"Good. We got some hide cats killed."

"Oh?" inquired Frodo. "You tell."

Beowulf shook his head. "Food first; then I tell all."

Even as he spoke, Pandora brought him some antelope meat. Ozma did the same for Anson and Littlejohn. Ray had tried to change this social behavior, but realized that to the dogs there was nothing "sexist" about it—it was natural, it was the way they preferred it and he couldn't get them to share such duties.

"They *are* still dogs, Ray," his training instructor had told him when he persisted in trying to make the dogs act more like human beings. "Their social order evolved out of millions of years of interaction; they do what works best for them. You're not going to be able to change that."

Ray had accepted it intellectually, but he never quite gave up trying to teach the dogs to act more like humans. Loving him and, well, being dogs, the scout dogs never held his modest attempts to reform their social structure against him. How could they? He was Ray; he was the Man.

"Before eating, we recite the Law," rumbled Beowulf.

They formed a rough circle.

"What is the Law?" intoned Beowulf.

"To place duty above self, honor above life."

"What is the Law?"

"To allow harm to come to no Man, to protect Man and his possessions."

"What is the Law?"

"To stand by Man's side—as dogs will always stand. Together, Man and dog."

"Let us eat."

★　　★　　★

"I'll take Roger," said the tall, raven-haired boy named Bill Roan.

"Mohammed," said Bobby Smithfield.

"Pablo."

"Jimmy."

Jeez, not again! Ray prayed. It wasn't like he was a *poor* athlete, he wasn't. He simply didn't play any team sports often enough to develop the sort of skills that come with repetition. He was small but fast; normally, for a sport like soccer, that would have been enough reason for a captain to choose him. But, since he rarely played or even practiced keeping a ball on his foot when he was by himself, he wasn't the most skillful player in the neighborhood.

"Francis."

"Akira."

The available pool was rapidly growing smaller and Ray realized that eventually it would be down to Margaret Dysan and himself. The other remaining boys were chosen, the pace slowing down as the sides for the soccer game were filling up.

Soon, it was just Ray and Margaret. "Margaret," Bill Roan said finally.

As the only one left, Ray was automatically on Bobby's team. As he started to walk toward the line of players who'd formed up behind Bobby, the team captain, his face hot with shame for being picked last again, Ray suddenly halted. "Well, get your ass in gear, clubfoot," Bobby Smithfield said.

"I don't think so," Ray said. "I got better things to do than kick a little ball around." Despite the hoots and catcalls directed at him, Ray turned and walked away, his eyes blinking rapidly as he swallowed the lump in his throat and fought back the churning feeling in his stomach. *Last again*! he told himself. *Picked after a damn girl*!

In a meadow in the shadow of Rattlesnake Mountain, Ray tossed the stick as far as he could. Eager to please, Tajil, Ray's purebred Irish setter, gleefully retrieved the piece of wood time after time, seemingly willing to play the game forever. "Atta boy, Tajil," Ray said, taking the wet stick from Tajil's mouth. "Yuck," he said, "dog slobber!" Tajil responded by licking Ray's face with his long tongue. "More dog slobber," he laughed.

"You're the best friend a guy could have, aren't you, boy?" Tajil barked and backed off a few feet, indicating by his actions that Ray should throw the stick again. Ray just laughed and complied with his pet's wishes. As the big red dog ran after the stick for the umpteenth time, Ray pulled a blade from the slowly browning grass carpet around him, stuck the end in his mouth, leaned back against the tree he was under, and pulled out the paperback he'd bought at the rare books/comics emporium out at the mall. His dad would shit a brick if he knew how much he'd paid for the old classic: thirty credits. The cover price, however, was thirty-five cents. He thought a moment . . . that was thirty-five one hundredths of a pre-Federation "dollar," an archaic form of paper money. He whistled through his teeth and said in admiration, "You *are* a find, aren't you?" The book was *Time in Advance* by William Tenn. Ray ignored the stick that Tajil dropped at his feet, absorbed in examining his treasure. The cover art was kind of abstract and artsy-fartsy and the cover blurb read: "The future is coming! Four prophetic and astounding novelettes from one of today's most brilliant young writers." At the bottom there was a picture of a red rooster and the inscription: A Bantam Book. On the back was a photograph of the author: a goateed man with a pipe in his mouth and wearing glasses—another giveaway to the book's age. He smelled the book, inhaling its musty, ancient odor.

Tajil whined for Ray to toss the stick again. "Sit, Tajil," he commanded, reluctant to cease his contemplation of the book. "You're a time machine," he said, holding the book and gently leafing through its yellowed pages, "a freakin' time machine to the past, the long dead past." He opened the book to the first story, entitled "Firewater," and began to read. Soon he was engrossed in a world that made more sense to him than his own—a make-believe "future" world he could go to any time he wanted, or needed, to.

Ray both hoped and expected that things would change when he went to college. They didn't. Realizing he was an anomaly, and wanting to understand himself and others better, Ray decided to study sociology and anthropology. He learned a lot . . . but not much about how to go about making friends.

If people were out, however, who or what was left?

II

"Come on, Larkin," Stan D'Aloiso, the director of the scout dog breeding facility, told him that warm day he'd arrived at the breeding crèches to pick out his dogs. "I've got three dozen nearly grown pups for you to choose from."

Ray Larkin hesitated at the entrance to the crèches. "I . . . I'm a little nervous, I guess," he admitted.

"Hey, well, sure," agreed D'Aloiso, "but you can bet the dogs are nervous, too. They've grown up here, knowing only the staff, and now some stranger is going to take nine of them away from the only home and humans they've known."

"Thanks for making it easier," said Ray with a rueful grin.

Ray walked into a large room, a combination show area and holding pen. There were nine holding cubicles—the staff detested the word "cages"—with four dogs each in them. It was clearly a meeting of reluctant suitors; the dogs looked at Ray with as much evaluation in their eyes as he held in his upon seeing them.

"Gosh, you've really got some beauties here," Ray said.

"You okay, too, mister," one of the pups said.

Astonished, Ray just threw back his head and laughed. "Sorry. After all my training, I still have trouble remembering you guys can talk—and at such a young age." He peered at the pup who'd spoken and asked, "What's your name?"

"I have no name yet, Ray. I am Chaucer and Margarite's son. If you choose me, you will give me my life name."

D'Aloiso looked at Ray in not-so-private amusement. "We

told the pups who was coming today—that's how they know your name."

"I see." Turning back to the holding cubicles, he said, "Well, son of Chaucer and Margarite, you are now called 'Beowulf' and you're my first choice."

"Thank you, Ray," said Beowulf as several of the other dogs in his group surged about him, offering their congratulations by nudging him good-naturedly and licking him.

Feeling pleased with himself—he'd wanted to make a good first impression on the dogs—Ray chatted briefly with each of the other thirty-five dogs there for him to see. He knew that if he couldn't put together his team from these three dozen, more would be brought in for him to see, but to require more showings was considered bad form by both the breeding staff and the dogs themselves.

Ray saw one little female looking at him with bashful eyes. Whenever he caught her staring at him, she would look away quickly, embarrassed. "And how are you, little one?" he asked.

The small female shook slightly as she answered, "I fine . . . Ray."

"Do you think you would like to join Beowulf and me?"

"Oh, yes!" she answered quickly.

"Well, then, come on out . . . Grendel," Ray said.

Ray's third choice was another female, one he named Mama-san. His fourth choice was a handsome young male pup who seemed both eager and bashful at the same time. Noting the spark of interest in his eyes when he interviewed him, Ray accepted him almost immediately and decided to call him Anson—after the middle name of one his favorite old-time authors, a writer from before the "crazy years," Robert Anson Heinlein.

The next two dogs came as a sort of matched set. The two he eventually called Ozma and Littlejohn both seemed attached to each other. Rather than break up their special fondness for each other—their "puppy love," as Ray whispered to D'Aloiso, who promptly burst out laughing—Ray took both of them.

Number seven was a dog who seemed a bit standoffish to him, but who, nonetheless, showed the gumption and intelligence Ray was looking for. "So," Ray said to him, "do you think you'd like serving under me?"

The dog looked him in the eye and said, "You probably good as anyone."

When a few of the more conservative puppies gasped—Ray noted their numbers and marked each of them unsuited for his needs—Ray nodded at D'Aloiso and said, "There's my Frodo."

Dogs eight and nine were two similarly colored beauties with reddish-brown and white coats who kept bounding about the confines of their holding cubicles. Ray decided their energy and enthusiasm would be pluses and took them, naming the male Sinbad and the smaller female Pandora.

"I guess that's it," Ray said to D'Aloiso after making his final choice.

"Fine. Now if you'll give me and the other handlers and trainers about an hour, we'll muster your new team for you in one of the training areas."

"An hour?" Ray asked.

D'Aloiso looked a little sheepish. "These aren't ordinary dogs," he explained. "They develop relationships with their trainers even though we all know they're going to go off and join a survey team when they reach the right age." He stared frankly into Ray's eyes. "Look, Ray, I guess what I'm trying to say is that we'd like a little time to say our final goodbyes to the dogs we've raised and trained. Soon they'll be your team and it'll be like you've never *not* known each other . . . but since their birth, they've been ours."

Ray was genuinely touched by the man's concern for the dogs. "Of course. I should have realized. Take all the time you want."

"Thanks," said D'Aloiso. He looked at the ground and then back up at Ray. "Take special care of Beowulf—I like the name you've given him—because he was one of my dogs."

Ray took D'Aloiso's hand in his. "I will. Thanks for everything."

"What you think of this Ray?" Littlejohn was asking Frodo.

"I hope he's tougher than he looks," Frodo said. "He's not very tall."

"Ho," said Anson. "You think need be tall to be tough; I not the biggest of us, but I'll bite ass on any of you think he can push us little guys around."

"Big talk little dog," sneered Sinbad. Immediately, Anson charged him and knocked him over with a shoulder shove. Snarling, Sinbad leapt to his feet, ready to tear into Anson and teach him a lesson. Beowulf got between the two combatants and said, "Enough. Anson proved his point."

"Who made you boss?" said Sinbad.

"I did," replied Beowulf. "You want to try someone your own size?"

"Ray picked Beowulf first," said Mama-san. "Ray is our new master and Beowulf is his second-in-command. Anyone not agree with that can wait and join another team."

"Mama-san's right," said Littlejohn. "Ray's our team leader and rest of us better learn that fast—and learn to start thinking like a team."

Even Sinbad grudgingly agreed with that assessment and the dogs walked around nuzzling each other and vowing friendship and loyalty. They were taking the first steps in becoming a man/dog team.

When Ray returned to see the nine dogs for their first private talk, he could sense they'd already settled something among themselves. "So," he began. "Now the hard part starts. We've got to build ourselves into one cohesive unit—a scout team second to none. The training you've had up to now has been tough but it's nothing compared to what we're going to go through together on the way to becoming that cohesive unit.

"I picked you guys because you seem to me to have the right stuff; you seem to feel that way about me. It's going to take a while but we're going to become close friends.

"Beowulf," he called, "please come here."

When the burly puppy waddled over to him, Ray embraced him and said, "Hi, Beowulf—I'm Ray and I think we're going to be great friends." At that, the other dogs began crowding around Ray, wagging their tails and trying to lick his face. "Hmm, salty," said one.

Tears of happiness flowing down his cheeks, Ray said, "It's gonna be awful easy to love you guys."

The sun shone down cruelly on the nine dogs and one man making their way through the obstacle course. "C'mon, guys,"

Ray said, aware that he was huffing and puffing like the little engine that could. "We just gotta get over the water obstacle and we're home free."

Running smoothly and effortlessly beside Ray, Frodo glanced up at his master and said, "Littlejohn says you twenty-eight years old. That right, Ray?"

Throwing the big scout dog a puzzled glance, Ray said, "Yes, that's right, Frodo. Why?"

Frodo looked back at Pandora and Sinbad, close on his heels, and asked mischievously, "How much that in dog years?"

Ray made a choking sound and pulled up, clutching his side. As the dogs swarmed around him, he half-laughed and half-wheezed. "Oh, you dog-breath bastard! I'll get you for that!"

"Not on those two legs!" teased Frodo, bounding away a few strides.

"Water next," said Beowulf. "Let's go!" The other dogs tore off in pursuit of the massive Beowulf.

"Jeez," said Ray, stumbling after them, "who's in charge here?"

At least they had the decency to wait for him at the water hazard, Ray told himself. Catching his breath, Ray grasped the thick rope and carried it back as far as he could stretch it, then ran forward, lifting his legs off the ground and launching himself across the six-meter width of the water obstacle. Landing adroitly on the other side—amid the cheers of the dogs—Ray turned and nonchalantly swung the rope back across for Beowulf to catch in his teeth. "Okay, Beowulf," he said, "you're next."

Beowulf ran in a semicircle and leapt into the air, swinging around wide and then across the expanse of water. When he was over dry land, he opened his mouth and let loose of the rope, dropping to the ground. Ray again sent the rope back across and, one by one, grasping the rope between their powerful jaws, the dogs successfully swung themselves across the water hazard to join Ray.

"D'Aloiso and the others taught you well," Ray admitted. Breathing a little more easily now, he said, "Now comes the fun part—our daily ten-K jog." Looking down at the happy canine faces staring into his, he added, "Hey, if it's just too much for you today—it's a real stinker with that hot sun—why, we'll walk back to the barracks and start fresh tomorrow."

"You so funny!" said Pandora, falling in behind Frodo, who'd already moved out onto the running trail with the other dogs close behind.

"That's me," said Ray, rushing to catch up. "Mr. Funny-bones!"

III

It was cold. Bitterly cold. Ray could see his breath steaming from his mouth each time he exhaled. It was the same with the dogs. Ray knew that a certain amount of his I'm-freezing-my-ass-off sensations were psychological; the cold-weather gear he wore was designed to keep him warm and safe at temperatures reaching minus eighty degrees Celsius. Beowulf and the dogs had been bred to endure almost any kind of weather conditions, from blazing heat to freezing cold, and so the low temperature did not pose any danger to them, snug in their snap-on body wraps, but they much preferred a warmer climate.

Ray and the dogs had been hired by Cryo-Corp. to provide security for its network of a half-dozen scientific research and manufacturing outposts on the ice world of Amundsen. The self-contained encampments faced few threats more dangerous than boredom, but there were several hostile indigenous life-forms on the planet which usually avoided the humans but were potentially dangerous. Ray's team, called "virgins" since they hadn't done a job before this opportunity came up, was hired because most veteran teams turned up their noses at the low-paying, ten-month contract the corporation was offering. Ray was glad for any offer, eager to get his first job behind him.

Although a minimally manned mothership equipped with shuttle craft circled in a geosynchronous orbit above the planet, the inhabitants of the camps had to make do with various hovercraft—sleds, scooters, and the like—to transport themselves and their equipment because the planet's erratic magnetic fields played hell with the navigation systems of more sophisticated vehicles.

The job had been routine until three days ago. A small contingent of scientists went down somewhere on Amundsen's vast southern ice shelf when their hovercraft lost power and crashed. A series of ice and magnetic storms prevented the bases from sending out any sort of aircraft—or anything with a motor.

Assuming he found them before they died of exposure, Ray was to do little more than provide minimal first aid, food, water, and shelter. When the storms passed, he was to send up a message. In response, a shuttle craft would land and take the survivors and the man/dog team up to the mothership and safety.

Linked as pairs, except for Beowulf who strode by Ray's side, the dogs pulled four small sleds loaded down with food, explosives, clothing, and communications gear. Because the ice was rough and uneven, their progress was slow. The sled runners all too often got wedged in cracks in the ice or the sleds had to be hauled over chunks of ice the size of boulders.

By the third day, they were still a hundred kilometers away from the spot most likely to contain the downed scientists. "I don't like it, Beowulf," Ray told his scout dog leader. "We're not making very good time across these sheets and floes."

"Yeah, rough," Beowulf agreed.

Ray looked up into the gray sky, full of swirling snow and ice pellets driven by the wind. "From the air, the ice pack looks smooth, as smooth as the surface of a billiard table," he muttered, his voice half lost in the howl of the wind. Beowulf didn't know what a billiard table was—but if Ray said it was smooth, then it surely was. "The only problem, big fella," Ray added, scratching behind Beowulf's ears, "is that we're not *flying* over the ice, we're walking across it."

"We make camp soon, Ray?" Beowulf asked.

"Yeah, I guess so," Ray replied. "It's getting dark, although night doesn't really descend in these latitudes. C'mon, let's get the other dogs out of their harnesses."

Ray fed the dogs and then started a fire. The fire burned meagerly in the oxygen-poor atmosphere of Amundsen. As Ray warmed his hands, he mused about the surroundings. "I guess this place has a rough kind of beauty, but I miss the colors—the greens and yellows, the browns and reds of a jungle or a desert planet. Here, it's all white."

"Sure, Ray," rasped Sinbad.

"Huh?" asked Ray.

"Colors—you're talkin' 'bout colors again," Sinbad elaborated.

"Oh, yeah," Ray said, remembering. "You guys have been genetically altered in a lot of ways, but you still have dog vision: black and white. Forgive me."

"Hey, it's okay," Anson said. "You see these things called 'colors,' but we can see better in dim light."

"I guess it's a trade-off, eh?" Ray said.

"Yeah," began Beowulf, but suddenly he stopped and sniffed the air. The other dogs immediately followed suit.

"What is it?" Ray asked, glancing about for his energy rifle.

"Doan know, Ray," Beowulf said. "Smells like some kinda animal. Maybe like—"

Ray later wondered if it was the dry air—a less reliable carrier of scent than warm, moisture-laden air—of the ice shelf that kept the dogs from smelling the creature. In any event, a huge white monster, all teeth and claws, exploded out of the swirling snow and was among them in the blink of an eye. Five or six meters tall when it raised up on its hind legs, the massive beast attacked the unprepared dogs.

When Beowulf and the others had gathered their wits, they fought back viciously. Although the creature's initial assault had caught the dogs by surprise, they quickly recovered and began fighting back. They worried the huge creature with their powerful jaws, but it was clearly winning the short, ugly conflict. It seemed only a matter of time until it would manage to seize and rend one of the much smaller dogs.

Ray, unharmed as yet, ran for his energy rifle. Grabbing it up, he whirled and fired point-blank into the looming mass of the white-furred monster that was savaging his dogs and sabotaging his first rescue effort. Aware that the awful bolts of energy imploding painfully into its body were coming from Ray's position, the creature whirled, flinging aside the huge scout dogs as if they were no more than a momentary nuisance, and strode to where Ray stood—covering the distance between them in several enormous steps.

It smashed Ray senseless with a sweep of its arm, sending him flying through the air to land in the icy waters at the edge of the sheet. "No!" screamed Beowulf as he launched himself at the beast's throat. Seriously wounded by the blasts from Ray's energy rifle, the creature succumbed to Beowulf's vicious attack. Feeling the life seep from the hideous beast,

Beowulf hobbled over to the edge of the sheet of ice and looked for Ray. There he was . . . floating helplessly in the water.

Beowulf leaped into the icy water and began swimming toward the unconscious Ray. The shock of the freezing water revived Ray and he became aware of his perilous situation. "Help! Help me, Beowulf. I can't move. I think some of my ribs are broken."

"I'm coming, Ray," Beowulf shouted. He paddled furiously and was at Ray's side in seconds. As Beowulf seized Ray's coat with his teeth, Littlejohn and Grendel leapt into the water to assist him. Together, they towed Ray to the edge of the ice sheet and dragged him up out of the icy waters.

"Piss and crackers!" ejaculated Ray angrily. "Who's going to rescue the rescuers?" Taking stock of the situation, Ray told Beowulf, "Get me over to the fire. I'm gonna have to get out of these wet clothes." He looked at the water dripping from Beowulf's coat and body wrap. "Jeezus, you three are soaked as well. Anson, Sinbad, Ozma—the rest of you—get over here and get between the wind and the four of us. You can shield us until I can build the fire up higher. Oh, and someone drag that thing's body over to the water and push it in—we don't want any more surprise visitors." Ray had one and a half sleds full of firewood with him to sustain the survivors once he found them, but he hated having to "waste" so much of it on himself and his team. Still, the warmth from the flames felt wonderful and he was able to slip off his water-laden garments and inspect his ribs.

"What's story?" asked Beowulf, himself soaking up the fire's heat.

Ray got out a roll of tape and began winding it around his rib cage, grimacing with the pain. "Well," he gritted out, "I don't think anything's actually broken. But it isn't going to be fun from this point on."

"What we do?" asked Frodo.

"We move out as soon as I'm done doing this and we're completely dried out," Ray said. "I'm going to stiffen up pretty quickly, so I want us to cover as much ground as we can before I start walking like the Mummy." (Later, Sinbad asked Littlejohn what 'the Mummy' was, but the other dog didn't know either.)

While Ray's hand-held magnetometer told him the magnetic

disturbances were continuing, the ice storms of the past several days abated and they were able to make good time. They got even luckier when Mama-san trotted back from her foray out ahead of the team with the news that she had spotted the wreckage of the downed hovercraft just a few kilometers ahead.

The four survivors had heard them coming and gave them a rousing welcoming cheer. "Thank God you're here," said one of them, a portly bald man.

Ray took his proffered hand, saying, "Doctor Livingstone, I presume?"

★   ★   ★

"But you have bee-aitch-dee," protested Beowulf. "Why you need go back to school—to get even smarter?"

Ray smiled: The dogs often had difficulty saying their P's. "First off," Ray explained, "schooling provides you with education and knowledge—it doesn't necessarily make you any smarter. Second, I'm in debt up to my eyeballs despite the Amundsen job I was able to get for us so far and I don't see any easy way out: It's not easy finding people willing to hire a one-mission team like us when there're veteran teams with six or seven missions under their belts begging for jobs."

"So school makes debt bigger, don't it?" asked Pandora.

"Technically, yes," Ray admitted. "But I can float a school loan, and two more courses in planetary colonization methods will get me my certificate and we can join a terraforming team."

"Where is this school?" asked Littlejohn.

"It's Cuiaba University, in Brazil," Ray said.

"Oh," said Littlejohn dejectedly. "A city."

"Yeah, I know," Ray said, shrugging. "I'm not thrilled by the prospect of locating near a metropolis either. Still, I can probably wrangle subsidized dog-team housing out in the sticks. It's Brazil, after all, not Boswash or any of the great City-States of the north where there's no dealing with the crowding and the filth. You guys'll have some fresh air and space, and the bullet trains will make my commuting time bearable."

"How long?" asked Beowulf.

"Two semesters—eight months," Ray said.

"Oh," said Beowulf tonelessly, dropping his head onto his front paws.

2

Instead of attending group gropes or cocktail parties, once he was settled in for his post-doc work, Ray much preferred staying at home playing complex mindbender games of his own devising with Cheng, his living complex's computer. (He did so even though he suspected that Cheng cheated.) His busy schedule was not conducive to meeting fellow students. He was at first surprised, then delighted, when a tall, skinny agrobiologist named Taylor Hollister became his first and only real friend at the university. Like Ray, Taylor was taking post-graduate courses to get his terraforming certificate. Talking about their mutual interests led them to a bar after class, and that led to their finding out how much they had in common, especially their shared sense of humor.

The new drinking buddies didn't spend *all* their time together—Ray was still too much the loner for that, as well as having the dogs to care for, and Taylor had begun seeing a young woman named Mary Elizabeth Brennan who was getting her terraforming certificate in chemistry and xenobiology.

But, despite the intrusion (as Ray considered it) of this young woman into their friendship, Ray and Taylor still had plenty of time to go bar brawling . . . plenty of time.

"You heard me, sport," the squat, red-haired man was saying loudly, "Scout dogs are freaks of nature!" He reconsidered. "No, they aren't even that—they're test-tube freaks."

19

"Thanks for repeating your considered opinion," Ray said, sliding off his bar stool gracefully. "Sometimes when I hear wind break I don't know which asshole it came from; it helps to know."

The red-haired man's two friends guffawed, appreciating Ray's insult. A little the worse for wear and feeling the effects of the beer too much to think as straight as his companions, the red-haired man slowly absorbed Ray's words. The others, not nearly as piss-faced as he, and sensing an outbreak of hostilities, backed away from the bar. Finally, like a slow-acting drug, Ray's words reached the red-haired man's booze-soaked brain. "Hey . . . why, you son of a bitch!" he slurred, coming up swinging.

Ray just sidestepped his clumsy charge and drove a short, efficient right hand into the center of the man's face, which was bunched with anger. As the blow knocked the red-haired man backwards, Ray turned to Taylor and said out of the side of his mouth, "For a guy insulting scout dogs, that's a helluva great pun: 'son of a bitch.' Unfortunately"—here his hands flashed as he lightly beat a tattoo on the head of the red-haired man who'd risen from the floor and again charged—"this bozo's too drunk and too stupid to realize he cranked out an amusing *bon mot*. I, however, will save it in my diary."

Taylor chuckled appreciatively; as always, he was Ray's best audience. His laughter cut off quickly, however, when he noticed that the red-haired man's friends were giving every indication of joining the altercation. "Oh, shit," he said softly, sadly. Ray's big mouth and inability to suffer fools gladly was once again going to pull him into another bar fight. Still, he would wait a tad—allowing the red-haired man's two friends a free shot at Ray before stepping in to rescue his diminutive buddy. It seemed unfair, but Ray would protest if Taylor came to his aid too quickly. Mighty Mite had to be convinced he *needed* rescuing.

As the four of them thrashed around on the floor, fists and arms emerging from the bunched bodies only to dive back in again, the bartender reached for the phone to call security. Taylor laid a hand on the man's arm. "Don't," he said. He had a smile on his face.

The bartender saw something in Taylor's smiling face and relented. Still, he was a big man himself and asked, in

Federation-standard English, "Just what are you gonna do about this?" He pointed at the roiling mass of kicking, biting, hitting humanity on the floor.

"I take it you have an argument-settler back there, don't you?"

"Yah, so what?"

"Gimme."

Reluctantly, the bartender reached under the bar, found what he was looking for, and withdrew a padded baseball bat. Taylor drained the last of the beer in his glass and set it down as he wiped the foam from his lips. Picking up the bartender's persuader, Taylor approached the combatants and said, "Fore." Then the bat flashed quickly, four times, and the mass was motionless. Handing the bat back to the bartender, Taylor said, "Works every time," and slid back onto his barstool.

"Christ, you did your buddy, too," said the bartender.

"So I did," agreed Taylor. "Another cerveza, por favor."

"Jeezus, Taylor," Ray said, his left hand holding a towel full of ice cubes to his head while his right hand cupped a steaming mug of black coffee, "you just about knocked me into next week!"

"No, just into tomorrow," said Taylor, glancing at his wrist chronometer and yawning.

"Yeah, mate," said the red-haired man, grinning a gap-toothed smile, "you're a crack batsman. You could play for our side in the next test match, if you're willing."

"Cricket?" asked Taylor. "I thought that old game disappeared back in . . ."

"Don't *you* start now!" warned Ray. "My head can't take another 'inning'!"

"Yes, please!" said one of the red-haired man's two friends.

"I think the exchanging of names is in order," said Ray before sipping some of his coffee. "I can't keep calling you the red-haired guy and his two cheeks."

"Cheeks?" asked one, puzzled.

"Ray!" said Taylor sternly.

"Okay, I made you behave, so I'll stop, too," promised Ray. "As you may have deduced from our exchanges, the two of us are Ray and Taylor. I'm Ray Larkin, scout dog handler, and this is Taylor Hollister, agrobiologist extraordinaire. We're both taking post-fudd courses at the university."

"Fudd?"

"Ph.D.," explained Taylor.

"Pleased to meet you, lads," said the red-haired man, taking first Ray's proffered hand and then Taylor's. "I'm Syd Farnum, Engineering Officer Second Class, of the *City of London*, best damn merchantman in the whole starfleet."

"My name's Alf Kinnock," said the taller of Farnum's friends, the one whose open and cheerful face looked like an unmade bed. Offering his hand, he added, "I'm a ship's cook on the *City of London*."

When Ray and Taylor looked at the third man expectantly, he responded by saying, "Me? I'm Geoffrey Hanesford, Purser."

"Tell me, lads," said Syd Farnum, leaning across the table conspiratorially, "do you often get yourselves into these sorts of dustups? I mean you both being college nerks and all, and . . . " His earnest inquiry was interrupted by the arrival of the waitress bringing their order of grilled stickies.

"What in the hell have you blokes ordered for us here, then?" asked Kinnock as the waitress—looking like she had been hired for the job right out of central casting, anachronistic beehive hairdo with a pencil behind her ear and all—placed the plates containing their food in front of them.

"Grilled stickies," said Taylor. "They're just buttered cinnamon rolls heated on the short-order cook's grill," he explained. "The Aries Lounge is famous for them—they freeze 'em and ship 'em offplanet to aficionados everywhere."

Using his knife and fork, Syd Farnum cut off a piece and gingerly inserted the bite-size portion into his mouth. "Well?" asked Ray.

"Call me a turnip and paint me blue!" marveled Farnum. "It's good!"

"Really?" asked Hanesford, unconvinced.

"Oh, try it, you stupid burke," roared Farnum. "You've eaten ship's food, haven't you, so what're you worrying about?"

"Come on, now," protested Kinnock. "I'm one o' the bleedin' cooks now, ain't I? Don't be knocking my food or you'll be findin' yourself swallowin' your teeth!"

When the red-haired Farnum looked like he might actually respond to his friend's comment, Ray said, "What's the time getting to be? I bet it's nearly six A.M."

"Eh?" said Farnum, looking at his chronometer. "By George, the wee lad's right! It's five forty-eight—we've got just twelve minutes to get back to the shuttle craft."

The three crewmen wolfed down their grilled stickies, gulped their tea and coffee, and offered their apologies for having to leave so suddenly. "It was lovely havin' a dustup with you lads," said Farnum, "but me mates and I have got to be on our way."

"Take care," said Ray.

"Bon voyage," said Taylor as he and Ray shook hands with the departing sailors.

"Well, that was pleasant," Ray said after their new friends had left. "I enjoy these little fisticuff parties—you get to meet the most fascinating people."

"I thought you didn't like people," said Taylor.

"I don't much, usually," Ray said. "But this is such a great way to get to know strangers: First you mutually rearrange each other's facial features, then you down a few beers together." Ray grinned. "What could be better than that—you've gotten those who-is-this-then? hostile feelings out of the way up front. It's now *possible* to be friends."

"Yeah, sure," said Taylor, yawning. "I'm getting too old for this sort of thing."

"Huh?" questioned Ray. "Why, you were hardly involved in the fight."

"The fight, no," agreed Taylor. "But it is *still* almost six in the morning; I never even gave Mary a call."

"She'll live," Ray said, his face clouding because Taylor's concern for this Mary had reminded him that the dogs would be needing attending to this morning.

Taylor sighed. "You know what I mean—here's *another* night the two of us have gone out for a drink and wound up nursing twenty-parsec coffee with a trio of space rummies burning up their back pay."

"Speaking of pay, I think this is yours," said Ray, handing Taylor the check.

Taylor had been seeing Mary for about six weeks when Ray finally asked, "Isn't it about time I get to meet this mystery woman, Taylor? You aren't keeping anything from me, are you? I mean, she has the requisite number of arms and legs, hasn't she? There's no gaping hole of horror where her nose should be, is there?"

"Of course not," laughed Taylor. "It's just that—"

"It's just *what*?" challenged Ray.

"It's just that I was planning to invite you to dinner at her apartment tomorrow evening, that's all."

Suspicious of this sudden invitation, Ray asked, "Why now, why all of a sudden?"

"I want you to meet her; I want to hear your opinion of her."

"Why should my opinion matter?" asked Ray.

"I'm going to ask her to marry me," Taylor said softly.

For once, Ray was speechless.

★　　★　　★

"Oh, I hope I look all right," Mary Brennan said, staring at her reflection in her makeup mirror as Taylor hovered nervously nearby.

"You look fine," he said.

"Fine. *Fine*?" she asked.

"Er . . . you look wonderful, *beautiful*," Taylor stammered. He bit his lip nervously; he was still learning how to speak "woman."

"You're sure?"

This time Taylor did not stumble. "I'm sure. Ray's eyes will pop out."

Just then the door chimed. "That'll be him," said Taylor. "Let me get the door."

"Okay, hon."

Taylor opened the door to find a freshly depilated, smartly dressed Ray waiting expectantly outside. He'd even trimmed his mustache. "Kowabunga!" exclaimed Taylor upon seeing his friend. "I didn't know you had anything but charity ward clothes in your wardrobe. Come in."

"Thanks," said Ray, trying to appear as suave as Cary Grant—a short Cary Grant—always was in those old sinny comedies.

Closing the door, Taylor said, "There's someone I'd like you to meet." He ushered his friend into the center of the room where a tall slender young woman waited nervously.

"Ray, I'd like to introduce you to my fianceé, Mary Brennan. Mary, this is Ray Larkin."

"I'm pleased to finally meet you, Mary," said Ray.

"And I, you," she said, taking his proffered hand.

Ray *was* pleased to meet Mary. Parted in the middle, her chestnut hair cascaded down to her shoulders (in a hopelessly dated style, Ray noted), enchancing a light dusting of freckles ("chocolate jimmies," Ray recalled Taylor calling them) that was compellingly sexy. *Old Taylor here has gotten himself a handsome woman,* Ray told himself admiringly as he took in the curves and hollows of her lithe frame.

Mary had never felt anyone's gaze examine her with such intensity as Ray's; his pale blue-gray eyes seemed to bore into her soul and her left hand involuntarily fluttered to the opening at the top of her blouse as if to pull it together for modesty's sake. She became aware suddenly that she was still shaking his hand up and down. Blushing slightly, she broke contact with his hand, hers still tingling from his touch, and said, "Why don't you two get comfy in the living room while I fix some drinks?"

"That sounds like a good idea, Mary," said Taylor, unaware of the jolt of sexual energy that had passed between his fianceé and his best friend.

Once Mary returned and they were seated, Ray raised his glass and said, "Here's to you two guys. May your marriage be long and happy."

"Thanks, Ray," said Taylor, touched. He raised his glass to his lips.

"Wait, that's not all," Ray said. He added, "And here's to me as well—this gin and tonic is my last drink—well, actually, my final one of the evening will be my last drink."

"You're giving up drinking?" Mary asked. "That's wonderful."

Ray grinned. "Yes, I know Taylor will agree with you. He's gonna be a married man now and he won't have the time to be pulling me out of bar fights."

"I'm not going to keep him under lock and key," Mary insisted. "He can still go out with you if he wants." She thought about that for a moment and then amended her statement:"*We* can go out with you; I want to be a part of the gang, if you'll have me, that is."

Sipping his drink slowly, Ray looked her over carefully. "Sure, I'll have you."

Mary reddened slightly, and Taylor didn't understand why.

II

Since Taylor had introduced him to Mary, Ray returned the favor one day by introducing Mary to the dogs. "Fellas—guys and bitches," said Ray, making Taylor laugh, "I'd like to introduce you to a new friend—Mary Elizabeth Brennan. Mary, the dogs."

"How come you got three names?" asked Frodo.

"Well, a lot of humans do," explained Mary. "Elizabeth is my middle name; it was my mother's name."

"She dead?" asked Ozma. Ray looked helplessly at Taylor. The dogs could be *so* rude with their questions; in all innocence, of course, but rude nonetheless.

"Yes," replied Mary after a moment's hesitation. "How about yours?"

"No, but we with Ray now; he is the Man."

"The man?" Mary said. "Can a woman be the man, so to speak?"

"Woman!" chortled Sinbad—who was immediately butted by Pandora.

"Ah, well . . . " began Ray, unsure how to put it delicately. "You see, scout dogs prefer a male leader." He shrugged, opening his hands in a palms-up gesture. "That's just the way it is," he said. He added, somewhat lamely, "Most scout cat teams are led by women, however."

"Cats!" said Anson disdainfully.

"You don't like cats?" Mary asked.

"Oh, I guess they okay," Anson admitted. "If Ray say so, we work with them, sure enuff."

"You must like Ray a lot."

Beowulf looked at her in shock, his blue eyes expressing his bemusement. "*Like* Ray?" his basso profundo voice boomed. "We *love* Ray." Mary looked at Ray—who just grinned back with a butter-wouldn't-melt-in-my-mouth look.

"I see," said Mary finally. "Well, I love Ray, too—as a friend, of course."

Mary coughed as both Taylor and Ray enjoyed her discomfort. Looking at Beowulf, she said, "I'll bet you're Beowulf, right?"

"That's right," beamed Beowulf. "How you know?"

"Just a lucky guess," said Mary dryly. "I'm pleased to meet you. And you," she said, looking at Anson, "you're . . . ?"

"I am Anson," the big dog said proudly.

"Nice to meet you, Anson."

Mary went down the line, introducing herself to each of the dogs in turn. Then they crowded around her, sniffing her and letting her know she was accepted as one of them.

"Oh, jeez!" said Ray when Frodo stuck his nose between Mary's legs and up to her crotch. The dogs were just being themselves, just being dogs, and he hoped Mary understood. She did, much to Ray's relief.

Thus reassured, he whispered to Taylor, "Hey, Taylor, it took you three dates to get—"

Taylor was on top of Ray before he could utter another word, getting him in a headlock. Laughing, they rolled around on the ground while Mary and the dogs could only watch them in amusement. "That Ray," said Mama-san dolefully, "he *never* gonna grow up!"

III

The jungle outside Cuiaba had been driven back and the land cleared. Even so, the forest was relentless in its attempts to reclaim its primal domain. While the city of Cuiaba itself was on the flat, featureless lowlands, in the Mato Grosso, Ray and the dogs lived more than one hundred and fifty kilometers to the east, where foothills began pushing up from the vast tropical plain that lay at the heart of Brazil. While the dogs were comfortable in almost any weather conditions which allowed human activity, Ray was glad for the relief from the heat and humidity the hills and mountains afforded.

Each day, assuming he wasn't meeting anyone in the city or on the campus of the university, Ray took the dogs for two exercise runs, one in the early morning and one in the late afternoon or early evening. His bungalow, with its detached kennel for the dogs, was one of several in the area providing housing for a scout dog team. Inevitably, he would encounter another team or two on a similar exercise run whenever he and the dogs went out. This day was no different.

With Littlejohn in the lead position (Beowulf, a gracious—and shrewd—leader, often allowed the other males to have the privilege of leading the team), Ray and the dogs jogged down a gravel-and-dirt road. As the foliage on either side gave way to clearings, Ray could see that they were going to merge with another team where two paths came together to form one. "Looks like Wah and his team," Ray said out of the side of his mouth to Beowulf, running easily beside him.

"Happiness is," said Beowulf. Neither Beowulf nor Ray liked Tsuneo Wah very much, finding him and his dogs insufferable braggadocios.

"Ray, hello," Wah called out as he and his dogs angled toward Ray's team.

"Hello, Tsuneo," Ray said with as much simulated sincerity as he could muster. Then, seeing the green-eyed scout dog at his side, Ray added, "Hello, Mao." The big dog just grunted, too superior, in his own mind, to further acknowledge a human not his master.

"You'll have to forgive Mao, Ray," Wah said. "He's feeling a little crabby and out of sorts today."

"Just today? Hunh!" grumbled Beowulf, sotto voce.

Wah, aware that Beowulf had mumbled something, but unsure just what, frowned before saying to Ray, "So, tell me, have you heard the big news?"

"Big news?" said Ray. He knew Wah wouldn't have mentioned it if he hadn't been sure Ray was ignorant of his scoop. "No, what's up?"

"The Bureau has its eyes on a new planet some light-years away; as a matter of fact, there's never been an attempt to terraform a planet so far from our own system before. The word is that this planet—I think it's called Chiron—is the pet project of the Triumvirate."

"The Triumvirate?" Ray just whistled.

"That's not all," confided Wah. "People are whispering that the General himself is overseeing the Planetary Colonization Bureau's efforts." Ray shook his head in wonder. If the General was involved, then this Chiron *was* important, damned important.

Wah scratched Mao behind the ears and continued. "This

project is taking precedence over everything else. They're signing up all the top teams; that's why I'm putting in my application first thing tomorrow morning." He looked disdainfully at Ray's dogs, running easily and freely ahead of them, mingling with his own team. "You could always give it a shot, too—you never know, they might be taking anyone."

"Gosh, thanks, Tsuneo," Ray said in a voice dripping with so much sarcasm that anyone else but Wah would have noticed it. Instead, the other just replied, "My pleasure." Then he angled his head and said, "Chiron . . . I wonder what that means, if anything."

"Chiron?" said Ray. "Well, in ancient history, Chiron was the name of Achilles' tutor."

"That's a bit obscure, isn't it?" commented Wah. He thought for a moment, considering this new bit of information and then said, "Since the General is involved, the project is probably military in some way—maybe this planet is supposed to be our Achilles' heel, our vulnerable point?"

Ray laughed. "I doubt they'd be so obvious about the name, then. There's another possibility." He patted Beowulf and said, "Chiron was a centaur."

"A centaur? You mean one of those man and hors—"

The forest had closed in on them again and, at a bend where the trees overhung the path, a dozen green and brown shapes had hurled themselves from their places of concealment, one leaping on Wah with a savage growl.

"Jaccamore!" Beowulf howled.

"Jesus H. Christ!" a shocked Ray screamed as he saw the Jaccamore rip out Wah's throat with its fangs. Ray was drenched by a geyser of blood from Wah's torn carotid artery. In the blink of an eye, a furious life-and-death battle was joined between the two teams and the attacking Jaccamore. Vaguely apelike, the carnivorous Jaccamore were a fearsome combination of ability, strength, and viciousness. (Later, on Chiron, Ray would compare the hide cats' mindless belligerence to that of the awesomely ferocious Jaccamore.) Ray could smell their rank odor, like tomatoes left to rot in the hot summer sun.

As Beowulf and Frodo, acting in concert, tore apart one Jaccamore with their powerful jaws, Ray raised his right arm and pointed it at one of the attacking shapes as it hurled through the air at him. By contracting a voluntary muscle in his wrist by a conscious movement of his thumb, Ray fired the needle gun strapped to his arm. The weapon coughed and a small, explosive ceramic shard punched into the attacking Jaccamore's skull and exited the back in a scarlet shower of blood and brain; the creature fell dead even as Ray turned to locate another target. Again he quickly, almost reflexively, pointed and fired. And again the explosive needle brought instant death to one of the attackers, blowing a hole in its chest the size of a plum.

Ray saw one of Wah's dogs go down, a Jaccamore holding its jaws shut with its powerful grip and trying to sink its fangs into the dog's throat. The other dogs from Wah's team leapt to their comrade's defense and between them tore the attacker to bits—causing Ray to avert his eyes.

Another Jaccamore rode the back of one of Wah's team like a short hairy cowboy, shrieking and gibbering as it simultaneously tried to maintain its position and somehow do damage to the dog it sat astride. Mao came up beside the two and snatched the howling Jaccamore right off his companion's back with a snap of his powerful jaws. He threw the apelike thing down and ripped it open, pulling out its innards as it thrashed helplessly.

Having mindlessly attacked two full teams, the Jaccamore were quickly and efficiently dispatched by the much larger scout dogs and the attack subsided almost as quickly as it had begun.

With all the Jaccamore dead or dying, Ray bent to examine Wah's still form. Wah lay by the side of the path, his sightless eyes staring at the canopy of the forest overhead, and his torn neck dribbling blood. "Sorry, Tsuneo," Ray said, reaching out and closing the dead man's eyes. Wah's team had suffered two fatalities as well. Ray made a note to return with an armed escort to retrieve their bodies.

Mao hobbled over, his right front paw injured. "Our Man . . . our Man is dead?"

"Yes," Ray said without elaboration. Then: "Come on, I'll see you back to your place." Ray picked up Wah's body—it seemed to weigh nothing at all—and slung it over his shoulder.

"What are these Jaccamore, Ray?" asked Pandora.

"They're alien predators," he explained. "They're contraband, supposedly quarantined and not permitted on Terra.

Unfortunately, some asshole, a big-time drug dealer, imported several to use as 'guard dogs.' Well, what *can* go wrong *does* go wrong, and they escaped and began to breed. They're considered vermin, to be shot on sight, but they may never be eradicated from these forests." He sighed. "This is the first I ever heard of any being this far east, this close to the mountains."

"Oh. Thank you, Ray."

"You're welcome, Pandora."

"Ray?" It was Mao.

"Yes?"

"We be good team," Mao pressed. "Good team for you."

"I know," Ray agreed. "But I have my hands full trying to see that the ten of us don't starve. I can't take on another team." He reached out and patted the top of Mao's massive head. "Don't worry, I'll do what I can."

"They split us up?" Mao asked, the concern showing in his raspy voice.

"I don't know, Mao," Ray said sadly. "Maybe . . . I just don't know."

★　　★　　★

"Three months!" moaned Mary. "Three whole months!"

"Yes," confirmed Taylor. "Well, only twelve weeks, if that sounds better." He squirmed uncomfortably. "Mary, you know that all I need at this point is my Bureau certificate in cholo handling for us to qualify as a terraforming team. The training is free, and at the end of the twelve weeks my only obligation is three years service for the Bureau at the standard contract fee. It's too good a deal to pass up."

"I know," confessed Mary, "I know. But I don't have to like it."

3

This was a mistake, Ray thought as he watched Mary silently eating her meal. *Taylor's only been gone two days—it's too soon to be doing this*. "How's your steak?" he asked.

Mary looked up as if startled by the sound of his voice. "Fine. It's done just the way I like it . . . a bit charred on the outside, yet pink in the middle."

Ray shook his head. "I like to know that what I'm eating has truly kicked the bucket." Mary's fork paused in midair, halfway between her plate and her mouth. "Oops, sorry about that," Ray apologized.

"That's okay," Mary responded. "For a second there, though, I had a mental image that wasn't very pleasant."

Go ahead, *Ray*, he chided himself, *put your foot in your mouth*, *why don't you*? Aloud, he merely said, "My fish is wonderful, quite tender and flaky." Then he laughed as if he'd said something absurd.

"What?" asked Mary.

"I'm a sparkling conversationalist, aren't I," Ray said, still laughing at himself.

Mary's features softened. "I haven't exactly been holding up my end, either."

Ray shrugged. "More wine?"

"Please." Watching the clear liquid rise in her wineglass,

Mary said, "Are you sure you can afford this—that's a 2165 bottle of Kolln Vineyards Seyval Blanc, isn't it?"

"You forget that I've run a mission already," Ray responded easily. "I'm Daddy Warbucks."

"You and your obscure popular culture references!" Mary scolded. Then she said, "We're going Dutch on this tonight." Ray started to protest but shut up when she added, "Taylor left me a few credits for tonight, so don't let's argue about it."

"As you wish." Secretly, Ray was more than willing to allow Mary to pick up part of the tab. The Cristobal, a *very* expensive revolving restaurant, was located atop a one hundred and twenty-five-floor building in the heart of the city. Ray had made reservations weeks ago, after learning of Taylor's planned absence.

In the ninety minutes they'd been there, the restaurant had made one and a half full revolutions. Looking out at the lights of the city below them, Mary said, "It's a spectacular view, isn't it?"

"It had better be," Ray said. "We're paying for it as much as for the food."

Mary put down her silverware and took Ray's hands in hers. "I really appreciate your bringing me here tonight, Ray. I know it's hard for you," she said. "It's hard for me, too. I want us to be best friends—as close as you and Taylor."

"Me too," said Ray. "But tonight's too soon to begin, isn't it?"

"I think so," agreed Mary.

Although they still ordered coffee and dessert, Ray knew that the evening was over and he told Mary he'd drop her off at her place. They took the drop tube down two floors to the waiting area. The fact that more and more people worked and traveled with animals meant that there had to be facilities for them, but few places, especially fancy restaurants, allowed them on the actual premises.

"Hi, Beowulf," Ray said. "Hi, Littlejohn." The two dogs struggled up from their positions on the low couches where they had been talking quietly to each other and another dog, wagged their tails, and trotted over to greet Ray and Mary.

"Food good?" Beowulf asked.

"Yeah, I suppose so," Ray replied. "How about you guys?

I hear they have a special biscuit that's supposed to be wonderful."

"Was okay," Littlejohn conceded.

Mary said, "Sounds like all four of us were underwhelmed by the cuisine."

"Yeah," said Littlejohn, looking around. "And the food not so hot, either."

Mary laughed and then looked quizzically at Ray. "Is he for real, or did you teach him to say things like that?"

"Huh?" asked Littlejohn.

"Me teach the dogs?" Ray said. "Sure, but not what to say; whatever comes out of their mouths is pure canine." He raised his hands, palms outward, to indicate his innocence.

"Huh?" repeated Littlejohn.

"I think you made joke," Beowulf patiently explained.

"Me?" Littlejohn said. He beamed and proudly stated, "I made joke." Then he frowned and asked Beowulf, "Uh, what *was* joke?"

"Never mind," said Ray. "Let's get out of here."

As they left, the remaining dog, a pretty bitch, called out, "Goodbye, Beowulf. Goodbye, Littlejohn." Her voice was higher than either of the two males'.

"Goodbye, Gretchen," they chorused.

Several people in the drop tube looked apprehensively at the two huge scout dogs but said nothing. Surreptitiously, Ray sniffed the air in the stuffy drop tube. He could smell nothing apart from Mary's delightful perfumed scent and he breathed a sigh of relief. He'd helped both Beowulf and Littlejohn bathe that morning but it was just like the dogs to find something long dead and completely repulsive to roll around in; fortunately, they'd heeded his words about staying relatively clean.

Sensing that Ray was sampling the air, Mary leaned over to him and whispered, "It's called 'Angel's Desire.'"

"Huh?"

"My perfume—it's called 'Angel's Desire.'" Mary repeated. "I noticed you becoming aware of it."

"Yea, it's very nice," Ray said. He was silent for a moment as he considered whether or not to say something else. Shrugging a what-the-hell shrug, he said, "I know several scents I'd like to suggest. What you're wearing is wonderful, but the dogs are sensitive to certain ingredients in perfumes and since you're going to be around them a lot more, I'd like you to consider using one of the brands I recommend."

Ray cringed. *Jesus, what an asshole I must seem—telling her that her perfume is all wrong and suggesting she change it!*

Mary, who'd spent years finding the perfect scent, just nodded thoughtfully and said, "Of course, Ray, if it's for the dogs' sake."

The sidewalks of Cuiaba teemed with people out enjoying the relative coolness of the night air. Venders hawked candy, drugs, watches, scarves, windup toys, flavored ices, and other typical street fare. Acrobats, guitar players, magicians, street preachers, prostitutes, and bewildered tourists filled the streets with life, color, and vitality. "Don't you just love the city?" Mary asked.

"Yeah," said Ray dryly, "I just love it."

Linking his arm with hers, Mary said, "You can take the boy out of the farm, but you can't take the farm out of the boy."

"I'm no farm boy," Ray retorted. "I just prefer fewer people in my life, that's all."

"Uh-huh."

As usual, when they were in the city with Ray, Beowulf and Littlejohn took up protective positions—Beowulf in front, clearing the way, and Littlejohn in the rear, watching for any danger from that direction. "Do you think all this is necessary?" asked Mary, indicating the dogs' precautions.

"It's habit," Ray said. "The dogs are used to assuming a protective stance in the wild; I don't see any harm in their continuing the practice in an urban situation."

"Cuiaba's a safe city," Mary insisted.

"Yeah, tell that to the thousand people who get mugged every day," Ray retorted.

Mary just sighed and let the matter drop. As a matter of fact, she *did* enjoy the way people moved out of their way.

Ray looked at his watch. "A hover cab's not gonna be able to take the four of us, so we better hie ourselves over to the subway."

On the subway, the other riders tried to ignore the couple flanked by the two immense dogs sitting patiently on their haunches and panting in the heat. "The air-conditioning is always broken, it seems," Mary said. Ray just grunted in acknowledgment.

The subway dropped them off a few blocks from Mary's apartment. "This looks like a good place for a murder," commented Ray cheerfully. "With all the students and professors who live in this area, you'd think the city would extend the subway to this neighborhood."

"It does, usually," Mary explained. "But one of the tunnels is being repaired and the end of the line is now more than two kilometers from the apartment building where I live. It's just temporary."

"So's the universe," said Ray dryly.

As they walked up an apparently deserted street, filled with blowing papers, empty beer bottles, broken glass, and all the standard filth of a decaying inner-city block, the dogs kept a wary watch. Beowulf stopped to sniff something on the sidewalk and was still busy running his nose over the asphalt as Ray and Mary approached. "What is it?" asked Ray.

"Doan know."

"Then get the hell up ahead again," Ray said.

When Littlejohn brought up the rear, he found himself so entranced by the odorous patch on the sidewalk that he fell behind as he ranged over the appealing spot. Similarly, a noise from a distant alleyway attracted Beowulf and he trotted ahead to investigate. For the moment, at least, Ray and Mary were on their own, or so it would appear to any onlooker.

"Well, what have we got here?" said a tall, powerfully built man wearing a torn jacket as he stepped out of a doorway. Ray quickly noted the two shapes stepping out beside him.

"We don't have very much money," said Ray reasonably, "but what we have is yours."

"No kidding," said the tall man, stepping out into the dim light. A lightning-bolt scar ran up the side of one cheek.

"Fuck the money," said one of the first man's companions, a chunky man with a shaved head and a walrus mustache. "We want some of that pussy you got."

"It's the bitch got the pussy, dumb ass," said the third man, staring at Ray. "Me, I want to see what shorty's got hangin' 'tween them legs of his. He's cute."

Ray wished he'd had his needle gun with him, but restaurants generally frowned on that sort of thing and he'd left it at home. Instead, he pulled his bush knife from his calf scabbard.

"Look," said the tall man with the scar. "The twerp's got a

blade." He smiled menacingly. "I'm gonna shove that so far up your ass, shorty, that you'll be able to pick your teeth from the inside."

Ray returned the man's smile, slipped the small brass whistle between his lips, and blew. When the three thugs heard no noise, they assumed Ray's whistle was broken and started toward the two of them. "Bye, bye, asshole," the tall man said a split second before Beowulf's one hundred and fifty kilograms, with twenty meters of momentum behind it, crashed into him with an impact so stunning that his head cracked open like a ripe melon when it smashed into the wall of the building behind him.

At nearly the same instant, Littlejohn bowled over the other two assailants and immediately ripped out the throat of the one nearest him on the ground. After a few shakes of the lifeless body convinced him his prey was dead, Littlejohn dispatched the second man.

Blood flowed across the dusty sidewalk, turning into a mauve mud, and the tall man's brains slowly oozed down the wall as his feet skidded out from under him and he slid down the wall to end up splay-legged on the sidewalk. "Oh, Christ!" said Mary, turning away and expelling the half-digested remains of a very expensive entree.

Ignoring her for a moment—Ray knew she was unharmed physically—he turned to the dogs and asked, "Are you okay?"

Both were a little shaky. "Yeah, Ray, we okay," Beowulf said, speaking for the two of them.

"Mary, how are *you*?"

"Fine. How should I be?"

"This may sound callous now, and I apologize for that," Ray began as he comforted her by putting his arms around her. "But the dogs are conditioned to value and respect human life above all else. They were able to override their conditioning because our lives were in danger. Even so, the shock of what they just did is going to be severe. I've got to get them to a specialist the first thing in the morning to prevent any lasting psychological damage. Therefore, I've got to see you home and then catch the first bullet train back to the compound." He squeezed her hand. "As much as you may need me, I've got to attend to the dogs first."

Mary's breath was coming in short gasps, yet she was

clear-headed enough to understand what Ray was saying.
"I . . . ah, I understand, Ray."

"Let's get you back and call someone to come over and
spend the night with you—a girl friend, perhaps. Is there
someone like that who you can call?"

"Yes."

"Good. Now let's get out of here."

"But," Mary protested, "these three men—we can't just
leave them here, can we?"

"I can't get involved with the police," Ray said. "Besides,"
he added grimly, "trash pickup is in the morning."

Ray and the troubled dogs took Mary home and stayed with
her until a pale-skinned girl named Gretchen arrived to spend
the night with her. As jumbled as his thoughts were, Ray still
thought, *Gretchen . . . why does that name sound familiar?*

Later, walking quickly down the mean streets with the dogs
at his side while he took a roundabout way back to the subway
station, he heard the whoop of distant emergency vehicles.
"Sounds like they discovered the mess we made," he said.

Consoling and reassuring Beowulf and Littlejohn, Ray
caught the last train out. He and Mary would try again. *Christ,
what a night*, he thought as he patted both dogs' heads. *What
a "first date."*

▌▌

As Taylor's extended absence stretched into weeks, Mary *did*
grow used to spending time with Ray. More and more she
found herself catching a bullet train out to where he lived, far
away from the noise, filth and overcrowding of the city. Mary
spent long hours with Ray in his living quarters, listening to his
unique repertoire of scout dog folklore. One night she felt
brave enough to ask him if his lack of feeling for everyday
human interaction was why, perhaps, he felt such a kinship,
such a bond, for his dogs.

"Yeah, I suppose so," Ray agreed. "Hell, it's even kinda
obvious, isn't it? My dogs are trained from birth to obey me,
to accept me as their leader, but not necessarily to give me their
love—though they do, asking nothing in return." He nodded
thoughtfully. "That's the most important thing, the asking for
nothing in return."

"But you can't only *take* love; it's no good if you don't give as much as you receive," Mary protested.

"Look," he said in a reasonable tone of voice, "I haven't gone around begging people to love me. If anyone did—hey, great. And if no one did, why I could survive that, too. But everyone"—and here Ray flushed, for he realized she knew he was including her in that everyone—"wants something in return. That hardly seems like true giving, if you know what I mean.

"I've made it a policy all my brief but event-filled life to accept nothing, not even love, that carries with it a note saying 'Pay to the bearer on demand!' "

Mary looked immeasurably sad. "You poor jerk. You must have had a pretty lonely life."

"No," Ray said too quickly. "No, not at all. Hell, I've had my share of lovers. I've been friends with lots of people, too: my parents, a few teachers, and several women—including you." He smiled. "And besides, as I said, the dogs love me."

"Of course they do." She shook her head. "You're so blind, Ray. Can't you see that they love you because they know you love them?"

"You don't know my dogs," he said.

"And you, obviously, don't know the first thing about love," she retorted.

"Well, if you're such an expert, you could always teach me," Ray said, the words tumbling out before he realized it.

Mary's gaze caught and held his; Ray held his breath until he thought he was going to explode. "Taylor said you were to take care of me, didn't he?" she asked, although it was more a statement than a question.

"Yes-s-s-s," Ray said, the air slowly leaking from him.

"Let me ask you something, Ray," Mary began. She took his hands in hers. "Do you *like* me?"

Ray's brow furrowed. "Do I like you?"

"You met me through Taylor and I sometimes have the feeling you only put up with me because of your friendship with him . . . and yet . . . and yet there's an electric tingle that goes through me every time you touch me, or when you look at me as if you want me as much as I want you."

"Er, well . . ." Ray was flabbergasted at the turn the conversation had taken. "Sure I like you, I just thought that—"

Suddenly, Ray's eyes widened and he asked, "Did you just say what I thought you did?"

"Jesus and Mohammed!" Mary exclaimed. "I thought Taylor was dense, but you're even worse."

Ray slumped back, his brain whirling. "Damn it, girl, you're the sexiest and most gorgeous woman I've ever known and I'm just . . . well, I'm just me. Look at me—who'd suspect that you'd think *I* was attractive?"

Mary just shook her head and sighed. "I think we've both been ignoring the signals because we couldn't believe they could possibly be for real."

"You're sure they *are* for real?"

"Why don't you kiss me and we'll find out," Mary suggested.

Slowly, Ray leaned forward and put his arms around Mary. He did it tentatively, carefully—fearful any sudden move might cause him to awaken from a dream. He gently pressed his lips on hers and kissed her. His touch was light at first, but, as she kissed him back, he intensified the pressure. Mary, despite her protestations, had one or two serious boyfriends before she met Taylor and she had kissed guys on dates. Yet she had never experienced such a sudden explosion of nerve-tingling sensations. The passion and feeling in Ray's kiss stirred something deep and primal in her and in the moment she forgot everything except the man holding her in his arms.

Ray pulled back and then lay his head on her shoulder, burying his face in her hair. He breathed in the sweetness of her, glorifying in her womanly musk, and feeling her breasts pressing against his chest. "I . . . ah . . . Christ," was all he could get out.

"Please," Mary said. "Could we try that again? I need to know something."

Without a word, Ray kissed her again. And again Mary felt her insides melt with passion and desire. This time she pulled away first. "My god," she gasped. "My god."

What happened next was inevitable. And neither of them, for a single moment, thought of Taylor.

"Well?" the other dogs asked Sinbad when he returned from peering in through the living room window.

"Yep," Sinbad said. "They sexing each other."

"Are you *sure*?" asked Frodo. "They do it differently—face to face."

"That's why I'm sure," replied Sinbad.

After the other dogs cheered and laughed, making good-naturedly lewd comments, Ozma said, "I'm 'fraid of this. What about the other Man . . . what about Taylor?"

The others considered that for a moment; then Mama-san broke the silence by saying, "They just like us now, the humans—they take more than one husband or wife."

"So then it be okay!" yelped a relieved Anson.

"Yeah, it be okay," agreed Beowulf, "if it okay with Taylor."

"Oh," said Anson, his glee dying.

They started to walk away, back toward their kennel, when Pandora stopped and stared over her shoulder at Frodo. "Where you goin', Frodo?" she called to him.

"Up to the house," Frodo replied, as the other dogs stopped and turned to stare at him as well. "Heck, I never seen humans do it."

The others looked at each other in wonderment. "Hey, Frodo, wait up," one of them called, running to join him. The rest quickly followed suit.

★   ★   ★

"You mean, while I was all alone on Armstrong and studying my ass off to learn how to handle choios, you two were back here playing house? My best friend and my wife!" Taylor sneered.

"How'd you like my fist in your face?" Ray said, rising.

"Sit down!" commanded Mary. Turning to Taylor, she said, "And you—don't play the hurt and outraged husband. You knew how we felt about each other, yet you went ahead and placed us both in an impossible situation."

Taylor sighed and looked at the floor. When he looked up again, he asked, "Do you love him?"

"I thought that's what started all this," Mary said. "You know that I do."

"And I love Mary," Ray said.

"So, what are we to do?" asked Taylor.

"Well . . ." Here Mary looked at Ray, who nodded, and

continued: "I love Ray—but I love you, too, Taylor." She sighed. "There seems to be only one solution."

"And that is?" questioned Taylor.

"Don't be dense. You're making this harder than it needs to be," said Ray. "A triple. Mary's suggesting a triple marriage."

"A triple?" Taylor said slowly, as if rolling the idea around in his head. "I don't know. What's wrong with a standard two-person marriage?"

"Hey, I agree," said Ray quickly. "Apply for a divorce and clear the way for Mary and me to have one."

"I guess he's serious," Taylor said, turning back to Mary. "But are you?"

"Yes, I love you both," Mary said. "But please don't make me choose."

Taylor shrugged. "Then I guess all we have to do is make it official."   •

"That's right," said Ray, taking Mary's hand and then Taylor's.

"The Three Musketeers," said Taylor, finally smiling.

"One for all and all for one," said Mary.

Ray, in the midst of their three-way hug, didn't believe a word of it, didn't think things would ever be the same between them. *But*, he told himself, *I'm willing to give it a try. Who knows, maybe it'll work out; stranger things have happened.*

III

Ray yawned, not bothering to cover his mouth with his hand, while Melvin Nhroma, a round man with gleaming ivory teeth, and the career Planetary Colonization Bureau official in charge of recruiting contract terraformers for Chiron, droned on with his briefing. Ray felt a little pity for the man. His was an almost impossible job because terraformers, as independent entrepreneurs, Ray knew, could be touchy if treated as "hired hands."

". . . Yours is a very important job," Nhroma was saying in his most officious drone. "The gee-wave stations must be totally self-supporting: Chiron's too far away for us to be sending food and other supplies every month or so."

Sitting across from Nhroma, with Taylor and Mary, Ray fidgeted in his chair. He wished the man would cease his endless lecturing and get to the signing of the retinal contracts.

"Yes, indeed, Chiron will be a marvelous scientific outpost and colony world for us. Of course, the soil must be altered ever so slightly to favor Terran plants, and the oceans must be sown with microorganisms that will prepare the way for Terran-type sea farming, but that is where you and many others like you will come in.

"It's a great responsibility: In as short a time as possible, you must prepare much of the northern continent for eventual colonization and agricultural exploitation. It won't be easy." Ray just lowered his chin onto his hands resignedly; he knew a full-bore bureaucrat when he met one "There will be wild animals, disease, wind, cold, but eventually you will succeed."

"For Chrissakes, Mr. Nhroma, we're not dime-novel heroes making the West safe for schoolmarms and civilization," interrupted Taylor. "We *are* getting well paid for our efforts."

"Certainly," acknowledged Nhroma, somewhat taken aback by Taylor's words.

"I have a more substantial matter to raise with you, Mr. Nhroma," Ray said impatiently. "Our contract has a clause which I've never seen before in any Bureau contract."

"Er, what clause is that?" asked Nhroma nervously.

"I believe," put in Mary, "that Ray is referring to the one which states that at the direction of the Triumvirate we may be placed directly under the control of the Cadre. Since when is the Cadre interfering with PCB business?"

Before Nhroma could say anything, Taylor joined in, saying, "Yes. None of us is particularly adept at serving an authoritarian leadership such as that represented by the Cadre—that's why we're in the business we're in, that's why we work for ourselves."

Nhroma looked put upon. Finally he asked, "Do you wish a completely frank answer?"

"That would be refreshing," acknowledged Ray.

"I have absolutely no idea," Nhroma said flatly. And there was something about his new demeanor which bespoke candor. Lying through his teeth, Nhroma looked benignly at Ray.

"Damn your eyes!" marveled Ray. "I think I almost believe you!"

* ★ *

It wasn't until the twelve of them, including the nine dogs of course, had boarded the F.S.S. *Gorbachev* that Mary admitted to her husbands that she had never been on a starship before.

"Really?" said Ray.

"Really."

"You're in for a real experience, then," said Taylor enthusiastically. Then, unaware of the implications of juxtaposing his next sentence with what he'd just said, he asked, "Did you take the anti-nausea pills?"

"Not yet," Mary admitted. "You said we wouldn't be jumping until we had put a few hundred thousand kilometers between us and Terra."

"That's right," Taylor said, looking at his watch. "But that's going to be in about two hours."

"I'll be ready," said Mary.

Ray looked at Taylor. "After the two of you are comfortably strapped in for the jump, I need to go back to the dogs."

"You're going to leave us?" asked Mary, her concern showing.

Ray looked unhappy as he said, "They're like big kids—well, like little kids, really. They're smart as a whip, but the jump into hyperspace is the sort of thing that scares the bejesus out of them; they need me."

"I understand, dear," Mary said. She kissed Ray and told him, "Go to them, go now."

"Thanks," said Ray, relieved that Mary was being so patient with him where the dogs were concerned.

"It's about five minutes to jump time now," Ray said, looking at his watch. The area in which the dogs were required to stay, while not as luxurious as the human accommodations, was certainly comfortable and as psychologically relaxing as possible. The muted color scheme was not only pleasing to the human handlers but also produced soothing shades of black and white. Ray guessed that the pleasant smell in the cabin contained specially chosen pheromonal molecules to calm and reassure canine sensibilities.

Each of the dogs had his or her own curved acceleration couch (*Why are they called that*? Ray wondered. *There's no acceleration to speak of*), and Ray had strapped each in securely yet not so tightly that they would feel confined.

"How long now?" asked Mama-san.

"Two minutes," said Ray, after a quick glance at his watch.

"Tell us again what is 'jumping,'" Frodo said.

Ray sighed. As far as he could tell, the conceptual and theoretical aspects of jumping were beyond the ken of the dogs. They were intelligent but still dogs. Yet, they still liked to hear Ray describe what happens during a jump, in some way exorcising their fear the way a small child might prefer to have his night fears explained away by a confident and in-control—to the child's eye, at least—parent.

"Okay, here goes. Space is folded and curved even though it appears straight to our limited senses. A spaceship traveling at the speed of light in normal space, in a straight line, takes a long time to go from point A to point B—or C, D, E, or even Z." Ray licked his lips and continued. "But when a ship punches a hole in the fabric of space where it is folded and touching, it can leave normal space at point A and reenter normal space at point B without any time passing. No time has registered on timepieces on board, yet the ship has traveled trillions of kilometers, exiting and reentering normal space in the same nanosecond."

"Magic!" whispered Sinbad.

"I agree," said Ray. "I know a little of the basic theory, but it seems like magic to me, too." He glanced at his watch. "Okay, here it comes," he said. Even as he spoke, a series of muted chimes resounded throughout the ship.

The ship jumped.

Ray and the dogs experienced a momentary feeling of nausea. Looking at the dogs—staring back fearfully at him—Ray saw, or imagined that he saw, them ripple and waver. His insides felt as if every cell in his body had, for just a second, bulged outward against its walls. Then the feeling passed.

"How long?" asked Beowulf.

"It's a nine-minute jump to Armstrong," Ray replied. The dogs just looked at each other; in less than nine minutes, when the ship exited hyperspace, they would reexperience those disorienting physical sensations. Ray did not bother to look at his watch. Although the passengers and crew would experience that nine minutes—they could eat, drink, give birth, or die during that duration—their timepieces would not register the passage of any time whatsoever and they would be returning to the normal-space universe at the same instant they left it, albeit in a different location.

"Are you okay?"

Mary gagged, but did not vomit. After the wave of nausea passed, she managed to blurt out, "Yes, damn it, I'm okay!"

Taylor smiled. If she was testy enough to swear at him, then she was doing fine. "Here, this will make you feel better," he said, pressing a damp cloth to her forehead.

"Jesus, is it always like that?"

"The first time is the worst," Taylor soothed. "You'll do better when we pop out."

"Ohmygod!" Mary shuddered. "I forgot—we're going to go through this again in a few minutes!"

After the dogs pleaded and cajoled, Ray agreed to their going down to Armstrong's surface with Taylor and him. At the cholo breeding facility Ray sternly admonished them: "Now, don't go far—and don't get into any trouble."

"Yes, Ray," agreed Beowulf, leading the exuberant dogs off on the run.

"They're big kids," Ray said to Taylor. "Just big kids, and—Jeezus!!"

"Impressive, eh?" asked Taylor, enjoying Ray's reaction upon seeing his first cholo in the flesh.

"Impressive isn't the half of it," Ray said, marveling at the pasty-white creature before him. Then his nose wrinkled. "That odor, what is it? It's . . . it's almost like, er, like—"

"Like freshly baked black bread?" finished Taylor.

"Hey, yeah, that's it."

"Shit."

"Ah-h-h, I beg your pardon?"

Taylor laughed and explained. "I mean, it's a cholo's natural waste excretion, its feces—you know, shit."

"Oh. Oh-h-h."

Ray slowly walked over to the untouched grass parallel to the track of the cholo. It was the first one he'd ever seen outside of a holo, and it was indeed an impressive sight. Only a great blue whale from the Terran oceans could equal it in size—but there were no more blue whales on Terra, of course.

"Say, how much of does one of these porkers weigh?" Ray asked.

"Oh, approximately fifteen metric tons," Taylor replied. Pleased to be asked about his cholos, Taylor continued. "They're twenty meters long by three meters wide and are four meters tall. They eat the equivalent of their own weight every twenty-four hours, Terra-standard time. They were created over one hundred and fifty years ago in the Bureau's labs. They're artificially engineered creatures specifically developed from earthworms to range over the surfaces of Terran-like planets unable to—" He stopped, shaking his head. "I'm sorry, I'm afraid I'm beginning to lecture."

Ray waved a hand at Taylor. "Oh, please don't stop. I find this all very interesting."

Taylor looked dubious but was glad to continue. "As I was saying, they're put to work on planets unable to support Terran plant forms in their unaltered state. For instance: On Chiron the cholos will eat great swaths through the local vegetation and topsoil and excrete a waste that is as deadly a poison for the original native plants as it is a highly efficient fertilizer for the Terran crops that will someday be growing after they've passed."

He pointed to the bare earth left in the wake of the cholo. "With the fierce winds on Chiron, soil left like that would soon blow away. The last thing we'll be trying to create is a dustbowl, so to 'hold' the newly transformed soil for the Terran plants, we'll sow Terran grasses behind the cholos."

That was Ray's introduction to the cholos he and the dogs would be protecting in the near future.

4

The front end of a hyperspace jump was no big deal and could be initiated almost anywhere. Exiting hyperspace was another matter, however. A prudent captain, ensuring that an error in astronavigation did not result in his or her ship's coming out of hyperspace in the middle of a sun or planet, always came out some distance away from the system which was their destination. The most time-consuming portion of any starship journey was the final leg of the trip. Thus, it would take the *Gorbachev* a week to reach Chiron.

The terraforming teams spent the week on board ship getting to know one another. Once on Chiron, the chances that the majority of them would see one another again were slim, considering the size of the northern continent they and their cholos would be transforming.

The group Mary, Taylor, and Ray got to know best was the Khorsegai/Tanaka/Evans team, not the least for the fact that they'd be only a few hundred kilometers apart. Vaslev Khorsegai, the group leader, was, by appearances at least, in his early fifties, a remarkable fact considering that terraforming raw new planets was normally a young person's game. Miya Tanaka and Jenna Evans were the other two members of the group. They were all singles, unlike Ray's group, and Ray could not help but wonder what the arrangement was between the older Russian male and his two younger female partners.

I'd ask if it weren't rude and none of my business to boot, Ray thought.

Poring over a holomap of the northern continent and consulting their sector assignments, the two teams remarked how close they would be by the end of a year or so. "We're starting off way below you and to your left," Mary said, looking at the map. "As we move up and you move left, we start to converge."

"Let's meet and have a reunion," Miya Tanaka said.

"Sure," said Taylor. "That sounds like a good way to celebrate the near-completion of our work."

"Think we'll have to invite any of those folks?" asked Khorsegai, nodding his head in the direction of a black-uniformed Cadre regular passing through the lounge.

"I know what you mean," said Ray. "There are an awful lot of them on board, aren't there?"

"I don't think there are to be any Cadre or regular military personnel stationed on Chiron, however," Jenna Evans said.

"That's what they've told us," agreed Ray. "But I wonder . . ."

"These gee-wave stations must really be important," said Khorsegai.

"Yeah," agreed Ray, telling everyone about the conversation he'd had with Wah back on Terra concerning the General's interest in the project.

Jenna Evans frowned. "The General . . . why would the First Consul himself be bothering about gee-wave stations, I wonder?"

"Forgive me for being stupid," said Miya Tanaka, "but I'm just a poor little Ph.D. in biology and not up on much of anything outside my area of expertise. Just what *is* a gee-wave station?"

"Wanna take this one, Vaslev?" asked Taylor, tired of playing the role of lecturer.

"My pleasure," said Khorsegai, clearing his throat and beginning. "Simply put, a gravity-wave detection system consists of a planet—Terra, for instance—and a string of seismic stations, monitoring the motion of the planet's surface. By proper harmonic analysis of the planet, it's possible to observe the resonant vibration of the planet, excited by a passing gravitational wave."

"Are there a lot of those to detect?"

Khorsegai laughed. "Well, the monitoring stations built so far have been used to detect the pulse of gravitational radiation created by the mass of a starship emerging into real space at the end of its journey," he explained. "Thus, human star travel provides valuable benchmarks for calibrating detector systems, and providing information on the propagation of gravitational interaction."

Evans scratched her head. "As a scientist myself, I'm not one to question the value of basic research, even when there is no known immediate payoff in results," she said. "But why are the General and the Cadre so interested in such a basic scientific project?"

"That's a good question," admitted Khorsegai.

Mary bridged her fingers and asked, "Is there anything else a gee-wave station might accomplish, any other use to which it might be put?"

Khorsegai was silent for a long time, apparently deep in thought. Then he looked at Mary, started to open his mouth as if to say something, and stopped. "What . . . what is it?" Mary asked.

"I *had* a thought," admitted Khorsegai, "but it's too wild, too unlikely to even consider."

"So tell us," said Ray. "We'll be the judge of that." He shrugged, "Maybe you're right—maybe we'll laugh at your fancy notions . . . but maybe not."

Khorsegai rolled his eyes in a you-asked-for-it-so-don't-blame-me fashion and said, "Gee-wave stations detect starship 'signatures'—*any* starship signatures, right?"

"Yeah?"

"Well, why would you need to build a gee-wave station so far from the center of the galaxy to detect human starship signatures?"

"*Human* starship signatures," said Taylor slowly. "You mean . . . ?"

"That's right," said Khorsegai. "I think this new gee-wave station is intended to detect alien starship jumps, if any."

"That's preposterous," sputtered Taylor.

"Is it?" said Ray, running a finger along his mustache. "What if the Federation has detected starship gravity disturbances from many thousands of light-years away? Our present

Terran-bound systems would be unable to provide a large enough baseline to determine the exact location of signals coming from a more distant corner of the galaxy."

Mary frowned. "But an alien civilization thousands of light-years away would be—oh, my God!"

"Yes," agreed Khorsegai. "Signals from such a race would mean that they have possessed star travel for at least that many years, a thousand or more—the time it takes for the waves to reach Terra. Who could begin to even estimate the progress they might have made since that time ten centuries in our race's past?"

"Damn it, Vaslev's right!" said Ray. "The Triumvirate might be concerned with the possibility of the Federation being discovered by an alien civilization whose technology is far superior to our own and who might not be nice guys. One need only look at our own early Terran history for an example that demonstrates all too clearly the inevitable outcome of such an encounter."

"And what example might that be, pray tell?" asked Miya Tanaka.

"The Aztecs and Incas were powerful and well-entrenched civilizations when they were invaded and conquered by 'aliens' possessing a more advanced technology—the Spanish forces of Pizarro and Cortez," Ray explained. "How much less prepared are we, then, to repel an invasion originating from another star system, another galaxy?"

"We don't know that they'd be hostile, do we?" asked Mary.

Ray smiled grimly. "As the Incas and the Aztecs found out, what you don't know *can* kill you," Ray said. "Death is the universe's answer to ignorance—it is *not* a survival factor."

There was a long silence. Then Jenna Evans laughed nervously. "You folks really had me going there for a moment," she confessed. "You're all just kidding." When no one replied, she insisted, a pleading note in her voice, "You're joking . . . aren't you?"

II

Mary Elizabeth Brennan Hollister-Larkin was disgusted at the interior of the self-propelled hover van that served as both a mobile lab and as their living quarters. It was a mess. Not a filthy mess, but the sort of disarray that any working area falls into when more concern is expressed for the work being done than for appearances. The place hadn't really had a good cleaning in the more than two months they'd been on the surface of Chiron, and it looked it. At least, it looked bad to Mary; Frodo, sitting patiently on his haunches and watching Mary clean, didn't see what Mary was so upset about.

"This not seem dirty to me," Frodo told her.

"Uh huh," Mary grunted. "I don't accept housecleaning advice from someone whose idea of fun is rolling around in an antelope carcass."

"You do female work real good," said Frodo, meaning it as a compliment—which, in dog terms, it was.

Mary threw him a look. "If either Taylor or Ray had spouted that nonsense, I'd remind him of my black belt before bouncing him off the walls and ceiling. I do most of the cleaning not because it's 'woman's work,' but because the lab is essentially mine and I feel responsible for it."

Mary knew, though, that both Ray and Taylor would complain that putting things in some semblance of order would cause notes and papers, normally right at hand, to lose themselves under miscellaneous headings in the files. Once again she chided herself and her husbands for allowing the papers to mount up by not taking a few minutes each day to read them into the computer's memory where they could be stored as magnetic impulses and not centimeter-thick files. Each time she brought the subject up, they all three agreed that keeping up with things day by day was the only way not to be overwhelmed—and each time they all promptly forgot their vows. *Well,* she told herself, thinking of Ray's and Taylor's reaction to her efforts to get things squared away, *they will just have to scream. But where to start?*

Roughly half the van was lab/work area, with the remaining half devoted to human needs. In the extreme rear of the van was the bathroom with its sonic shower and chemical toilet facilities. Then came the sleeping quarters and a series of tiny closets which were totally inadequate to the needs of three people who still had favorite sweaters and other clothes from their undergraduate days with which they were unwilling to part.

The living room, at least, was fairly spacious. It had a

deeply piled carpet, aborigine sculpture from the colony world of New Australia, and body-heat furniture. Built into the walls were various audiovisual entertainment facilities to cut boredom into manageable slices and to aid in reducing any feeling of being removed from the everyday contact with the rest of humanity. While Mary preferred viewing her collection of romance holotapes, Ray watched over and over again his SF and horror sinnys, and Taylor viewed his assortment of Shakespearean dramas and Busby Berkeley sinny musicals from the mid-twentieth century. All three of them—for reasons they couldn't explain, not even to each other—enjoyed their vast assortment of professional wrestling holos. What added to their sheepish delight in them was the fact that the dogs liked them as well; it always discomforted Mary to have her tastes in entertainment, or anything else for that matter, shared by the scout dogs.

All the reading material, equal to a fair-to-middling public library in a mid-sized city, was in the computer and, via the small stationary communications satellites above the planet, could be exchanged with the other groups busy terraforming other parts of Chiron's gigantic northern continent. They were all omnivorous readers, but their duties on Chiron had, so far, allowed them little time to curl up with their favorite authors. The dogs had their own library of audiotapes, folktales and children's stories, read by various professional actors. Like children, the dogs had four or five stories which they would listen to endlessly without tiring of them.

At the midpoint of the van, situated to serve both working and living quarters, was the small electronic kitchen. They all took turns cooking, but it was agreed that Taylor's and Mary's culinary abilities were better developed than Ray's. As Ray once put it, "The dogs'll eat anything I make—I don't know why you guys are so fastidious."

The front of the van was devoted solely to Mary's scientific instruments and measuring devices. As an anthropologist, Ray felt intimidated by Mary's gear and avoided her work area as much as possible. Taylor, on the other hand, liked to watch Mary work and tried to pick up new skills by doing so. Even so, his chemistry was too poor for him to do much more than operate some of the equipment under Mary's watchful eye.

Mary was nearly done cleaning up when Taylor came in, his

mud-brown hair disheveled by the constantly blowing wind and his lanky frame hunched against the cold of that wind. "Hello, darling. Hello, Frodo."

" 'Lo," said Frodo.

"Welcome home," Mary said and kissed him. "How are the cholos doing?"

"The cholos? Okay, I guess."

"You guess?" Mary was shocked at his nonchalance.

"Well, Godzilla still has that crusty patch of skin on his right side," he said, calling the cholo by the nickname the three of them had given it. Officially, it was known to the Bureau as "XYZZY/Hol-Lar.17." "I have no idea what it is, although it doesn't seem to be spreading."

"Maybe it's a fungus."

"Could be." He shook his head in sudden exasperation. "Damn it, I knew I forgot something—I wanted to get a sample to bring back to the van for analysis."

"No problem, hon. We can do it tomorrow."

"Yeah, tomorrow," he agreed. He rubbed the heels of his palms against the lids of his slightly bloodshot eyes. "Say, how about a drink?"

"What's bothering you?" Mary asked.

"Why do you ask?"

Mary considered, then said, "Well, usually if you want to unwind you smoke a happy stick or pop a 'laxer because Ray's been nagging you about drinking too much. Therefore, if you ask me to fix you a drink, something must be bothering you."

"Jesus, you missed your calling, Sherlock! Maybe you ought to be bossing a squad of robocops."

She tossed her hair back with a snap of her head. "I'm Irish enough but I don't have the right voice."

"Oh, really? Ever heard yourself when you're angry?"

Mary gave him a not-so-soft love tap to his jaw and said, "Somehow I think I'm losing control of this conversation. It seems to me, if I remember correctly, that we were discussing what's bothering you."

He shrugged. "Not really; we hadn't gotten that far yet."

"So—here we are *now*."

Taylor put up his hands. "I surrender, officer. You've got me cornered. So what's bothering me? Nothing . . . and everything. The windy season is approaching. If we don't get to the base of those low rock piles ahead that pass for mountains on this planet on time, there's likely to be a good chance little pieces of this van and its inhabitants will be raining down on the other contract groups for the next three months."

"We'll make it," Mary said. She poured his drink and crossed over to him with it. "I haven't had a totally perfect day either, you know."

His features softened. "I'm sorry. Guess I was so wrapped up in self-pity that I didn't notice."

"That's okay, babe. I enjoy standing over a hot Bunsen burner all day," she said, using the archaic term for the laser torch in hopes of making him laugh.

She succeeded. "So tell me about it," he said with a smile.

"You really want to hear about my day?"

"Hell, no, lady—I'm just making small talk!"

"I ought to kick your butt out of here until you get sick of hanging around your damn cholos." Her eyes blazed in mock fury. "If you only knew how difficult it is to try to do the work of months in just weeks. The tests I'm used to conducting over months are being demanded by the control base before I can even recheck my figures. I wish I knew why we're in such a god-awful hurry!"

Taylor lifted his shoulders as if to say, "Hey—don't look at me, kid, I just got here." When he did speak, he said, "I guess they just want the gee-wave station built as quickly as possible."

Since they'd landed on Chiron, they'd talked often about Khorsegai's theory, pro and con, but lately they'd let the subject drop, given that they had no way of determining its veracity. Yet the continuing pressure from the Bureau to get the work done as quickly as possible kept alive in their minds the possibility of Khorsegai's wild flight of fancy being true.

"Without confirmation one way or another, we've got no alternative but to get Chiron habitable and self-sufficient as quickly as we can."

"Sure, but why?" she persisted.

He leaned over as if to confide in her, whispering in a low voice: "Sorry, Mary—you've only got a B-1 clearance, the Triumvirate won't let me tell you."

"You bastard—think you're smart, don't you?" She took his glass from him and put it down, snuggling into his lap. She brushed his long hair back into place with her slender fingers, finishing the job he had started. He looked at her and smiled through his weariness. She kissed him—softly at first, then long and hard. Their lips parted slowly and he hugged her to him in his long arms. His touch didn't inflame her like Ray's did, but she felt safe in his embrace.

"Ohh-h-h," she moaned, "I like that."

"Me, too. I don't know why I don't do it more often."

"I know," she said, "but I can't tell you."

He pulled back a moment, puzzled, looking her in the eyes. "Why not?"

She smiled slyly, a cat-with-a-bird smile: "You've only got an A-2 clearance, turkey."

Frodo lay down, head on his paws, watching with interest.

★　　★　　★

"What is it, Anson?"

The big dog had just trotted back from his position as point. "Centaurs been here—nosing around, Ray," the dog replied.

Ray then saw the marks left by the hooved feet of the Centaurs. "Yeah, I guess you're right. They're still curious about us. Can't say I blame 'em."

"Hah!" said Beowulf. "Anson is hurried up—"

"Anxious," corrected Ray.

"Yah, anxious, then, to get back to camp today. That why he first to smell Centaurs. Mebbe Anson *anxious* see someone."

"Mebbe Ozma," suggested Littlejohn.

"What you know!" snapped Anson.

"Well, now," Ray said, "I've noticed, too, how you've been sniffing around Ozma a bit more than the other females—you wouldn't be having a little romance, would you, Anson?" Ray knew the scout dogs were not normally monogamous.

"We are almost there," said Anson stonily. The others laughed at his obvious discomfort, but not for long or with any viciousness.

Ray left the dogs to proceed on into camp on their own and headed toward the line of cholos. The cholos never ceased to amaze him, and he often stopped off on his way back to the hover van to watch them methodically eating their way across the continent.

It was rapidly growing dark and Ray nearly stumbled when

he emerged from the heavy grass onto a bare patch of soil. Completely devoid of grass, the area was wide as a country lane and snaked away through the grass. Ray followed the "road" with his eyes, up to the point at which it ended by running right up to a huge "rock" lying across its path. The rock was not really a rock but a cholo. The road through the grass was a result of the cholo's passage just minutes previously.

The cholo's size became readily apparent as Ray approached it from behind. Ray walked forward until the rear of the gray-white mass of the creature's body loomed over him. "Hello, good lookin'," he said as he approached. He had no fear for his life because of his proximity; a cholo couldn't move in any direction but forward and was harmless unless frightened. Even then, Ray knew, he'd have to be standing directly in front of one to be injured by it.

The square, blunt "tail" of the cholo scraped over the bare ground, leaving it moist and slightly steaming in the cool evening air. Since Ray's introduction to the cholos on Armstrong, he never tired of watching their endless mealtime as they ate their way across the windswept plains of Chiron, even though they were no longer a novelty to him.

He walked to the front segment of the cholo and watched it attack the grasses with an insatiable appetite. The cholo's mouth was a gaping hole into which the tall grass disappeared. This cholo, like the others, never stopped eating; cholos possessed no muscles to close their mouths. They were eating machines, pure and simple. Still a collector of ancient SF novels, Ray called the cholos "grass worms" after the fictional sandworms of *Dune*.

Ray lit a happy stick and stared at the creature's featureless visage. The mouth was really all there was to differentiate the cholo's front from its rear. The huge slug was eyeless—Ray's dogs served as all the eyes the cholos needed.

Each dog carried a small transmitter on a collar around its neck. Similarly, each of the cholos had a small receiver implanted in its flesh on both the right and left sides of its body. Slaved to the transmitters, the receivers imparted a brief, sharp stab of pain whenever one of the dogs got within ten meters of one. This made it easy for the cholos to be driven in any direction Ray and the dogs desired. Each of the twenty-five cholos also had a small electronic "eye" in its forehead sending back images to Ray's pocket receiver and to one in the van. By choosing any channel between one and twenty-five, Ray could monitor what any particular cholo was "seeing"—or facing, actually.

Ray coughed and mused that his was not an easy job. He had a hover scooter and nine dogs—one of which was pregnant and due in a month or so. The ten of them were supposed to guard and guide twenty-five cholos. This meant keeping away hide cats and curious Centaurs. The Centaurs seemed content to leave the cholos and dogs alone. For the time being, anyway.

Ray carefully ground out his butt, aware of the danger of a grass fire, and headed back for the van, noting that the air was getting noticeably chiller. Discreet, as always, he rapped sharply on the screen door.

"Yes, who is it?" came Taylor's voice from inside the van.

"Very funny," Ray growled as he came in.

"Hello, Ray," said Mary, getting up from her seat beside Taylor and walking over to greet her second husband. Ray, his eyes still adjusting to the glare of the lights, was vaguely aware of the change Mary had wrought in the van's interior appearance, but devoted his attention, momentarily at least, to the warm young woman who slipped into his arms and welcomed him home with a kiss.

Ray hugged her tighter. "Oh, you're so cold," she laughed.

"Yes," he agreed, "but it's so warm in here." Then his eyes, adjusted now to the light, fell on Taylor's drink. "Ah-ha, back on the old joy juice again, eh?"

"Oh, please don't start," Taylor pleaded. "It's been a long day."

Ray looked mock-hurt. "Hey, what am I, a nag? Look, if I were a nag—which I most wholeheartly assure you I'm not— I'd say alcohol is none too good for your liver, to say nothing of your onions, and that it burns little holes in your brain if you drink too much." He stared hard at Taylor. "I admit, that's a tough one—how could we tell the difference? And your nose grows large and red enough to lead Santa's sleigh, and you fall down a lot. Of course," he reiterated, "I'd only say that if I were nagging you, which, obviously, I'm not."

Taylor, despite himself, laughed. Then he made a minor clapping motion. Ray took a small bow.

"Knock it off, you two clowns," Mary told them. "I'm getting hungry and it's *your* turn to cook, Ray."

"Okay—I guess everyone's forgotten the food poisoning incident, eh?"

"I'll cook," said Taylor.

Ray winked at Mary. "Works every time."

After the meal, Ray leaned back contentedly and said, "Shall I tell you how the dogs and I handled those hide cats again?"

Mary rolled her eyes and said, "No, Ray—four times is plenty. I wouldn't want you to spoil us."

"Wel-l-l," Ray said, slightly disappointed, "okay. But I do have something new to pass along."

"What's that?" asked Taylor.

"Anson caught the scent of some Centaurs just outside the camp."

"Is that a problem?" Mary asked.

"That's hard to say," replied Ray. "So far, this is as close as any of them has ever come. I guess they're just curious about us. After all, we've only been on Chiron for something over two months; we're something new in their experience."

"I hope that's all it is," said Taylor flatly.

Ray arched his eyebrows. "Want to elaborate on that just a bit?" he said.

"Sure," Taylor responded easily. "There are a few dozen other groups on this continent, working the land just like we are, right? Well, some of them have started having more run-ins with the Centaurs than we were told was likely."

"I see," said Ray slowly. "Think it might get serious?"

"You tell us—you're the anthropologist and animal behaviorist. But you and the dogs better be extra careful from now on."

III

The dogs were happy. Littlejohn, Ozma, and the now-pregnant Mama-san had to remain with the cholos to keep watch, but the other six had permission to go hunting on their own. The freedom made them puppies again.

"Hah," said Pandora. "Is fun to chase antelopes once more." The other dogs, moving in a loose pack, agreed.

"Frodo," said Sinbad, "you better stay in rear—you too fat to catch antelopes."

"Yeah," agreed Grendel. "Frodo's belly drag on ground; ha ha!"

While Grendel was laughing, Frodo suddenly leapt at her, knocking her down with a well-placed shoulder block and giving her a nip on the rump as he did so. "Ha, I not too fat to bite *your* ass, Grendel!"

All the other dogs laughed—except Sinbad, who just moved farther away when Frodo turned to stare in his direction.

They continued on their way, telling dirty jokes and boasting who was the most spectacularly endowed when it came to sexual equipment.

"You can talk," said Grendel, "but Littlejohn not little where it counts."

"Ho-o-o," said Beowulf. "Mebbe that's why Ray make Littlejohn stand behind—he too tired carrying great weight around to chase antelopes."

"I bet Littlejohn not too tired to chase Ozma or Mama-san," guffawed Frodo.

Pandora added to Grendel's pique by saying, "Why you think Littlejohn have to *chase* them?"

The snickering had died down by the time Anson, who'd gone on ahead to scout, returned.

"What is it?" asked Beowulf, seeing the joy in Anson's eyes, "hide cats or antelopes?"

"Antelopes. Just over the hill." Panting, his tongue hanging out, Anson caught his breath and continued, "Wind's blowing this way; ought to catch their scent soon as we move closer. 'Bout ten of them."

"Good," rumbled Sinbad. "We take one same way as usual?"

"Why not?" replied Frodo. "It works."

"So, let's go," said Anson, the thrill of the impending chase burning bright in his eyes.

Grendel and Sinbad moved out to the right, to flank the unsuspecting antelope. Pandora and Beowulf took up the left flank, leaving Anson and Frodo to proceed straight ahead. The two dogs in the center waited for the others to take up their positions, then moved ahead slowly. They topped the slight hill, moving toward the antelope through the natural cover of the high grasses. The antelope continued grazing until the two dogs were all but on top of them. Then, suddenly, one of the antelopes raised its head and snorted in alarm. Like a shell-burst, the antelope scattered in every direction, bounding across the plains in great, twisting leaps.

As soon as the antelope broke, Frodo and Anson leapt up in pursuit. Frodo flung a brief burst of words in Anson's direction and the two of them decided on just one of the scattering antelope, ignoring the others. They forced the chosen one in the direction of Grendel and Sinbad on the right. Just as the antelope reached the grass concealing the two, they burst from hiding and charged. Almost flinging itself around in mid-air, the startled antelope changed direction. Now moving at right angles to the hiding place of Pandora and Beowulf, the antelope again was forced to change its line of flight when they burst across its path. All six dogs were now in pursuit, driving the frantic antelope back and forth between them.

In the mad ecstasy of the chase, the dogs were barking furiously, human speech forgotten completely. They were enacting an ancient ritual of pursuit and death that predated even their ancestors' association with the shambling primate that was to become Man.

The terrified antelope would run flat out in what it hoped was the path to safety only to have one of the dogs loom up, teeth bared, forcing it to change direction. Built for speed but not for endurance, the antelope soon began to tire. The dogs closed in. Its tongue lolled grotesquely from the corner of its mouth as it sought some escape from the circle of dogs.

Flanks heaving, the antelope stumbled in fatigue and immediately Pandora leapt on its back. The assault knocked it to the ground and the other dogs were soon tearing and slashing at its throat. It thrashed and kicked in mindless terror as its lifeblood spurted out in pencil-thick streams. The antelope gave one final shudder and its eyes glazed as its life poured out onto the grass and into the ever-thirsty soil.

There was blood everywhere. The dogs were covered by blood and it dripped like scarlet rain droplets from their teeth.

Sinbad raised his muzzle to the sky and, from deep within his throat, issued an ancient howl that was both a cry of triumph and a challenge to whoever might dare dispute his prowess as a hunter. Then he joined the others in tearing the antelope to pieces in an absolutely glorious orgy of mindless, primitive bloodlust.

The fire Ray had built for them blazed high in the dogs' camp near the now-stilled cholos, and Littlejohn, Ozma, and Mama-san listened eagerly while each member of the hunting party gave his or her account of the antelope hunt.

"Yes," Beowulf concluded, "was good hunt."

"Ho," urged Littlejohn, "give us a song, Beowulf."

"Yes, a song," chorused the rest of the dogs.

"What would you have me sing, then?" Beowulf asked.

"A song about us and Ray—about dogs and Man," suggested Mama-san. "I will give birth soon and the little ones will have to learn our ways."

Beowulf thought for a minute, then began to sing, his bass voice filling the stillness of the night air.

> Man serves an unseen God
>   but dogs serve God in Man.
>
> Man from God descended
>   dogs from wolves ascended,
>   both each the other to meet.
>
> Man to dogs gave fire and shelter
>   and food and love uncounted.
>
> Companionship and loyalty gave
>   dogs to Man,
>   Always by his side to stand.
>
> Man and dog, dog and Man,
>   joined together 'til time is done.

When Beowulf had finished, Mama-san said, "Thank you, Beowulf."

Standing in the darkness, meters distant, Ray drew deeply

on his pipe and smiled as he felt tears well up in his eyes. "You big mangy bastards!" he said softly. "I do love you so."

"I guess it's my turn to clean up after meals today," Ray said as he started clearing away the remnants of their breakfast. "Funny, isn't it," he observed while scraping the leftover bits of foods into the disposal hopper, "that the very same stuff that five minutes ago was *food* is now *garbage*. I mean we look at it now as if it's contaminated but it's just leftover food."

"And people still ask if philosophy is dead," deadpanned Mary from the front of the van.

"That's the trouble with this marriage: No one wants to broaden his or her mind by examining everyday things from new perspectives," said Ray with a shake of his head.

Taylor returned from the lavatory just then and said, "Mary—and Ray—I want to talk to you both about this Centaur business."

"What Centaur business is that?" Ray asked suspiciously.

"I was concerned after our recent discussion, so yesterday while you were out with the dogs, I got in touch with a few of the other groups. They indicated that their contacts with the Centaurs are becoming more numerous and more violent."

Ray frowned. "You mean the Centaurs have been attacking some of the other groups?" he asked.

Taylor nodded grimly. "Exactly. Oh, no one's been killed yet, but it looks as if it's only a matter of time if the attacks continue."

"Is it that serious, Taylor?" Mary asked, coming back from the front of the van to the kitchen area.

"Some dogs have been ambushed—and Ben Wing says he lost one of his cholos to a deadfall trap of some sort. I'd call that serious."

"A deadfall trap?" said Mary. "Constructing a trap is a pretty good indication of intelligence."

"Wait a minute, Taylor," said Ray, his forehead creased by the lines of a puzzled frown. "You say you talked to some of the groups yesterday and you're only telling us about it now?"

"Perhaps I should have told you immediately but I decided I wanted to think this over myself first. It means a lot to us, but particularly to Mary and me."

"Taylor!" Mary objected.

"Forgive me, honey, but it's true—you and I put up most of the money that went into the cholos and the van. Ray has much less to lose; ten thousand at most."

"Oh, I see," said Ray in a tone that clearly indicated he didn't.

"We are *married*," Mary snapped, "all three of us." She glared at Taylor. "And if I ever hear such asinine talk from either of you again, I'll—"

"Okay, okay," Taylor agreed in a tired voice.

"Now that that's out in the open," Ray said without visible emotion, "why don't you go on? I want to hear the rest of what you have to say about this matter of the Centaurs."

Taylor nodded gratefully. "We *all* have a lot at stake if the Centaurs decide to get nasty with us. We don't even know how many of them there are. We *do* know how many humans there are on Chiron: a grand total of one hundred and thirty-seven. And we'll be at that strength until the Federation sends in the construction crews . . . and the soldiers to guard them."

"And Vaslev's group, the group nearest to us, is over three hundred and fifty kilometers away," murmured Mary.

"It's a damn big continent."

"What's your point?" pressed Ray.

"Do you know how I've been driving the cholos?"

"Sure—I've got eyes; normally in a line about one to two kilometers wide."

"That's correct," Taylor said. "Obviously, this is not nearly compact enough for them to scour each and every square meter of vegetation, but that's not necessary—given a toehold, our tough Terran grasses spread out slowly from the cholos' original paths and displace the weaker native grasses."

Ray, his sense of humor returning, said, "Thank you, Melvin Nhroma."

Taylor waved a hand at Ray. "So I'm lecturing; this is important. Now, for the time being, I see no reason to change this pattern. But, if we have any run-ins with the Centaurs, I want to move the cholos in closer. They won't be as efficient, but you and the dogs can better guard them."

"I hope so, I really hope so," said Ray.

Taylor was attending to Godzilla, about a kilometer beyond the hover van. "This is going to hurt you more than me," he said to the bulk of the cholo looming over him. He took a can of spray antiseptic and cleaned an area on the surface of the cholo's leathery skin. When he was satisfied it was sterile, he took the immense syringe he'd carried out to the cholo and plunged it deep into the creature's flesh. When it was all the way in, Taylor pressed the plunger and injected the amber liquid that would hopefully correct the cholo's hormonal imbalance. "There, Godzilla, you big sissy. That didn't hurt much, did it?" Taylor looked guiltily around after he'd spoken to the cholo. "I'm starting to talk to you guys too much, I think," Taylor admitted to the mute bulk of the cholo. "I know Ray talks to the dogs, but that's different—they can talk back." He laughed. "I'm doing it again, aren't I?"

He was just putting the syringe back in his case when he saw Anson trotting over to him.

"Hello, there, ah . . ."

"Anson."

"Yes, Anson." Then Taylor asked, "What is it? Ray got a message for me?"

"No, I on way to see Ray when saw you here. Thought I tell you first."

"Tell me what, Anson?"

"Centaurs."

"Centaurs?"

"They been watchin' us'n the cholos for long time," the big dog rumbled.

"Are you sure?" Taylor pressed Anson.

"Yep. They kept back, but we knowed they watchin' us."

"A long time, you say." Taylor knew the dogs had trouble with the concept of time, but they were getting better, and if Anson said it was a long time then at least five or six hours had probably passed. "We've had Centaurs stumble across our path and become curious enough to investigate closer, but never for such a long period of time. Tell me, did *they* know that *you* knew they were watching?"

"Huh? Oh, no, don't think so."

"Okay," Taylor said to Anson, "you'd better get back to your post. I'll see what Ray has to say about this."

★   ★   ★

Ray saw the imminent attack almost by accident. He was routinely scanning down through the channels, monitoring the cholos, when a blur of motion caught his eye. Ray flicked back up to the channel, not really expecting to see anything more threatening than blowing grass. Instead, the small screen on his viewer revealed four or five of the Centaurs slowly approaching number eight, the cholo Taylor had named Quasimodo.

"Sonofabitch!" Ray swore. "Beowulf! Anson!" he shouted. "Get your asses over to Quasimodo as fast as you can!" Ray leapt back on his hover scooter and followed the dogs.

The interval between Ray's discovery of the attack and the arrival of the first of the dogs allowed the Centaurs enough time to seal the fate of the unsuspecting cholo. Its body quickly came to resemble a pincushion as it was filled with short spears. Reacting to pain unlike any it had ever before felt, the cholo shuddered and tried to escape by the only means open to it—it charged forward.

One of the Centaurs, caught unaware by the beast's sudden and unexpected spurt of speed, tried to get out of its path. It was too late. The huge creature lunged forward in fear and pain, knocking the Centaur off its feet. Screaming, the Centaur tried to regain its feet, but before it could, the entire front segment of the cholo came down on it like a dark shadow and cut off its screams abruptly.

As Ray topped a small hillock, he saw the dogs arrive at the scene of the attack. The Centaurs formed a crude circle, facing outward and assuming a defensive position. The dogs, shouting comments back and forth between each other, darted in and out at the Centaura, snapping and barking furiously. Well versed in combat strategy, the dogs easily avoided the Centaurs' short spear thrusts. Ray quickly got out his camera—he wanted to take some holos.

One of the Centaurs—probably the leader, Ray surmised—made a motion and the small band of attackers wheeled and galloped across the plains. Ray arrived at the scene and ordered the dogs not to give chase.

"Why not?" asked Beowulf. "They 'tacked a cholo!"

"I want to know what we're up against, first," Ray explained. Then he spoke into his communicator. "Taylor, Mary—home in on my signal and bring the van up. Quasimodo's been killed and I need help moving his body."

"Why do we need to move his body?" asked Mary's voice.

"Because there's a dead Centaur underneath."

"Christ almighty!" swore Taylor as he stared at the mutilated body of the dead cholo Ray and Beowulf showed him. The cholo, stuck full of sharpened sticks or spears of some sort, looked like a great mass of white dough that had settled and spread out under the influence of gravity. "I guess there's no mistaking what killed it," Taylor said, pointing at the spears.

"It was the Centaurs all right," agreed Ray. "The dogs and I witnessed the attack."

He looked at Beowulf and the big dog lowered his head in shame. "We got here too late to save Quasimodo, Ray—sorry."

Ray waved his apology off. "It's not your fault, Beowulf. You dogs can't be everywhere at once. Besides," he added, examining the grass flattened by the imprint of many hooves, "it looks as if the Centaurs planned this attack in advance, made their move, and got away quickly. There was nothing you could do."

Beowulf just nodded, thankful that Ray understood. Not only was Ray the Man, but he was also fair.

"I suppose you recorded the attack via the visual sensor in the cholo's forehead?" Ray asked Taylor as Mary climbed out of the hover van to join them. Taylor nodded.

Looking at the dead Quasimodo, Mary said, "I guess it was just our turn." She looked at the spears sticking from the dead cholo's now-stilled body. "Unintelligent, my ass!"

"Hey, language!" said Ray, forcing a smile and pointing at the dogs. "Little pitchers and all that."

Mary laughed, then said, "Well, let's get moving. I want to start the autopsy as soon as possible."

PART TWO

Runner-with-the-Wind

5

Mary covered her work surfaces with plastic sheeting, set up and focused extra lights, got out her instruments, adjusted the recording devices, and said, "Okay, let's start."

Ray and Taylor carefully laid the body of the Centaur on the dissection table and stepped back. "I'm sorry to disappoint you two, but you're going to have to assist me," she told them. Reluctantly, they rejoined her.

"I'm recording everything we say, so be careful," Mary warned. "This dissection is for the official records."

"Okay, we got you," Taylor acknowledged.

"Yeah," added Ray.

"We've made holochip recordings outside," Mary began for the benefit of the recording's eventual viewers, "of the Centaur's external appearance, but I'll run down the physical description once again." She coughed. "As you can see, these creatures are a curious mixture of hooved mammalian and reptilian forms of life. We'll probably find that they bear their young alive from an internal womb like Terran mammals. I say that because, as you see"—here Mary reached down between the Centaur's legs and spread them to reveal a penis—"this male has all the equipment to deposit his fertilizing sperm in a vagina. One of the other teams reports seeing youngsters being fed from teats located on the underside of the females' bodies—just where they're located on a horse or a cow."

"Ugly SOBs, aren't they?" Taylor said.

"They might say the same of you if they could speak," said Ray.

"*Please*," said Mary, gesturing at the recording devices. The creature's head was tucked into its chest and Mary carefully grasped it and pulled it out, arranging it for the benefit of the cameras. "Their hairless skull is remarkably humanoid and, as anyone can clearly see, they possess two ears, a nose of sorts, and a mouth with . . ." Mary pried open the mouth. ". . . with the sort of teeth one might find in any omnivorous lifeform, including human beings.

"The rest of their humanoid upper torso appears to be little more than an enlarged, heavily muscled neck. I doubt that there's room in there for their lungs, heart, and digestive organs. Those are probably in the 'horse' part of their bodies. We'll find out for sure when we go inside."

Straightening the Centaur's ears until they were fully erect, Mary said, "Their ears don't appear to be particularly large, but they're slightly pointed and I would guess that they rotate to catch and focus sounds." After pulling the corpse's eyelids back, revealing its large eyes, Mary paused, looking intently down at the dead Centaur's "face."

Seeing her hesitate, Ray joined Mary in contemplating the creature's all-too-human visage. *Well, that's not it*, Ray mused. *It's not that this thing looks human, really, so much as it looks . . . what? Intelligent. With those damned eyes open, it looks too damned intelligent.*

"The 'man' part of their anatomy seems to be covered by a tough, reptilianlike hide," Mary continued. She ran her hands over the dead Centaur's greenish-yellow skin for the sake of the devices recording the dissection. "I can report that it doesn't feel at all scaly or anything like that, merely leathery."

Ray, feeling the Centaur's rough skin, agreed and said, "It feels like it's good protection against the elements." Then, as he ran his hand over the Centaur's flank, his fingers felt something. "What's this?" he said.

"What's what?" asked Taylor.

"I felt something . . . something rough and raised up," Ray said, bending down for a closer look. His eyes widened. "Jeez, look at this!"

"What do you see?" asked Mary. "What is it?"

"Scars," said Ray simply.

"Scars?" a puzzled Taylor repeated.

"Not just scars—*decorative* scars," Ray explained, the anthropologist in him coming out. "The sort primitive people give themselves to confer status or rank. This fellow's probably wearing the self-inflicted scars of a mighty warrior or a great hunter." Glaring involuntarily at the unblinking lens of one of the recording devices, he said softly, "Animals don't do this to themselves."

"Well," said Mary as she readied the laser scalpel, "it's time to open him up."

They sat around the fire Ray built just a few meters from the van, each lost in his own thoughts as dusk began giving way to night. Looking like three people who'd just gotten bad news, they were a picture of passivity. Ray sipped a bourbon and water, his first in nearly a year. Both Mary and Taylor had watched him go to their small bar and pour out the drink, but neither had said a word at the time.

Mary, still wearing the smock she'd put on for the dissection, finally broke the silence that had fallen over them. "They're intelligent," she said. "They're intelligent and the Bureau either knows it or suspects it."

"We don't know that for sure," said Taylor. "Maybe the Bureau doesn't really understand the situation. I think that's why the Bureau says they're just animals."

"Oh, yes—'the Bureau says.' . . . Heaven knows, the precious Bureau would *never* promulgate an untruth!" Mary laughed mirthlessly. "Well, since Taylor's brought up the Bureau, let me think out loud, rather like Vaslev did." She paused a moment, searching for the best way to proceed. "You both know as well as I do that intelligent alien lifeforms whose technology is inferior to our own are protected by the Planetary Colonization Code."

"Yeah, so?" said Taylor.

"So," said Mary, drawing out the word and giving Taylor a hard look, "the Code mentions only *officially* recognized intelligent lifeforms. The Centaurs have *not* been officially recognized as intelligent and, if all the terraforming teams keep their distance and ignore any evidence to the contrary, there is no reason why they should ever be."

"You mean . . . ?" began Ray.

"Yes," Mary continued. "For whatever reason, maybe even the one proposed by Vaslev, the Triumvirate has deemed the completion of these gee-wave stations so important that they're going to conveniently overlook one of the prime directives of the Code."

"I must admit," conceded Taylor reluctantly, "that would explain how and why the Judge Advocate could allow this project to go forward when it clearly—if *unofficially*—contravenes the laws of the Federation."

Ray and Mary digested Taylor's admission. The Judge Advocate, the powerful world-wide computer that oversaw the day-to-day functioning of the Federation, functioned as an incorruptible administrator of the legal system and was designed to stop any obvious illegality. It was splitting hairs, as Mary suggested, but as long as the Centaurs weren't officially labeled as intelligent, and the Judge Advocate's office had no evidence to the contrary, the computer and the pseudo-priesthood of Programmers who tended to the giant machine might be content to not examine the situation too closely.

"Damn it," whistled Ray. "I think we're about to learn what it's like to be between a rock and a hard place."

"Yes, the dissection proved what we've known all along," Mary explained to Taylor. "The Centaurs are carnivores—they're predators who hunt and kill their food. It's likely that they subsist mainly on the antelopelike creatures we've seen roaming the plains."

Taylor nodded. "Sure, that much seems obvious."

"Then, if they're intelligent, we're in a hell of a fix. In a very vulnerable position, to paraphrase Ray," Mary said.

"How so?" queried Taylor.

"Since the Centaurs are not unintelligent, they'll soon understand what the cholos are doing to the grass that the antelope herds eat," Mary explained. "It won't take them long to see that the antelope can't eat the Terran grasses we're sowing in place of the original native grass."

"Yeah, and?" challenged Taylor.

"Jee-zuss!" exploded Ray. "Are you *trying* to be particularly dense today or what?"

While Taylor colored, Mary said, "If someone was destroying your source of food, you'd do everything in your power to stop him. You'd kill to protect your life and the lives of your family." Mary looked down at the fire, then up again, and continued, "How many thousands of Centaurs must there be in our sector alone?"

Ray pulled out the holos he took of the retreating Centaurs, choosing the one where he'd zoomed in on the Centaur leader looking back over his shoulder at Ray and the dogs. He grimaced and then put the pictures away. Even so, in his mind's eye, Ray could still see the creature's bold, challenging look directly into the camera that had captured its image and he suddenly knew—he *knew*—that what he had seen burning in the Centaur's eyes was more than the spark of intelligence. It was determination . . . and hatred.

As the hot sun glared down, Ray climbed a small hillock and stared down at the sight unfolding before him. To his right was the hover van and directly in front of it, by about two or three hundred meters, were the cholos. They stretched across the prairie in an uneven line, eating the gently flowing grasses as they progressed. If Ray turned back to look in the direction they'd come from, he could still see the body of the dead cholo, lying where the Centaurs had killed it.

" 'Lo, Ray." Ray turned to see Littlejohn looking at him.

"Oh, hello, Littlejohn. What are you doing up here?"

"Just wanna see if'n you want anything," the big dog answered gravely.

"Thanks, but I'm okay—no, wait," Ray said as he changed his mind. "Mosey on over to Beowulf and Grendel's point and see what's happening. I doubt the Centaurs are done with us and I don't know what we'll do if a large party of them attacks us. So, what good it'll do us I don't know, but you'd better see if Beowulf and Grendel have seen anything."

"Right, Ray," the dog said as he ambled away.

Ray checked his energy rifle's charge.

★   ★   ★

"Cold, hunh?" Grendel asked Beowulf as they continued their routine patrol of the area around the cholos.

"Yah, but spring coming."

"So are big winds, Ray say," Grendel reminded him.

"And they not make our job any easier," Beowulf acknowledged.

Grendel looked down the line of cholos. "Littlejohn coming," she announced.

"What is it?" Beowulf asked when Littlejohn reached their position.

"Nothin' much. Ray sent me to see what happening here," Littlejohn informed them.

"It's quiet," replied Grendel. "For you?"

"Same," said Littlejohn.

"I'm worried," Beowulf said.

"Oh, why?" inquired Littlejohn.

"Centaurs be back for sure," Beowulf said with a shake of his great shaggy head. "And there not 'nuff of us if bunches of them attack us."

"Funny," marveled Littlejohn. "That what Ray said, too."

"I smell them, too," said Littlejohn as Mama-san trotted over with a warning. "Something up. Better warn Ray."

Mama-san had not gone ten paces before she heard Littlejohn cry, "Fire!" She turned to see a wall of flame rushing down on them like a tidal wave.

The dogs leapt into action immediately. The cholos had to be turned or they would head right into the path of the fire, sensing the heat only when it was too late to escape.

The other dogs, posted at irregular intervals around the line of cholos, were reacting too. Dashing in close to the still blindly eating cholos, they started the great beasts turning back away from the fire. To the dogs, it appeared as if it would be a very close thing.

In the hover van, Taylor was the first to notice the fire's approach. "Son of a bitch! I'd better get this van turned and moving," he explained to Mary as he slipped into the control couch. "The dogs will start turning the cholos on their own and Ray has the hover scooter."

"All right," said Mary. "I'll batten down any loose material I can."

"Damn it!" Ray shouted into the wind as he stood between the cholos and the van and watched the fire sweep closer to the beasts.

He climbed onto his scooter and dashed about, shouting orders at the dogs, trying, futilely, to *will* the fire to halt its all-too-rapid progress toward them.

There was just enough smoke to obscure visibility beyond forty or fifty meters. Ray failed, in the confusion, to consciously note the distant figures moving through the smoke like shapes flowing across a dreamscape.

Aware now that something was wrong, the cholos felt the first tentative touch of heat from the advancing flames and started to move faster and faster. They were no longer eating—a remarkable turn of events under normal circumstances. Instead they were moving away from a danger they as yet could only recognize as something to be feared.

Suddenly, a great jagged streak of lightning tore across the darkening sky, followed immediately by a hollow clap of thunder. The wind began to rise. Then the wind turned back on itself momentarily and, for an instant, the tidal wave of flame was checked as if by an invisible dam. Then the dam was breached in several places as the revived wind sucked parts of the fire up and literally hurled them forward among the virgin grasses ahead of it. For the first time Ray understood the term "holocaust."

One of the slower-moving cholos was overtaken and enveloped by a sheet of flame. Ray heard an incredibly deep rumble of sheer terror and pain explode from the trapped cholo—the first sound he'd ever heard one of the great eating machines utter. But he had no time to consider the novelty of the event as the doomed cholo's pulpy, corpse-flesh body sizzled and popped like that of a fat and juicy caterpillar in a campfire. The unlucky cholo writhed in an unbelievably violent spasm of death.

"Oh, sweet Jesus!" Ray moaned, turning away from the horror of the sight. A smell of burnt flesh, bearing an uncanny resemblance to charred rubber, reached him as he turned his scooter and joined the other cholos in their mad retreat from the onslaught of the flames. He gagged, but willed the rising bile back down his throat and kept driving.

Ray sensed the dogs all around him now. The cholos, in full flight, needed no more urging from their canine drivers to run from the fury of the fire.

"C'mon, Ray," Beowulf shouted at him.

"I'm coming, but I want to stay as close as possible to the cholos. But you fellows are faster than the cholos—get ahead where it's safe."

"Okay, Ray. G'luck!"

Their backs rippling, the cholos raced across the plain. The dogs had pinched them in toward a common center and occasionally they would collide and rebound from each other as they ran before the hot breath of the death-carrying wind.

Small animals and an occasional antelope or hide cat could be seen among the cholos and dogs. No species paid any attention to any other; the fire was a common enemy to all.

Ray saw the van disappear into the ravine and waited for it to climb out the other side. When it did not reappear, he panicked for an instant, imagining that the van had become stuck at the bottom. Then he hit upon Mary and Taylor's probable plan—to remain at the bottom of the ravine—and approved its boldness and optimism.

He refused to look back—all he could hear, even above the roaring of the fire, were the death screams of cholos caught by the flames.

Suddenly, Ray was at the ravine. He bounced roughly over the lip and guided the scooter down the steep side of the wall in a sort of controlled skid. He hit the bottom and almost lost it, but managed to keep the scooter upright by sheer muscle.

Ray intended to linger in the ravine no longer than it took for him to be sure that both Mary and Taylor were uninjured. He passed slowly in front of the windscreen, waving like mad when the two faces from inside pressed up against it. Then the scooter lurched as he applied power, and it was climbing the other side of the ravine—a wall not nearly as steep as the first. Still, something about the van's position gnawed at him—what was it? The cholos . . . !

Ray turned just in time to see one of the cholos hesitate at the lip of the ravine, then press forward as a tongue of flame licked hungrily at it. It tried to pick its way down but quickly lost traction on the loose soil of the steep slope and skidded sideways. The cholo hit a small outcropping of rocks, flipped, and began to roll madly. It careened onto the ravine's floor and smashed into the rear of the van with tremendous force. The cholo's impact slewed the rear of the van drunkenly around, the vehicle striking the opposite wall of the ravine and over-turning—shearing off all the communication antennae in the process.

There was nothing Ray could do at the moment. Other cholos were braving the ravine at various points along its length, and the fire was right behind them. He *had* to get away, praying that Taylor and Mary had survived the awful collision.

In seconds the flames had reached the ravine and leapt across it, borne by the gusting wind. Ray and the few surviving cholos ran before it as they had done earlier.

Again and again lightning crackled across the darkening sky. The wind began to act erratically; now driving the flames forward, now pushing them back onto themselves.

Heavy drops of water, each the size of a small stone, fell from the sky. The rain began to fall faster and the wind now shifted, blowing the fire back toward the devastated plains it had just swept bare of all life. A victim of its own earlier voracious appetite, the fire now had nothing to sustain it and began to collapse inward on itself.

Ray looked about for the dogs. He could see only one or two. The others, he assumed, were probably trying to run down and halt the still fleeing cholos that had survived the holocaust.

He was turning the scooter to head back toward the ravine when he heard the sound of hooves.

Anson saw the Centaurs rushing in on Ray and reacted instantly. Even as he bounded across the charred prairie, he saw a bololike throwing weapon knock Ray from the hover scooter. The sight infuriated him. He now gave no thought to his own safety: A *Man*—Ray—had been attacked!

Anson's attack was so swift, so silent, that they did not hear his approach at all. He was in the air, fangs bared, when the Centaur he'd chosen for his first victim turned toward him. It was a fatal move, for it presented Anson with a clean shot at his slender throat.

Screaming a battle cry only at the last instant, Anson felt his teeth tear deeply into the Centaur's throat. Blood, the hallmark of success to an attacking scout dog, filled his mouth and gushed between his teeth to spill down the Centaur's body.

Knowing that the wound he'd inflicted was fatal, Anson loosened his grip on the Centaur's throat and attacked another one of the damned six-limbed creatures. By this time, the others in the group had recovered sufficiently enough to realize death was in their midst. Anson no sooner had his fangs in his second victim's throat than he felt the first spear enter his back. Its only effect was to make him bite down harder, the better to force the life out of this monstrous creature that dared to try to harm his master. More spears pierced his body and he felt his jaws release the almost-dead Centaur's throat.

"I HAVE OBEYED THE LAW!" Anson screamed as the leader of the Centaurs drove his spear through his heart, killing him as he lay bleeding on the ground.

II

"Here is Anson, Taylor," said Littlejohn. Taylor looked at the pitiful sight of Anson's body, pierced by a dozen short spears. Nearby lay Ray's hover scooter, turned over on its side with Ray's energy rifle under it.

"Did anyone see what happened to Ray?" Taylor questioned.

"Only Anson," said Frodo, "and he dead."

"But you think Ray's alive?" persisted Taylor.

"Yes," said Frodo.

"Why?"

"His body not here, is it?" snapped Beowulf. Then, a little more reasonably—Taylor, after all, *was* a Man, if not *their* Man—Beowulf said, "All signs point to Centaurs taking Ray prisoner. His scent is here, mixed in with scent of many Centaurs. They took him, all right, Taylor."

"I see. Have you tried following them?"

"Of course," said Frodo. "But they smart animals—took Ray to stream. In water, we lose their scent and Ray's, too."

"Okay," said Taylor. "Sorry to jump at you like that. We've got to find him, but it'll have to wait until we get the van righted."

"We may lose Ray if'n we do that!" protested Littlejohn.

"Well, what do you suggest?"

"Let me, Frodo, and Beowulf keep looking; we find him," Littlejohn said. "And when we do, we come back for you and Mary."

Taylor ran his fingers through his hair. "I guess that makes sense—I don't need all of you to round up the cholos and to help right the van. But stay in touch, okay?"

"Okay, Taylor," said Littlejohn. Then he asked, "Where you two been since the fire?"

"With the van," Taylor explained. "We also had to put a few of the cholos out of their misery. What a hellish day!"

"You right 'bout that," Littlejohn agreed.

Taylor patted the small mound a few last times with his shovel and stepped back from the grave he'd dug for Anson. He felt awkward, as usual, with the dogs and uncertain as how to begin a chore he dreaded.

"I didn't know . . . ah, Anson all that well, only through the work he did on behalf of us all. But based on that alone, I know what a fine and loyal member of our team he was. Anson knew his duty and he did it—even at the terrible cost of his life." Taylor smiled wanly. "Anson is one of Chiron's first colonists; his body will give nourishment to a soil which one day will be growing Terran plants."

Beowulf looked up at Taylor, his expressive dog's face lined with sorrow. "Thank you, Taylor." Then Beowulf, looking uncomfortable, paused before continuing with, "We like to be alone with Anson now, okay?"

"Of course. I understand," Taylor replied immediately. He swung the folding shovel up to his shoulder and turned back to the makeshift camp he and Mary had constructed near the hover van.

The dogs surrounded the small grave and lay down, their heads on their paws, staring silently at Anson's final resting place. They possessed no telepathic powers, unlike the smaller and more independent scout cats that served with special teams, but like all scout dogs they were markedly empathetic to each other's moods and subtle shadings of feeling. Their intelligence was secondary to their emotions. The idea might seem ludicrous, even distasteful, to someone not acquainted with mutated scout dogs, but it was remarkably easy for a sensitive human to love (almost *be in love with*) the dogs he or she worked with.

The pain the dogs were experiencing now over the unexpected loss of Anson was intensified by the fear they felt for the safety of the missing Ray. Terrible as it was, Anson's death was easier to deal with—it had a finality to it. But about Ray they did not know how to feel: Hope seesawed with despair. Plus—although it was in no way deserved—they blamed themselves for the apparent loss of Ray.

Beowulf rose stiff-leggedly to his feet. "Let us recite the Law.

"What is the Law?"

"*To stand by Man's side, as dogs have always stood.*"

"What is the Law?"

"*To place duty above self, honor above life.*"

"What is the Law?"

"*To allow harm to come to no Man, to protect Man and his possessions.*"

"What is the Law?"

"*To stand by Man's side—as dogs will always stand.*"

Beowulf looked mournfully at the other dogs, especially Ozma, and added, "Honor be Anson's, 'cause he 'beyed the Law; shame to us, 'cause we did not."

Then Beowulf raised his muzzle to the brooding sky, the silence almost audible, and voiced a long, drawn-out wolf's howl of sorrow. One by one the others joined him.

The chill wind took up the cry, too.

"Damn it," said Taylor, "I wish I knew Ray was okay!"

"I know, hon, I know," agreed Mary. "It's hard not knowing one way or the other."

"And I feel so guilty too," Taylor admitted. "How could I have been such a jerk to argue with Ray over something so inconsequential as the money we paid out for this heap of junk!" He shook his head. "If anything's happened to him, I'll—"

"Shush," Mary said. "Ray's fine. I know it—I can feel it in my bones."

Just then the wind carried the sound of the dogs howling to them and they looked at each other with a mixture of hope and despair.

III

As Ray slowly regained consciousness, he could feel the strips of leather that bound his arms and held him fast to a thick pole driven into the ground. Without opening his eyes, he balled his fists and then opened his hands, flexing his fingers. The itching, burning sensation that resulted was welcome news indeed; it meant his restraints hadn't fully cut off his circulation. With that worry out of the way, he plumbed his senses for other clues to his condition. From the way his head was throbbing, he knew he'd taken a nasty blow. Of course, that wasn't all conjecture; he could remember one of the Centaurs knocking him unconscious. The rest of him gave off no obvious signals of pain or injury; that didn't necessarily imply that he *wasn't* hurt—he could easily be suffering from shock, which would mask any symptoms. Still, he was willing to believe that he was essentially undamaged.

Ray decided to wait a while yet before opening his eyes. There was much he could learn just by listening to the sounds and noises around him, and no one had been watching him closely enough to observe him flexing his fingers or wiggling his toes inside his boots. What Ray learned almost immediately was that the Centaurs possessed a language—that they were anything but dumb animals. *That's dumb, as in deaf and dumb*, he told himself.

The Centaur voices he heard were high-pitched and squeaky; the males (or so he presumed) had slightly deeper voices, but they were still much higher than any human voice. As Ray's trained ear followed the many exchanges he overheard, he quickly got a sense of the rhythm of the Centaur tongue and developed an appreciation for its seeming complexity.

Ray was so engrossed in his blind research that he failed to immediately notice someone slowly moving closer and closer to his position. All at once, Ray sensed a presence just a few meters away; sensed it as well as smelled it—the Centaurs gave off a sweet, porcine scent that was strong yet not unpleasant.

As slowly and imperceptibly as he could, Ray opened his eyes. A tiny version of a Centaur—a small child, obviously— was staring in wonderment and awe at his face. Aware that Ray was looking at him, the small Centaur stood petrified.

"Hello," said Ray.

"Wa-a-a-a-a . . . !"

Runner-with-the-Wind, the leader of the tribe, had been summoned when the two-legged one had awakened. As he approached the place where the prisoner was bound, he saw immediately how the strange being had become the center of attention. The females kept their distance, but the children, especially those boys who would soon take the tests of manhood, carefully edged in closer and closer, dares and taunts from their friends forcing them beyond the closest point they might otherwise have chosen to venture.

The deformed one—as Runner-with-the-Wind thought of the prisoner—bearing hair on its skull and under its nose while lacking even a rudimentary tail, soon lost most of its curiosity value for the younger children, however. Even the toddler who'd confronted the monster face to face drifted away once he'd regained his composure. As for the warriors, Runner and the others kept their backs to the thing—indicating how little it meant to them as experienced and blooded warriors of the tribe.

"It speaks, Saminav," said his youngest wife, Sunchaser, to him.

"The *gnur* growl and roar," Runner replied. "That does not mean they speak."

"That is true, Saminav," said Sunchaser, averting her eyes, for she was about to contradict her husband, "but I think this strange one forms real words."

"Then I give it into your hands," said Runner. "Teach it what you can so that you might learn from it what you can."

Ray had been unsure what would happen to him, if anything, after his confrontation with the small Centaur. Fortunately, the males, the "warriors" of the tribe, had immediately seen that no harm had been done and quickly lost interest in him once they had determined that he was still securely bound.

After the warriors and the children had turned their backs on him, he was approached by a Centaur who was bigger than the young ones but smaller than the warriors; Ray guessed that it must be a she, a female. She kept returning to stare at him for what seemed like hours, her large brown eyes taking in every aspect of his persona.

At the midpoint of the second day of his captivity, and after some hesitation, the young female resolutely approached him, cut his bonds, and "introduced" herself. Pointing at herself she said, "Sunchaser" (well, she really said something else, something high-pitched and squeaky, but Ray soon put the two parts of her name together to come up with the correct translation). Ray, fighting the urge to say, "You Sunchaser, Me Tarzan," simply nodded—that seemed to mean the same thing here as it did on Terra—and said, "Ray," as he pointed at his own chest.

Sunchaser soon learned what Ray already guessed, having watched the dogs eat—that he could safely drink the water (called *bor*) and eat cooked antelope flesh (*leapers*, the Centaurs called them). Ray was glad he'd received the seemingly endless succession of vaccines and other injections before leaving Terra.

Looking at Sunchaser, Ray could not help but think how unattractive the Centaurs were, at least given the species-specific ideas of physical beauty imprinted in his brain. But, to another Centaur, she was probably *very* becoming. Her brown eyes were large and luminous, their size further accentuated by her small, flat nose. Ray noted that, unlike the male they'd dissected, her ears were cropped; probably a custom of this tribe, or, more logically, an indicator of her sex or her status as the "property" of her husband.

Sunchaser's neck was slender, as were her arms, and Ray could not help but think of a cobra with its hood extended when he looked at her upper torso. Shaking off that image, Ray noticed that she bore a series of expertly rendered decorative tattoos on her flanks. Again, Ray surmised, the tattoos and the way her tail was braided were probably cultural signals indicating to others her place within the society.

Boy, Ray told himself, *I hope I'm not as strange-looking to her as she is to me*, realizing as quickly as the thought passed through his mind that of course he was.

The next few days passed quickly as Sunchaser's intervention hastened Ray's process of familiarization with the Centaur language. With Sunchaser's help, Ray learned how words were constructed upon other words. *Shar*, for instance, the word for the short, thrusting spears the warriors carried, derived from *sha*, the word for the stone knives that were ubiquitous throughout the camp. Similarly—and revealingly, Ray thought—*sharnan*, which meant "taken by the spear," or booty, also meant wife.

Ray learned that Sunchaser was one of the wives of the chief of this tribe, one of his *sharnan*, captured in a raid, like all the wives were—"taken by the spear." *Marriage by raid is a good way to ensure the vitality of the race by going outside the local gene pool*, Ray thought in admiration.

The chieftain's name was Saminav—or "Runner-with-the-Wind"—and he and the others thought of themselves as "The People." There was nothing unusual in that, Ray reflected, since most Terran primitive peoples also had a name for themselves which meant "Mankind" or "The Human Beings." As a two-legged monster, Ray guessed that he probably didn't qualify as a real person in their eyes, but they were remarkably unhostile toward him. He had been stunned when Sunchaser cut his bonds.

Ray appreciated Sunchaser's lessons more than she might have expected; he knew his survival might depend upon his quickly learning what made the Centaurs tick.

As Sunchaser named common objects, Ray paid close attention, aware that even very fundamental acts of perception are culture-specific. Any intelligent being is conditioned to perceive life with an outlook heavy with cultural and social complexities. He knew that there were many things Sunchaser had been trained to notice, or to discard, or to cry out about. Or, conversely, that there were taboo things she'd learned not to notice or make any mention of.

Ray also discovered that the speech patterns of the Centaurs weren't so far removed from many of the other "primitive" languages he'd studied in school. There *were* differences, of course, but not as many as he might have suspected or feared.

He recalled that Professor Gomez had drilled into his pupils' heads the old proverb that went something like this: HE WHO TRANSLATES BETRAYS. Remembering that, Ray, like all anthropologists, tended less than other students of language to isolate speech from the total life of a people.

Ray could hear old Gomez wheezing, "Language completely interpenetrates direct life experience, helps one to categorize that experience, and becomes an instrument for action based on that categorization."

Okay, what do I have? Ray asked himself. *What does their language tell me about them so far?*

Well, he answered his own question, *they seem to have an almost unlimited number of words to describe the various kinds of grasses which might be encountered in their travels.* For instance: *Mehteve* was "thick grass"; *yoteve* was "tall grass"; *sharteve* was "cutting grass"; and *gnurteve* was "hide cat grass."

Nothing new there, he reminded himself. *If I remember correctly, there are more than six thousand different words for camel, its parts and its equipment, in Arabic.* To Ray, this was simply further proof that the language of a people cannot be isolated from their way of life.

Engrossed in his musings, Ray totally forgot about being "rescued" after his jittery first day as a prisoner had passed and he had plunged into learning the Centaur language. As far as he was concerned, he was in hog heaven. *It won't hurt my reputation to be known as the first anthropologist to really make a detailed study of Mierson's Centaurs, will it?* he told himself gleefully, unaware of the anguish Mary, Taylor, and the dogs were experiencing.

6

"You look better," Taylor said to Mary.

"I feel better today, too," she said. "This bump on my head isn't giving me the usual four-star migraine today."

"That's great," said Taylor. "Now if we can only find Ray . . ."

"The dogs haven't found anything yet?"

"They discovered a Centaur camp thirty kilometers from here but they don't seem to be the Centaurs responsible for all this destruction or for taking Ray," Taylor told her.

"I hate to say this," began Mary, "but it seems like the Centaurs aren't simply intelligent, they're a *lot* smarter than even we suspected. I hold Nhroma and the PCB responsible for Ray's capture. If only they hadn't lied to us about the Centaurs, Ray might be here now."

Trying to be charitable, Taylor said, "Well, maybe they didn't know."

"Or *want* to know," said Mary. "After all, we aren't supposed to study them at all. I always thought that restriction a little peculiar."

"Yeah," agreed Taylor. "I guess Ray's hunch about the Judge Advocate and the Programmers allowing things to go ahead on a technicality is right."

Just then Sinbad trotted up to them and said, "Cholos all back, Taylor."

"Good, thank you, ah, Grendel."

"I Sinbad," the dog said forcefully.

"Sorry about that." Taylor felt stupid, but then the dogs had always been Ray's province. As close as the two of them were before the triple, Taylor had, even then, been remarkably cool to Ray's dogs.

"Do you think this is gonna work?" asked Mary.

"I hope so," confided Taylor. "We need the van if we're to find Ray before . . ." His voice trailed away.

"Before it's too late," finished Mary.

"C'mon, the dogs are waiting for us."

"Well," asked Taylor, "whadda you think?"

"Gosh, it looks so fragile," Mary said, eyeing the immense harness Taylor had designed to be slipped over the front portion of a cholo. "Is it strong enough, do you think?"

"Sure," said Taylor, waving his hand as if to dismiss Mary's concern. "The molecular structure of this fabric is tightly interwoven; it could probably lift a small asteroid without giving way."

When the dogs guided the largest of the surviving cholos to a position in front of the overturned van, Taylor and Mary managed to slip the harness onto the great beast, named Monstro by Ray.

"Okay," said Mary to Beowulf, "do your stuff."

Beowulf and the dogs moved in, their collars transmitting directional signals to Monstro. Slowly, the cholo began to move forward, its mouth working.

"Watch it," cautioned Taylor. "Not too fast."

As the cholo moved away from the van, the cables connecting its harness to the van stretched, then tightened. "Careful, careful," Taylor said. Beowulf looked at Sinbad and made a face. Taylor was the Man now, in Ray's absence, but the dogs didn't much care for his leadership.

When he felt the unyielding pressure of the van holding him back, Monstro slowed, then came to stop. The dogs, barking suggestions back and forth between them, moved as one. "Littlejohn," Beowulf commanded, "you move in a little closer. Grendel, you join Littlejohn, too." The combined urging of Littlejohn's and Grendel's transmitters overcame the cholo's reluctance to move and again it began to creep forward.

"That's it, it's coming!" shouted Mary.

Slowly, the van was pulled upright, again sitting atop its hover engines. "Okay," Taylor yelled at Beowulf, "stop him so we can slip the cables and harness off."

"Thanks, guys," Mary said to the dogs. She turned to Taylor and commented, "As soon as we get the inside straightened up and things back in working order, you can tackle fixing the antennae."

Although things were lying about in total disarray, the indestructibility of modern materials meant that not all that much was broken. Of course, the inside of the hover van looked as if a small tornado had just passed through, but Mary and Taylor had expected worse. "Jesus," said Taylor, picking up a holochip recording lying in the middle of the living area, "it looks just like it does after Ray's lost something and gone looking for it." A split-second after the words left his mouth, Taylor regretted attempting to distract Mary by being funny; not that the effort was misguided, but his choice of subject matter just reminded her of the missing Ray.

"Oh, no," Mary wailed on seeing a five-thousand-credit piece of her equipment smashed to pieces on the van's floor. "I was hoping that soil analyzer had survived the impact, but"— she made a fist and struck her forehead lightly—"I forgot to pack it away before the fire."

"Mary, darling," soothed Taylor, "you could hardly have anticipated the fire or that a cholo was going to roll into the van and knock us over. It's not your fault."

"I know, but I still wish I'd put it away that day."

"Well," Taylor said, "why don't I start working on the communications equipment while you sort your things out here? I've got to raise at least one of the other groups as soon as possible."

"Sure, hon," Mary said. "Go ahead."

Taylor started to walk away, picking his way over the rubble-strewn floor, then stopped and turned around to say, "Mary—it *wasn't* your fault."

"I know, Taylor. Thanks."

★　　★　　★

Ray began to have real conversations with Sunchaser as he attained more and more fluency in the Centaur tongue. As they talked for hour after hour, Ray realized their conversations were a two-way street: She learned nearly as much about him as he was learning about her and her culture. Of course, there were often unbridgeable gaps between their worldviews.

"Why does your arm make noises every once in a while?" Sunchaser asked Ray.

Ray took a long time before responding, trying to come up with a way to explain that his watch was a way of measuring time. His problem was that the Centaur language seemed to have no real word for time—not as Ray and the culture he was from understood it. Finally, he resorted to showing Sunchaser the face of his watch and how it was marked off in twelve equal sections. Then he showed her the hands and how he knew what time it was by their position. While she found all that vaguely interesting, it was clear to Ray that she had no idea at all what he was talking about; nothing he said about the abstract concept "time" meant a thing to her. Still, Ray persevered.

"You see," he began, "when I am with my people, this tells me when I should be doing things."

"What do you mean, 'doing things'?" Sunchaser asked.

"Well, eating," Ray said. "With this I know when to eat."

Sunchaser found this amusing. "Don't two-legged ones eat when they are hungry? When *we* are hungry, we eat," she said proudly.

"Well, sure, we eat when we are hungry, too," Ray said. "That is, we eat three times a day and this tells us the proper time to eat."

"Very strange," Sunchaser murmured. "You say you eat when you are hungry . . . but only if that thing says it is permissible."

Aware that he was getting nowhere fast, Ray tried another approach. "It also tells when it is time to work."

"Work?"

Oops! Ray thought. *That's right—they don't seem to have a word that means the same as our culture's 'work' either*. "Er, 'work' means those times when I do what I must do to earn a living . . . that is, to provide for myself and my partners."

"Do you mean that you would not do those things normally? That if you did not have that thing you would not take care of your *teve* eaters?"

"Well, no, I don't mean that," Ray was forced to admit. In

desperation he said, "My watch helps me place myself in the middle of the unfolding of the universe—the rising and setting of the sun and moons and so on."

"Cannot you see the moons rise with your own eyes?" asked Sunchaser, indicating that she still understood nothing of what he'd said.

Later that day, in the heat of the afternoon, Sunchaser approached Ray and asked, "Is it going on now? That function of the universe which you measure—where is it?"

"I . . . ah . . ." Ray finally realized that there was no way he could explain what his watch did or what it was for. "I guess you're right," Ray admitted. "My watch really does nothing. Its hands move and it makes noise—that is all."

"I thought so," Sunchaser said triumphantly.

"Are all your people deformed?" Sunchaser asked him on the fifth day of his captivity.

"Deformed?"

"You have but two legs," she explained. "When the warriors first saw your camp, they thought that you were the servants of the four-legged leaper killers, not the other way around."

"Oh. Yes, we all have only two legs—a four-legged man would be the 'deformed' one in my land."

Sunchaser marveled at the wonders of a universe where such things could be. "How strange," she said.

"Yes," Ray agreed. Then he added, "Did you speak to Runner about what I told you?"

Sunchaser nodded solemnly. "I did."

"And?"

"My husband says he will not speak with a prisoner."

"But it may be the end of your people if you cannot see that we mean you no harm!"

Young as she was, Sunchaser all but laughed at that remark. "If you mean us no harm, why then do your monsters eat our *teve* and so befoul the land that nothing will grow but some hideous new *teve* that none can eat?"

Boy, she's got me there! Ray thought admiringly. Aloud, he replied, "There is much land here. We only want to share it with you." *Christ, what bullshit! Even I don't believe that anymore.*

Sunchaser's face hardened. "Runner says you cannot share what is not yours."

Having no good answer to that, Ray fell silent.

As dawn rose on the sixth day of Ray's confinement in the Centaur camp, he was aware that something was happening. "What's going on?" he called out to Sunchaser when she passed by without speaking to him.

Sunchaser stopped and returned. "Runner says the scouts believe that the monsters that guard the *teve*-eaters are getting too close to the camp and that we must move farther away. Besides," she added, "it is time to follow the great leaper herds as they move north."

"The leapers?" Ray said, momentarily forgetting the Centaur name for the antelope. "Oh, yes, the leapers. They are on the move?"

Sunchaser made a face that Ray recognized as a sort of amused smile. "You know so little. When the air grows crisp and biting, they follow the sun to the south," she explained. "The promise of spring draws them northwest, and the blessings of long hot days to nurture the *teve* once again lures them onto the vast plains of the north lands. That is why we must now move north with the herds."

"And you do this each year?"

"It is the rhythm of our lives, as compelling and constant as the beating of our hearts." Mischievously, she added, "We need no 'watch' to tell us this."

Ignoring her sarcasm, Ray said, "I see." Assuming that Mary and Taylor were attempting to find and rescue him, he added, "Perhaps if I spoke to Runner, I could convince him that . . ." He stopped when Sunchaser made the gesture that said no and just walked away. *Well, that's that, I guess,* Ray thought. *I'll just have to sit back and observe how this Runner handles his people.*

As Ray watched, devouring all the sights with his hungry eyes, the camp was struck and the meager tools and possessions of the tribe were placed on rude travois to be carried to their next encampment. Leaperstalker, one of Runner's lieutenants, was trying to make himself important as the tribe broke camp. He was dashing about yelling orders, pleading for haste, snapping a length of rawhide at *sharnan* slow to join the ragged line of march.

Ray smiled. *He's not so dumb, this Runner*, he thought. *He's content to allow his seconds-in-command to whip his tribe into line and draw the people's natural resentment down upon them rather than himself.*

Ray watched as an old and wrinkled Centaur ordered a young male to help him drag his travois into line. Earlier, when he had asked Sunchaser about this anomalous figure, for he had seen few other Centaurs as old as this one, she had told him that the ancient one was the tribe's *tanakiv*, their shaman.

Ray noted how Runner scowled at the sight. *That's interesting*, he thought. *Runner does not appear to care much for the tanakiv*. Reflecting on that, Ray guessed that Runner disliked having to share his authority with another, with being forced to have "political" decisions adjudicated by a holy man's reading of the signs to find the will of the gods.

Ray looked on as Runner's eight *sharnan*, fussing with children and with their belongings, jockeyed for position in the procession. Including Sunchaser, Ray knew the names of six of Runner's wives: Peo, Zarav, Kirinav, Nan-ha, and Nami, Runner's senior wife.

When all was ready, when the *sharnan* had sorted themselves in marching order according to their status within the tribe, and when the scouts had taken up their positions, Runner-with-the-Wind took his place at the head of the column and held high his *koro*. Runner's *koro*, Sunchaser had told Ray, was the visible badge of his leadership handed down first from his father to his brother and then from his brother to him.

All the males put their right fists to their foreheads, reaffirming their loyalty to the chieftain. With Ray observing intently, Runner acknowledged their salute by adding his *shar* to his *koro*, then dropping both. The tribe moved out—taking Ray even farther away from Mary, Taylor, and the dogs.

"Go ahead," Beowulf urged Mary, "ask him."

"Ask me what?"

"Beowulf wants me to ask you if you've repaired the communications antennae yet," Mary said. "Have you?"

"Not exactly."

"What does that mean?"

Taylor shrugged. "It means that our uplink to the satellite is gone until I can get some new parts or do a better job of jury-rigging a working system out of what we have. I've got enough power to cover six hundred to a thousand kilometers, however," he said, adding, "That's range enough to contact Vaslev and maybe one or two other groups if necessary."

"Why did you add 'if necessary'?" Mary asked. "Don't you think the situation warrants our calling in assistance?"

"Well, I . . . ah . . ." Taylor sputtered.

Mary put her hand on his shoulder and squeezed. "Don't get nervous—I didn't mean to imply anything terrible on your part," she reassured him. "As odd as it may sound, I don't think now is the time to let any of the other groups know what's happened to us."

Now it was Taylor's turn to be puzzled. "Why not?"

"Look," Mary began, "the only other group we know personally—and we don't really know them all that well, either—is Vaslev, Miya, and Jenna's team." She made a face that Taylor recognized as her I-know-this-may-sound-paranoid-but-trust-me expression. "Since we don't know anyone else, we don't know that there aren't spies or, at least, informants among them."

"Spies?" cried Taylor incredulously. "Spies!"

Mary put her hand to her face and sighed. "Look, this is a very important project—the General himself may be involved. I wouldn't put it past the General or the other members of the Triumvirate to have planted a few folks with big eyes and ears among the other terraformers."

"Jeez, Mary," Taylor said, "don't you think that's more than a little paranoid? Spies?"

"Wanna bet Ray's life that you're right?" Mary asked cynically. "Wanna bet *your* life?"

II

The wind howled constantly and Ray found it difficult to sleep more than ten or fifteen minutes at a time. Again and again he shifted position under the rude leaperskin blanket that was all there was between him and the cool night air. Nervously, he fingered the knife sheath at his belt. At first, he'd been incredulous that Runner would permit him to retain his knife, but then this was a society based on honor—and honor dictated that upon giving his word not to escape a warrior, even a prisoner, was allowed to keep his *sha*.

Ray kept imagining that a hide cat (he *still* couldn't think of them as *gnurs*) was stealthily creeping up on him. *What an active imagination I have*, he thought while reminding himself constantly that Runner, ever alert and fearful of an attack by Ray's tribe, always posted guards. Still . . .

Sometime later, he didn't know when, he heard a noise. Almost afraid to move, Ray slowly twisted his neck until he was looking in the direction from which the noise had come.

"Ga-a-a wha-a-a?" asked a pint-sized Centaur. Ray almost giggled in relief. It was Runner's firstborn son. Ray knew him well enough—the youngster was fascinated by Ray and followed him everywhere.

"Hey, you'd better get back to your hut before your mom misses you, little Runner."

"Ka-a-a . . . ?"

"Sure, you cute little bugger, but I said—" Ray stopped short when he saw the large shape materializing out of the night. It was a hide cat. A big one.

"Beat it, kid," swallowed Ray, pulling his knife and getting up to place himself in front of the youngster. The hide cat snarled and advanced. Ray wondered where the hell all those "alert" guards were. The child panicked and ran toward his hut and the hide cat was instantly attracted by his motion. Ray swore as the cat started toward the youngster.

"Hey! Here!" he shouted at the cat, but to no avail. The hide cat had its mouth set for young Centaur, obviously; it studiously ignored Ray.

"Okay, you bastard!" Ray intercepted the cat's rush and leapt on its back, grabbing onto one ear and locking his legs around the cat's lean body. That caught the cat's attention—especially when he drove his knife into its neck. The cat leaped straight into the air with a snarl and landed hard.

Clinging to the cat's back like his life depended upon it—and it did!—Ray was simultaneously telling himself that not only was he nuts but that also this was no time for false pride: "Help!!" he shouted at the top of his lungs.

Shapes started pouring from the huts, but he had no time to enjoy the results of his cry for help—he was too busy driving his knife home in the cat's neck and hanging on with his other hand. The cat suddenly changed tactics and whirled without warning. Ray found himself flying through the air—minus his knife, which remained embedded in the cat's neck.

This is it, he thought as the cat turned toward him, fangs seemingly growing longer even as he looked at them. The cat bunched to spring but then looked puzzled. It was puzzled by the sudden sprouting of a half-dozen *shars* in its back and sides. It made a weak mewing sound and toppled over onto its side, blood gushing from its multiple wounds.

Ray saw Runner staring down at him, looking concerned. "Thanks," he croaked, then passed out.

★   ★   ★

Since all the dogs but Anson survived the Centaur fire and attack while almost half the cholos were killed, Littlejohn, Frodo, and Beowulf had plenty of time to continue their search for the missing but presumed still living Ray. They had assumed that Ray would be discovered in a matter of a day or two, not counting on the cleverness and the resourcefulness of the Centaurs. Beowulf realized that the Centaurs had expected them to mount a search and had moved their camp far from the original point of capture. This made the dogs' task harder than they'd anticipated.

Harder, but not impossible: In the fifth Centaur encampment they'd examined, they found what they were looking for. "Look," said Beowulf as he joined Frodo and Littlejohn downwind of the camp. When the two did as Beowulf directed, they saw a figure on two legs moving about in the center of the camp.

"That be Ray all right," Littlejohn said. "No Centaur got only two legs, for sure."

"You right," agreed Frodo. "But look—he not seem be tied up or nothin'!"

"H-h-hm," Beowulf reflected, "I guess they think it impossible for Ray to slip away without them seein' him. And Ray not all that fast, he not be able to outrun a Centaur."

"Ha!" joked Littlejohn, relieved that Ray was alive. "He not able to outrun three-legged pig!"

"Think we ought to rush 'em?" asked Frodo.

"Oh, sure—and get Ray killed plenty quick," snapped

Beowulf. "No, you two go back and tell Taylor and Mary we found him; they know what to do."

"And you?"

"I stay and keep watch. Mebbe I can help Ray."

"You've learned our tongue quickly," Runner-with-the-Wind told Ray. The other council members nodded assent.

Ah, yes, Ray told himself, *Runner-with-the-Wind is the only one I need really consider. The others will assuredly follow his lead without question.* Aloud, he said, "I was trained in my . . . my land to learn to do so."

"I see." Runner paused. "I must again thank you for saving my son. You could have been killed; why did you not try to save yourself?"

"I could not allow a child to die when it was in my power to prevent such an occurrence," Ray replied.

"But will not many children die if your monsters strip the land of the *teve* that the leapers feed upon?"

Oh ho, a real GOTCHA, Ray thought admiringly. "Well, yes, if things go on unchecked," he admitted.

"Why then must this happen?" Runner persisted. "Can you not grow this evil *teve* of yours in your own land? Why must you take our land?"

Ray considered how he could possibly explain to Runner about the gee-wave station and what it seemed to mean to the Terran Federation. It seemed an almost insurmountable task. Perhaps he could satisfy Runner's question anther way.

"Our great chieftain, the General, sent us to take over your lands because"—*Oh, boy*, he told himself, *here's where it gets sticky*—"just as you did not at first consider me to be of 'The People,' he did not believe you were of 'The People' either—not as we use the term. You felt as you did because I and my people do not have the same customs as you, and because we are so physically different—I have two legs and you have four. Thus, also did the General reach the same conclusions about you: How could a real person have four legs instead of two? How could such a four-legged creature be anything but a beast—for only beasts have four legs in my land. These are the reasons, poor as they may seem, for acting toward you as we did."

There were murmurs from the other members of the council,

some of them clearly angry, but Runner did not immediately speak. Ray got the impression he was trying to digest what he had heard and make an intelligent and reasoned reply. Ray was beginning to admire this chieftain, this "Runner," more and more.

"Hm-m-m," began Runner finally. "What you have said makes sense. All ways and all bodies are not the same—yet are we not all the children of the Great Spirit? In saving my son you have proved that a man need not possess four legs to be a warrior both brave and true."

One of Runner's lieutenants leaned over and whispered something in Runner's ear. Runner listened, then whispered back. "I must act as the chieftain of my tribe now, two-legged one," he told Ray. "When I have meted out justice, we shall continue our conversation." Ray simply nodded and found a place to sit, trying to make himself as unobtrusive as possible.

Speaking to the assembled warriors, Runner said, "Nav-racer, Bor-run, and Shar-flight were on duty the night the *gnur* invaded our camp." He looked around the hut at the faces of his warriors, gauging their reactions. The three young warriors, Nav-racer especially, were not popular, at least not with the older members of the council, and what Runner saw in the faces turned toward the guilty trio was anger and dismay. *Good*, he thought.

"Nav-racer, Shar-flight, Bor-run: Step forward and receive your punishment," Runner commanded.

Sullen-faced and apparently unrepentant, the three reluctantly stepped before their chieftain. "For your failure to keep the watch as it must be kept, I order that you be stripped of a quarter of your *sharnan* and other possessions. They will be distributed equally among the other warriors of the tribe."

"You have no right to do this!" Nav-racer challenged Runner.

"No right?" Runner retorted. "Ha, you are fortunate no one, including the two-legged one, was harmed or killed. Were that the case, you and your shiftless friends would now be numbered among the Tribeless Ones. Now go. I don't want to see your insolent face again this day!"

"You will regret this, Runner," Nav-racer hissed. Pointing at Ray, Nav-racer said, "He is no warrior of the tribe, Saminav, and to bring him into the council hut is against the ancient prohibitions. I am not alone—others speak of your discarding of the traditions when it suits your purposes. Yes, you *will* regret your actions this day!"

One of Runner's warriors put his hand on his *sha* and stepped forward. "No, leave him," Runner said. "One so arrogant will meet his end soon enough and by his own doing. Then I will make a private song of it, to be sung at special times."

Nav-racer snarled an obscenity, whirled, and strode from the council hut.

"I fear Nav-racer spoke truly—you will come to regret your decision not to banish him and his friends," said a council member.

"Perhaps you are right," said Runner, staring at the aged *tanakiv*—who quickly looked away—"but the signs counseled against harsher action. Let us hope the gods are not playing with us."

Remembering he had a guest, Runner turned back to Ray. "Did you understand what just happened, two-legged one?"

"Most of it, I think," Ray replied. "I'm sorry to be the cause of so much trouble."

"Fear not," Runner replied. "If it were not you, Nav-racer would find another bone of contention with me and my leadership of the tribe." He put one of his thin-fingered hands to his face and rubbed it in a way Ray found strikingly humanlike.

"What are you thinking, my chieftain?" ventured the *tanakiv*.

"I am thinking that Nav-racer was right—about one thing, at least." He looked at Ray. "You have already demonstrated your courage, two-legged one, but are you willing to take the test of manhood? If you were to be made a warrior of our tribe, then Nav-racer would have one less thing to hold against you and your presence in our midst. And your words would carry more weight with the council."

"A warrior?" asked Ray, scratching his head. "Sure, why not? Tell me what I must do, Runner."

With the females banished from the ceremony, the warriors of the tribe gathered around the fire to sing one of several *gnur*-hunt songs that were traditionally sung before a young male embarked upon his test of manhood. The others were already in place when Ray joined them by folding his legs and sitting cross-legged on the ground in front of the fire and beside the *tanakiv*. Ray smiled as he noticed the way everyone intently observed the way he sat down—the Centaurs' anatomy called for a rather more complicated procedure of seating themselves, folding first this leg and then that one and so forth.

"To prepare you for your ordeal, Ray," Runner explained, "the warriors will sing a song of the killing of the *gnur*. I will sing the first phrase and then everyone will join in on the next." He looked at Ray as if evaluating his worth as a person and a warrior. "Do you understand?"

"I believe so, Saminav," Ray replied. "But tell me—am *I* allowed to join in the singing?"

Runner appeared nonplussed by Ray's request. "Why, yes, but surely you will have difficulty following the song."

"Perhaps," Ray said, "but perhaps not. I'd like to try if it's all right."

"As you wish."

Then Runner began to sing. Ray marveled at his high, pure voice. The warriors then joined in the singing and Ray attempted to jump in as well. *One thing is certain*, Ray thought. *I'm never gonna be able to sing as high as these guys.* I'll try it an octave lower.

When Ray joined the singing of the song, Runner got the oddest look on his face, a look Ray was, at this early juncture, unable to decipher. As soon as Runner's face took on this new and puzzling expression, the *tanakiv* began to make that choking, snorting noise that indicated he was laughing. It went on like that for the duration of the song: Ray following the lead of Runner and the other warriors, and the *tanakiv* beside himself with laughter.

When the song ended, Ray asked Runner what was wrong. Runner was evasive and unwilling to respond; not so the *tanakiv*. "I will tell you a story, two-legged one," the *tanakiv* said. "Once upon a time Runner's father, when he was the chieftain of the tribe, went hunting for leaper with the chieftain of another tribe. After a long and hard trek, they came upon several good-sized leapers and the other chieftain felled the largest of them with his *shar*. But hardly was the leaper dead before Runner's father rushed up to the fallen animal and began to kick it in the nose as hard as he could." His ancient face creased by a Centaur smile, the *tanakiv* continued. "So the other chief runs up to Runner's father and says, 'O great chief, why did you do that?' "

At that, the assembled warriors erupted into gales of laughter. *I guess that was the punch line*, Ray told himself, *but I'm damned if I know what the joke is!* Aloud, he said to the *tanakiv*, "I don't think I understand the point of the story."

"You don't?" said the *tankiv* to yet more laughter. "Well, you see, the chieftain was from another tribe—one that didn't know anything about eating leaper nose. He didn't understand that what Runner's father was doing was tenderizing the nose, softening it up by kicking it while it was still full of blood. But he was an outsider and didn't know that. So he asked why are you doing *that*?" Again more laughter; this time even Runner joined in.

Ray was lost. "Are you telling me this story because the other chieftain was an outsider and *I'm* an outsider, too?"

"Yes," admitted the *tanakiv*.

"It's my singing," said Ray. "Something is wrong with my singing—is that it?"

The *tanakiv* agreed that Ray was right as Runner and the others could no longer contain themselves and all but collapsed in laughter. Ray just sighed and inwardly observed, *There's something much deeper going on here with my singing than I can hope to understand*. He pursed his lips and began to appreciate anew the enormity of trying to understand another culture from the outside.

It was hot. The sun beat down mercilessly and distant features, like bluffs and low, stubby bushes, shimmered in the heavy waves of heat that curled skyward. Insects hopped, crawled, and flittered aimlessly through the grass and across the sun-baked soil, some attaching themselves to Ray's clothing for a free ride, while others were determined to taste his alien blood.

The grass rippled as a lazy wind drifted desultorily over the tops of the blades. It was fairly tall grass: *gnurteve*. The tubular blades reached nearly to Ray's shoulders and he moved through it as if he were fording a stream, his *shar* carried at chest level.

He had lost weight during his captivity and his clothes hung limply from his gaunt frame except for those places where they were plastered to his skin by a sticky, nervous sweat. He had reason to be nervous, he reflected—hide cats generally weighed one hundred to one hundred and twenty-five kilos, and he had to kill one with just his *shar* and a knife.

Ray swatted an insect that was trying to dine on his neck and recalled a more than slightly troubling conversation he'd had with Sunchaser at dawn of this very day.

"Here, WWhey," she said, still having trouble pronouncing his name correctly, and holding out something.

"What is it?"

"Take it," she commanded. "It is a vertebra from my father's spine."

Ray gulped. "A vertebra from your father's . . . *spine*?"

"Yes, it will help you find your way."

"To where the *gnur* is?" Ray asked.

"No. When the *gnur* kills you," Sunchaser said matter-of-factly, "my father will greet you as you enter the spirit world and guide you to the Plains of Eternity."

Thanks a lot, cobra neck! Ray thought. Then he looked in Sunchaser's sincere brown eyes and regretted this thought. "Thank you very much, Sunchaser."

"You're welcome," she said gravely. "I will also ask Runner to sing your death song tonight as well."

Ray smiled. "With friends like you . . ."

"Hunh?" she said, not understanding.

"Never mind," he replied. Reaching out slowly, he tentatively stroked her flank with his hand. "Thanks for thinking of me."

"You are welcome," Sunchaser again replied.

Ray had a sudden inspiration. "Say, Sunchaser, about last night—at the singing of the hunting songs?"

"Yes?"

Ray wondered how to put what he wanted to know. Finally, he asked, "Do you know what I did when I joined in the singing of the *gnur* song that was so amusing?"

Sunchaser's face brightened. "Oh, Runner thought it was funny, so funny."

"Yeah," agreed Ray. "But just *what* exactly was the funny part?"

"I do not know—Runner did not say," Sunchaser admitted. Then she brightened and said, "Why don't I sing the song and you can join in like you did last night?"

"That's a great idea, Sunchaser!" Ray exclaimed. Doing as Sunchaser suggested, he waited until she had completed the first phrase and then he began to sing as he had before—a full octave or so lower than her part.

Suddenly she stopped and pointed to him, almost collapsing in giggles herself. "What . . . what?" a perplexed Ray asked.

"You . . . you . . . made the men sound like *women*!" she said through her laughter.

"Like women?" Ray asked, confused. "How?"

"You sang lower than they did," Sunchaser explained. "By singing lower, you made *them* take the women's part."

Ray then told Sunchaser about the *tanakiv*'s story concerning the leaper nose and the other tribe's chieftain. *This* story made Sunchaser laugh even harder. "The *tanakiv* is very devious and sly," Sunchaser said upon hearing of this incident. "He told you a tale about an outsider to 'explain' why you could not sing properly, but in doing so he made fun of you as an outsider all over again." When Ray looked confused, she added, "Leaper nose is NOT a delicacy."

Suddenly, Ray understood everything: He had embarrassed the warriors by making them sound like women. An outsider, he did not realize the faux pas he had committed. So the wily old *tanakiv* told him a story about another outsider which not only "explained" that he'd committed an outsider's mistake but also underscored his outsider's status by pulling the wool over his eyes with a tall tale any member of the group would have immediately recognized as a whopper.

"Sunchaser," Ray said, "if I live through this, I'm never going to assume I know ANYTHING about another people and their culture."

Not knowing what to say, Sunchaser just nodded.

Ray shook his head as if to clear it—a curious musky smell had made him aware that this was neither the time nor the place to be daydreaming. He recognized the scent at once: It was that of at least one hide cat. At least one. . . . He tensed at the thought that there might be *more* than one just over the gentle rise of the hillock in front of him. According to Runner's scouts, the hide cat he was to kill was a young bachelor, driven from his family's pride when he had matured enough to contest his father's conjugal rights with the females. Ray felt he could handle a single hide cat—*Where the hell did that confidence come from?* he asked himself—but if the young male had already succeeded in attracting a female as a start toward his own harem, he didn't know what he would or could do.

Ray took a few deep breaths, wondering how he managed to get himself into these situations and imagining how he'd look if a hide cat ate his face. *Not very pretty*, he decided and shuddered. He felt his nose for reassurance.

Ray circled around the base of the low hill, careful not to make any more noise than he had to. He knew any of his scout dogs or any one of the Centaurs could have done it better, but he felt he was doing a fair job of getting within striking distance of the hide cat without its hearing him.

Slowly, with more caution than outright fear, he parted the stalks of grass directly in front of him. Just eight or nine meters away, doing a workmanlike job of stripping the flesh from a leaper haunch, was the young male hide cat he'd come after. It was *big*. He felt his meager store of confidence evaporating.

There was a sinus-draining smell of urine and decayed flesh, and the cat was surrounded by old, splintered bones. The grass was matted down in a rough circle surrounding the hide cat's body, indicating that the animal had slept here often and that this was indeed its current lair.

Ray could see no evidence of a second hide cat and he breathed a sigh of relief. Still, there was little else to be thankful for; he would have his hands full trying to dispatch a single cat.

CRUNCH . . . S-S-SNAP . . . The hide cat's powerful jaws bit through the bone it was chewing. Even watching the beast splinter the bone that occupied its attention, Ray was able to appreciate the creature's sleek beauty. *What a choice!* he thought. *If I don't kill this magnificent specimen, that means it'll kill me. And if I do kill it, I'm stealing the life of a wild animal.* He sighed; whatever he thought of his dilemma, it was too late to change it now.

Ray weighed the situation and pondered how best to take the cat. The young male was lying facing in his direction and it would be impossible to get closer by even half a meter without the cat's becoming aware of his presence.

Glancing up at the sky, he noted the sun's position. As hot as it was, it was not yet into the hottest part of the afternoon. Perhaps if he settled in to wait, the young hide cat would, like most Terran cats, settle in for a nice, long siesta. *No sense rushing things*, Ray thought, *I can get killed just as easily later as right now, so I might as well give the "nap time" plan a shot.* Gently, carefully, he eased himself down and waited for the big cat to get sleepy.

"Please, God," he whispered, "don't let *me* fall asleep!"

7

Ray's head started to roll forward and then snapped back quickly as he realized he was falling asleep. As he was rubbing his eyes he could hear a loud rasping sound: The hide cat was snoring. Figuring it was now or never, Ray gently got to his knees and then slowly raised up. Unfortunately, the grass was too dry and made minute crackling sounds. Each snap sounded like a cannon shot to Ray's ears. He couldn't see how the cat would fail to hear him.

He was right.

The cat snuffled in its sleep and one eyelid lifted lazily. The cat's breathing became more regular and less convulsive as its senses began to send danger signals to its brain. Unsure what had caused it to rouse from its sleep, the cat yawned and lifted its head to sniff the air.

Ray was stymied. Half crouched, half standing, he was in an untenable position. He had to do something. But what?

He finally used a very old trick: He found a small stone near his feet and threw it into the grass behind the cat. The hide cat leapt to its feet at once, whirled, and made ready to defend itself from an attack in the direction from which the noise had come.

With all the grace and agility of a pregnant leaper, Ray stumbled from his hiding place, raising his *shar*. The hide cat spun around to face the source of this new sound before Ray had covered even half the distance separating them. Ray didn't have time to feel fear; he just lunged forward in an earnest attack as best he could.

Berserkers by nature, hide cats, Ray knew, leapt into a fight without regard for normal predator cunning, and this one was no exception. The cat tried to mirror Ray's charge, but was stopped with the fire-hardened tip of the *shar* knifed into its breast. Ray had dropped to one knee and planted the butt end of the *shar* against the ground at a sixty-degree angle and, when the hide cat's charge took it into the tip, fell back and vaulted the impaled cat over his body.

The cat hit the ground and began clawing madly at the strange object which had mysteriously sprouted from its chest. As Ray watched in horror and fascination, aware that the cat no longer associated him with what was attacking it, the animal tried to pull the spear from its chest with its teeth but just couldn't. The *shar* had passed completely through the cat's body and the glistening red tip protruded from the cat's back.

Slowly, the cat's efforts grew more and more frantic and disjointed as its lifeblood flowed out onto the ground and matted grass. With a final shudder, its eyes went glassy and it coughed its life out—still trying to pull the *shar* from its chest.

Ray looked at his clothing with distaste; he was covered in the hide cat's blood. He wiped the blood from his clothes crudely with his bare hands, then wiped his hands on the grass. That done, he turned back to the hide cat's body. One of the tribe's requirements was that he sever the hide cat's head and take it back to the chieftain with him in addition to his *shar*, now honorably blooded in a fight to the death.

Standing over the hide cat's body, he put one foot on the dead animal's chest and both of his hands on the shaft of the *shar*. He took a deep breath and heaved. Nothing. He tried again, and again the *shar* refused to move a centimeter. *Well, this is ludicrous*, he thought. He spit on his hands, rubbed them on his trouser legs, and curled them around the shaft of the *shar* for one final all-out attempt.

"YARGH!!" He released a strength-giving yell and yanked as hard as he could. The only result was that his hands slipped completely off the blood-slick shaft and he went flying backwards to land rather solidly on his tailbone.

When Ray stopped hopping around, he conceded that the

shar was in there for good. *Little wonder the poor hide cat couldn't withdraw the thing with its teeth*, he thought. *I can't even pull it out with both hands*. Well, obviously the *shar* had passed through the hide cat's rib cage and brute force wasn't going to get it out. Then he stumbled onto the idea of wiping the blood from the tip and trying to push and pull the *shar* on *through* the body. Ray was about to try implementing that idea when he heard something moving his way through the grass.

Ray drew his knife and waited, looking wistfully at his *shar* . . . wedged between the ribs of a one-hundred-and-twenty-kilo hide cat where it could do him no good whatsoever.

He didn't have long to wait. A young female hide cat stepped lithely into the small clearing and then stopped when she smelled the blood. Her eyes, black pearls mounted in a sculptured gold head, passed slowly over the ruined body of her mate and then settled on Ray. The intense gaze she leveled on him seemed to bore completely through him, the black depths of her eyes reflecting her desire to avenge her mate.

Ray noted that the female was smaller than the male, but with only a *sha* to defend against her, that advantage added little to his chances of seeing his next birthday. He thought of running but gave that idea up almost as soon as it entered his head. Where was he to run to? Besides, the hide cat would be sinking her claws into his back before he could take a dozen steps.

Ray hefted his knife resignedly; he vowed to try to make a good fight of it. He stared at the cat as she bunched her muscles for a charge. *Papa Sunchaser*, he thought whimsically, *get ready to show a newcomer the way*.

"Ah-h-h-h"—he dashed forward suicidally just as the cat launched herself at him through the air—"shit!!"

Apparently lacking the experience needed to refine her offensive tactics, the young female overestimated the distance between them. She barely struck Ray's shoulder as she shot over him. Almost by reflex alone, Ray threw his arms across his face in a totally defensive motion that coincidentally put the knife blade in the proper position to rake the length of her body as she just glanced off his right shoulder and landed beyond him.

The cat hit the ground in a hissing, spitting fury and rolled to meet him. Ray landed on his back and did a fast backward roll to come to his feet immediately. Unfortunately, he was facing in the wrong direction. He whirled and met the hide cat's second charge.

It was one of those split-second things: He saw the open, gaping mouth full of razor-sharp teeth coming at him and acted instinctively. Instead of slashing with the knife, he held it steady and guided it into the maw of her mouth. The point dug into the roof of her mouth and the butt lodged against her tongue and lower jaw. Even so, her charge sent them both tumbling. Blood poured from her mouth—more as she struggled to close it—and covered his neck and arm. He twisted loose of her wildly slashing claws and rolled across the ground in an effort to get away. He succeeded, primarily because the tortured hide cat was now more concerned with the knife in her mouth than with her tormenter.

Unaware that she was only making things worse, she bit down harder on the blade and it finally penetrated the roof of her mouth to slice into her brain, ending her agony. She mewed weakly as a torrent of blood gushed from her mouth; she was dead before the blood hit the ground.

His breath rasping raggedly in and out of his open mouth, Ray stood up for a moment, had second thoughts about it, and sat down hard on the trampled grass. His right shoulder was bleeding profusely. At least he thought it was—it was difficult to differentiate between the hide cats' blood and his own.

Blood. Blood was everywhere. It dripped from the spindly stalks of grass, it ran like miniature rivers into quiet pools that drew ravenous insects to its warm promise of nourishment. The grass was trampled flat and littered by the bodies of the two hide cats, both giving mute testimony to their deaths by assuming contorted positions unknown to the living.

Ray felt himself growing nauseous and before he could move he gagged and ejected a stream of vomit. It was a necessary evil, he knew, but having to kill the two hide cats for no more reason than to prove his "manhood" made him ill. He rationalized that his successful hunt might save thousands of Centaurs and, yes, even hide cats, by preserving Chiron's environment, but the scene of carnage that lay before his eyes offered a mute but emotional rebuttal to his logic.

Ray stopped the harsh sound of his own breathing for just

long enough to confirm that again something was approaching the lair through the grass.

He looked at both of his weapons, their use denied him, and sighed. Life was unfair—he'd killed the hide cats for nothing; he was about to die, invalidating what he'd just "accomplished." All at once his predicament seemed blackly hilarious to him. "Well, screw you!" he shouted defiantly. "I still have my teeth and fingernails!"

The grass parted as the interloper arrived.

Beowulf thrust his huge head out. " 'Lo, Ray. We finally found you." He looked around, stepping into the clearing. "Some job you did on them hide cats."

For some odd reason, Ray almost felt . . . disappointed. Then he began to laugh.

"What . . .?" The big dog could see nothing to laugh about, nothing funny in the scene of blood and death.

"Oh, it's nothing," Ray giggled, "just a private joke."

▌▌

Ray's triumphant return to Runner-with-the-Wind's camp was, to say the least, a spectacle of no mean proportions. He rode into camp on Beowulf's back, managing to stay aboard by locking his legs around the hard body of the scout dog, carrying a hide cat head in either hand and covered from head to foot in dried blood. Women and children shrieked at the sight of Beowulf and warriors brandished their *shars*, but once they got over the initial shock of seeing the huge leaper-killer slowly padding into their camp, the inhabitants of the village crept closer to see this marvel up close.

Beowulf had wanted to send for help in order that the exhausted Ray might be returned to their own camp without further exertion, but Ray had refused, saying, "This whole episode was for the Centaur tribe's benefit; it was meant to convince them to accept me—and the others—as 'people' in their eyes. I have to go back. Further, I'm not going to pass up a great entrance scene. I know the stuff legends are made of. Let's do it right."

Ray was correct. The effort required of him to remain conscious, much less stay on Beowulf's broad back while juggling two hide cat heads and the now-freed *shar*, was apparently to be amply rewarded. At first, the silence was thick enough to cut with a *sha*; then, when his accomplishment became more apparent, Ray was surrounded by awed and cheering Centaur warriors. The *tanakiv* and Sunchaser looked on with bemused and rather stunned expressions on their faces. Recalling Sunchaser's words that morning, Ray knew they'd thought they would never see him again when he went off alone to kill the hide cat.

Having dramatically made his point, with an entrance as dramatic as Elizabeth Taylor's in the ancient sinny melodrama *Cleopatra*, Ray slipped from Beowulf's back with obvious enthusiasm. He held the two hide cat heads high and slowly made his way through the congratulatory crowd toward Runner's council hut.

Runner-with-the-Wind was standing outside, waiting patiently. When Ray approached him, the Centaur chieftain asked the ritual questions: "Is your *shar* blooded; have you proved yourself a warrior worthy of taking your place among The People?"

Ray knelt and placed the two hide cat heads on the ground in front of the council hut. Then he rose and presented Runner his *shar*. "My *shar* has tasted blood honorably."

A faint smile—Ray had learned to read Centaur facial expressions quite well by this time—crossed Runner's lips. "I see you have not only brought back the heads of two *gnur*, but also one of your leaper-killers."

"Yes," said Ray. "I have not talked to anyone else, but now that Beowulf has found me, the others will not be far behind."

Runner shook his head. "I wish my father were here now to advise me. The *tanakiv* has his bones and his leaper intestines, but I fear they are inadequate for such a complex situation."

"I understand. Perhaps—"

"Runner! Runner!" shouted a warrior, rushing in to interrupt Ray's words.

"What is it?" Runner asked patiently.

Fear showed in the messenger's widened eyes. "One of the two-legged one's possessions makes noises; it lives!"

"What are you talking about?" insisted Runner.

"It . . . it is no larger than this," continued the excited warrior, holding his hands a few centimeters apart, "but something is alive inside it—it made a noise like this: BEEP."

"That's a good impression of my communicator's attention beep," Ray acknowledged. "It was taken from me when I was captured."

"Then this thing of which my warrior speaks," Runner said, "it truly talks?"

"Not exactly," explained Ray. "It is a device my people use for talking over short distances—very short distances. It means my party is not far away and is trying to reach me."

"Come then," Runner said. "I would see this wonder with my own eyes."

You bet your ass, Ray thought. *If I don't answer that beep in about one minute, the shit's really liable to hit the proverbial fan in the form of an all-out assault on this place to free Beowulf and me!*

When Mary saw Ray she let out a shriek of happiness and ran toward him. Taylor, a big grin on his face, followed just behind her. Ray looked like another person to them: He was a little gaunt and he had a peach-fuzz stubble of a beard on his face. He had some kind of bandage on his shoulder, but otherwise he seemed not to be seriously injured.

Ray enveloped Mary in his arms and hugged her tightly. "Oh, Ray, dear, I thought I'd never see you again!" Mary sobbed into his shoulder.

"Hey," Ray said gruffly, afraid he was going to cry, too, "it takes a lot to kill us Larkins; we're tough."

"I never thought I'd be so happy to see your ugly face again, shorty—even with that fuzz on it," roared Taylor, sweeping *both* Ray and Mary into his long arms.

"Ouch!" said Ray as Taylor squeezed his injured shoulder. "It's wonderful to see you two. I love you both so much it hurts." Then he looked around and spotted the dogs, staying back but wagging their tails furiously.

"Littlejohn, Frodo, Grendel—all of you—come here!" That was all the urging the dogs needed to bound across the few meters separating them from Ray. Ray hugged Mary and Taylor again and then stepped back to allow the dogs to surround him and jump up to lick his face.

"Hey, take it easy," Ray cautioned. "You're going to lick my new beard right off with those rough tongues if you're not careful." As the dogs continued their happy assault on his person, Ray looked at them and asked, "Hey, where's Anson? Is he guarding the cholos or what?"

The dogs fell silent and Ray read their expressions and body language before Frodo confirmed his suspicions by saying, "Anson is dead, Ray. He died trying to prevent your capture."

Ray looked stunned. "You, you—"

"We did right by him, Ray," said Littlejohn. "He sleeps forever on prairie now, a hero."

Ray looked around at the canine faces full of anguish and said, "Let's make sure he didn't die in vain."

The dogs looked less than happy at being in the camp of the tribe of Centaurs which had killed Anson, and neither did Runner's warriors appreciate having in their midst more of the leaper-killers which had killed two of their number already. It seemed an uneasy truce.

"You're right," Taylor was explaining to Ray with an interested Runner-with-the-Wind looking on. "We thought we'd see if we could raise you before busting in here with energy rifles firing. You could have gotten seriously dead if we'd tried something like that without attempting to contact you."

"All I can say," replied a relieved Ray, "is that I'm glad someone got curious when he heard the beeping coming out of the hut they'd stashed my gear in."

"You're okay, then?" Mary asked, the concern in her voice showing as she glanced at his shoulder.

"I'm fine. As a matter of fact, Runner and I were just about to discuss the terms of an unofficial cease-fire," Ray said with a boyish grin.

"Who?" Taylor asked.

"Runner-with-the-Wind. He's the chieftain of this tribe," Ray said, pointing in Runner's direction. Runner had no idea what was being said but "smiled" politely.

"And we thought you were probably being tortured to death!" exclaimed Mary. Then she looked at Ray more closely and asked, "Just what *have* you been doing?"

"Oh, just getting in a little field research," confided Ray.

"Field research?" said Mary blankly.

"Hell's bells!" roared Ray. "We knew these pencil-necked geeks"—here he smiled warmly at Runner—"were intelligent before I was captured. Everything I've learned since then's been icing on the ole cake."

"That's what I was afraid of," sighed Taylor resignedly. "There goes the money we invested—and with it our futures with the Bureau."

"You have no choice but to continue your precious 'field research,' of course," Mary said. "But things are going to get a lot more dicey as a result. If the Triumvirate gets the idea that someone is evading the Bureau's orders to stay away from the Centaurs, someone who may just be stupid enough to prove that they are sentient beings protected by the colonization codes, who knows what the General and the others might do?" She answered her own question by saying, "They might unleash the Cadre." She smiled grimly. "It wouldn't take more than a handful of trained Cadre shock troops to wipe us out and eliminate the evidence."

"But . . . but . . ." Taylor protested. "That's crazy." He ran his fingers through his hair in agitation as he stared at the ground. Suddenly, a broad smile pulled up the corners of his mouth. Looking up, he said simply, "Cadre . . . what Cadre?"

"Huh?"

"I said what Cadre? Do you see any Cadre? I don't," Taylor said. "Look, Mary and Ray, we're virtually alone on this planet. The nearest Cadre outpost is a good sixty or seventy light-years away. No, the Cadre's no threat to us. Besides," he concluded smugly, "the Judge Advocate would never allow anything illegal to happen to us—certainly not assassination."

"If that's the case, then we have nothing to worry about, do we?" Mary said, placing a hand on his forearm.

"I know, I know," he admitted, "but I want to be able to bitch about it—a *lot*."

"Sure thing, Captain entrepreneur," giggled Ray.

Taylor and Mary looked at each other. "Are you *sure* you're okay, Ray?" Mary asked. "You seem a little . . . ah . . . *exuberant*."

Ray clapped his hands together. "*Mierson's* Centaurs, my ass! When *I* get done studying these guys I'll be the anthropologist of the century; I'll be—"

"A royal pain in the keister," Mary finished.

"Well, before you award yourself the Yannetti Prize," said

Taylor, "I think we've got to sit down together and discuss what we're going to do."

"I'm with Taylor on this," said Mary.

"Sure thing," Ray agreed readily.

There was a long silence which Runner broke by asking Ray, "You and your tribe argue?"

Ray smiled. "I think we're going to have to hold a council meeting of our own."

"Ah, yes," murmured Runner. He could see that he and this two-legged one were much alike in many respects. He shouted orders for a hut to be made ready.

Once they were inside the hut, however, Taylor and Mary turned toward Ray only to see his eyes close in weariness. "I think the galaxy's greatest anthropologist just went to sleep on us," Taylor said to Mary.

"Let's let him rest," Mary said. "We can go get the van and bring it over to the camp while he sleeps."

"Vaslev?" Taylor held the receive button firmly as the hover van's communicator crackled and hissed. He was rewarded by the tinny and distant-sounding voice of Vaslev Khorsegai.

"Yeah, Taylor, what's up?" Quickly, Taylor began outlining the series of events that had taken place in the past week or so, beginning with the fire and ending with Ray's subsequent capture and release.

"I . . . ah, what do you expect us to do, Taylor?" asked Vaslev.

"Look, we've had some very serious discussions about what's to be done about the Centaurs. We've come to the conclusion that we've been duped into passively accepting the directive forbidding any further study of their possible intelligence. Ray's preliminary findings, we think, are strong enough to warrant a first-class anthropological study of the Centaurs' way of life and cultural artifacts. We have no doubt that we'll be able to refute the original directive and force the PCB to reopen the issue—the Judge Advocate and its Programmers will surely see to that. The Centaurs have language, for Chrissake!"

"Hm-m-m," murmured Khorsegai thoughtfully. "If what you say is true, we're getting involved in something rather dangerous. How will the Cadre react? We've all got contracts, too."

Expecting the question, Taylor quickly replied, "You don't have to *do* anything; simply discuss what we're doing with the other groups. I think you'll find that we're not the only team concerned about the legal and moral dimensions of what we're up to on this planet. Try to set up an open forum; I think all the groups will support our decision."

"Okay, I'll see what I can do. I'll be in touch. Out."

"Right. Out."

"Well," said Taylor, turning to Ray and Mary, "that's that. Think they'll go along?"

"Oh, I think so, once they give it some thought," said Mary.

"I do, too," agreed Ray. "But it really doesn't matter if they do or don't; we have to do what we have to do."

"Speaking of doing what you have to do," said Taylor, "aren't you about to be made a warrior of the tribe?"

★   ★   ★

"Come inside, slayer of the *gnur*; the council will vote," Runner said to Ray outside the council hut. Ray followed Runner into the smoky and ill-lighted interior of the large hut and was himself followed by the members of the council.

When all were inside, Runner, as spokesman for the tribe, opened by saying, "I, Runner-with-the-Wind, have called this meeting of the council; therefore, it is my right and my duty to kindle and maintain the sacred fire—sent to our ancestors from the heavens in a flash of lightning as a divine gift from the gods."

Runner placed a glowing coal among the wood and leaper chips that had been patiently and painstakingly gathered for the fire. When at last the fire blazed high, bathing all in a warm, yellow-red glow, Runner rose from his task and looked at those present for a long time, saying nothing. Despite his nap, Ray was still so worn from his physically and emotionally draining fight with the two hide cats that he actually dozed on his feet.

Finally, Runner broke the silence by beginning: "We are all warriors of the tribe. All of us have undergone the ordeal of becoming a warrior by blooding our *shars* in combat against the mighty *gnur*. This one here"—he indicated the gently swaying Ray—"this two-legged one called Ray, has done no less than any of us. I see no reason why he should not be confirmed by your vote as a member of the tribe from this day forth. He has more than shown his courage. I do not speak only

of his hunting prowess—my son lives because of his bravery."
He made the motion that Ray translated as a shrug. "In council,
however, my voice is the voice of but one; now I would hear
from you, my brothers."

In accordance with a rigid protocol, the more important
members of the council of the tribe stood up front while the
younger or less experienced warriors stood in the back. It was
Leaperstalker, a warrior in the front, who spoke first. "Runner
speaks for us all, I believe. The two-legged one did as each of
us had done—and better than some. Let him then receive, as
we have received, the title of warrior, of member of the tribe."

Several more warriors spoke, all echoing Runner and
Leaperstalker. One of the warriors was Gnurfleet, the oldest
member of the tribe except for the *tanakiv*. "I have seen the
leadership not only of Saminav"—he nodded in Runner's
direction—"but also of his elder brother and his father. Like
them, Saminav is a great leader; I would do as he asks, for he
has the good of the tribe always in the mind."

"Who else would speak?" asked Runner-with-the-Wind.

"*I* would speak!" declared Nav-racer, pushing to the front
from his position at the back. Eyes blazing, he declared, "This
creature is not fit to be a warrior of The People and of this tribe!
So he has killed a *gnur*—that does not make a man of a
monster! And when he returned to the camp, it was on the back
of one of his killer beasts. I say he did *not* kill the *gnur*
honorably and by himself, but was aided by that beast. He is
not of The People—and you, Runner-with-the-Wind, are not fit
to be chieftain if it is your will that we blaspheme the gods of
The People by allowing him to participate in our rituals!"

There were shocked murmurs from the assembled warriors,
but Runner merely smiled grimly and said, "The purpose of a
council meeting is to allow each warrior to speak his mind
freely on the matter at hand. You have every right to vote to
refuse to accept the two-legged one called Ray as one of us and
to so speak, but you"—and here Runner looked hard at
Nav-racer—"have *no* right to question my authority as chieftain unless you are also willing to challenge me."

Nav-racer's eyes narrowed. He had wanted to strike back at
Runner by denouncing the two-legged one, but not to go so far
as formally challenging his chieftain. To do so meant a duel to
the death.

"*We* know you're unafraid of Runner," insisted a member of the small clique that had recently gravitated to the disgruntled Nav-racer. Nav-racer cursed his new follower's innocent faith in his abilities. Now, if he backed off he would lose the support of his friends, yet if he went ahead and challenged Runner he could be killed in the ensuing duel.

Runner sensed Nav-racer's dilemma and willingly pushed the proud young warrior over the edge. "If you are dissatisfied with my leadership, Nav-racer, yet are afraid to risk a duel, you can always leave the tribe branded a misfit and join the Tribeless Ones."

"You are no warrior, Runner-with-the-Wind!" snapped Nav-racer angrily. "You are without honor! I formally challenge you to meet me in combat to the death!"

"And I accept," said Runner in a matter-of-fact voice.

"What the hell is going on?" asked a stunned Ray.

Runner took Ray aside. "I'm afraid your induction into the ranks of our tribe must wait until after I meet Nav-racer in combat," explained Runner.

"But—"

"Do not worry," Runner assured Ray. "I will be back. Also," he added offhandedly, "the council meeting is not considered over until I throw dead ashes over the live coals of the fire. We will yet make you a warrior and a member of The People this day; I promise you that, my new friend."

"The hell with that! What about this duel business?" Ray demanded.

"It was something that was coming for a long time. Some of the younger warriors must have been goading Nav-racer to it," explained Runner. "I must meet it head-on today. Better a duel now than a *shar* in my back late some dark night." He put a hand on Ray's shoulder. "It is not really any of your doing, you must understand. Do not blame yourself, Ray."

III

A site had been chosen less than a kilometer from the camp. The warriors formed a large circle with their bodies and Nav-racer and Runner entered from opposite ends, perhaps twenty meters apart. Each carried a *shar*, a *sha*, and a whistler. There would be no quarter asked and none given. If both were so grievously wounded that neither could dispatch the other, the less seriously injured of the two would be declared the winner and the other killed by a member of the council.

"I don't like this," said a visibly disturbed Mary. "What if Runner is killed? Will we also be killed and our work left undone?" She frowned and added, "What a society—everything must be settled by violence!"

"As to what will happen if Nav-racer wins, I don't know," admitted Ray. "I doubt if Nav-racer, even in victory, could have us killed outright, but our research would surely be at an end—at least with this tribe." He glanced at Mary and said, "As to the Centaurs settling everything by violence, I seem to recall a certain person *you* wounded in a duel."

"That's different," Mary said defensively, biting her lower lip as she always did when confronted by something she'd done but would rather forget about. "That was a matter of honor."

"Uh-huh," said Ray in a tone that left no doubt how seriously he took Mary's disclaimer.

"Anyway, if Runner-with-the-Wind forced the issue as you say he did," argued Taylor as if to convince himself, "then he must believe that Nav-racer is no match for him."

"I hope so," swallowed Mary, pleased that the topic of her infamous duel had been dropped.

"Well, we'll soon be finding out," Ray stated. "It looks as if they're beginning."

As they watched, the two Centaurs walked toward one another warily, slowly swinging their whistlers at their sides so as to be able to suddenly speed up the motion and hurl the bololike throwing weapons in an instant. Runner and Nav-racer approached each other as gracefully and ritualistically as dancers and as slowly and full of purpose as fighting cocks. There was almost a discernible rhythm to the early stages of the duel: The two duelists would approach slowly, back off, circle, approach slowly again.

The two warriors eyed each other carefully, scrutinizing the other's motions, his way of holding his whistler and his *shar*. They sought any sign of weakness, anything which would indicate a possible opening, any advantage which could be seized.

And they played a waiting game, seeing who could better stand the building tension of waiting, of approaching, feinting and then backing off.

Runner waited.

Runner knew he was the older, wiser and more patient in the ways of combat. But, too, he must consider that Nav-racer was younger, full of brash confidence and likely to react in ways so obviously ill-considered that they would have the advantage of surprise.

Runner waited.

The day was hot. The sun beat down mercilessly and the wind hardly stirred the grasses. Insects hopped and droned monotonously. The watchers grew restless as the two antagonists continued their waiting game. The onlooking warriors representing both sides began to shout encouragement or derisive remarks: "Are you two going to fight or dance with each other!" and "One of you will die of old age. Come on, Nav-racer, mix it up with him." Runner calmly accepted both the insults and the support, whereas Nav-racer seemed to become nettled by some of the taunts hurled in his direction. He was young and had a youthful self-image to protect; he did not like to hear others questioning his bravery.

And still the sun continued its long, slow climb toward the top of the sky.

Runner waited.

Finally, Nav-racer could stand the waiting no longer. He edged in toward Runner and threw his whistler without warning. Half expecting the maneuver, Runner was able to avoid the weapon as it whirled past him. Unable to believe he'd missed, Nav-racer stood stunned. Runner smiled crookedly. Still whirling his whistler, Runner moved in.

Desperate, stricken with a feeling of helplessness, Nav-racer charged. Runner increased the speed at which he was whirling his whistler as Nav-racer rapidly closed the distance between them. The whistler's keening growing ever louder, Runner released the weapon in the direction of the charging Nav-racer, hoping it would catch him about his legs and hurl him to the ground where he could be killed—swiftly and without passion. But on this day, luck was with Nav-racer, too. Nav-racer was partially successful in avoiding the whistler—it struck his front legs, entangling them, but bound neither his rear legs nor his arms.

Runner dashed in, hoping to dispatch Nav-racer with a single thrust of his *shar*. But he was too slow: Nav-racer's arm rose and fell repeatedly as he slashed at the rawhide strips of the whistler with his *sha*. Desperately, taking what seemed to him an eternity, Nav-racer freed himself. It was none too soon, for Runner was upon him immediately. Runner thrust with his *shar* as Nav-racer stumbled to his feet, hoping to kill or cripple the young warrior before he could recover completely, but Runner was too late. Nav-racer lunged to one side and the *shar* did no more than glance along one flank, opening up a bloody but superficial wound.

With the strength of youth, Nav-racer fought back. He was so successful that his vicious counterattack actually succeeded in driving Runner back to the extent that the Centaur chieftain almost stumbled and fell himself. Unable to keep up the energy-sapping, all-out attack for long, Nav-racer was content to allow Runner to retreat a dozen steps or so. Both combatants needed a breather, a chance to rethink the situation.

Again the duel became a *danse de mort*, each of the two moving harmoniously in response to the slightest move of the other. Again they circled warily, again they reassessed the situation. Runner was the more tired of the two, but Nav-racer bore the shock of having been wounded and was losing blood—a factor in the outcome only if the duel became an even more attenuated affair, something Nav-racer had no intention of allowing.

Runner feinted several times, noting Nav-racer's reaction time and the defensive stance he went into in response to Runner's mock attack. Then, when he felt he could wait no longer, Runner rushed at Nav-racer with his *shar* at the ready. This time Runner was not feinting and he did not give away his attack.

It had to be good. Runner knew he was slightly larger and stronger than Nav-racer, but Nav-racer was young as well as strong. The two came together solidly, grunts forced from their mouths by the impact. They thrusted furiously and parried just as furiously the thrusts of the other.

Seeing an opening, Runner managed to drive his *shar* into Nav-racer's heavy lower body, his "horse" part. It was a poor thrust, however—penetrating only slightly. Nav-racer, shock registering on his face, jerked away so quickly that the *shar* broke off at the point where it had entered his body.

Bleeding, screaming with the maniacal rage that shock and

a pain-heightened sense of awareness can bring, Nav-racer lunged at Runner like some wild beast.

Runner willingly closed with Nav-racer. *Shar*less, he grabbed Nav-racer's *shar* with his free hand and stabbed at the young warrior with the *sha* in his other hand. The close quarters made it necessary for Nav-racer to drop his *shar* and resort to his *sha*, too, and the two whirled in a cloud of dust, locked in vicious hand-to-hand combat.

Runner smelled Nav-racer's fear-sweat and saw the look of wide-eyed terror in his face as he grappled with the other Centaur, trying to get in one good attempt at a vital killing point with his *sha*.

"So, Nav-racer, did you know it would come to this—did you see this fight in your dreams? If so, it will end as a nightmare, for I am going to kill you."

"Bold talk, old one," Nav-racer gasped. "It is you who is going to join your father and brother in the land of the dead this day."

Finally, Runner got the opportunity he was looking for and buried the blade of his *sha* in Nav-racer's neck.

"Argh!" Nav-racer screamed in fear and disbelief as he stumbled clumsily away and fell heavily to the ground. He tried to get up and fell again, blood pouring from the open wound in his neck. Runner picked up Nav-racer's *shar*, approached the dying warrior, and drove the tip of the spear into the back of Nav-racer's head at the point where it joined his neck. Nav-racer died instantly.

Immediately Runner was surrounded by his cheering warriors; Nav-racer's friends slunk away, not one of them staying to see to the body of their fallen comrade. "Always the bold warrior," said Leaperstalker.

Gnurfleet said, "A song will be made of this duel. It will live in the voices of the tribe."

"Ah," said Runner, "there are already too many songs of duels—let the memory of this one die with Nav-racer." Then Runner brushed aside the continuing congratulations of his warriors and patiently waited for the three humans to join him.

"Ah," he said when he saw Ray. "Now the council can vote to make you a warrior and a member of The People."

"What?" said a numb Ray. "Oh, yes, I nearly forgot."

8

As Mary and Taylor readied the van for the journey north, Ray considered the cholos. The eleven surviving cholos still ate their way through vast quantities of grass—that was unavoidable: they were cholos and unable to do other than their nature required. But Taylor was now sowing native grass seed in the wake of the cholos to restore the soil to its former state, so the damage the cholos did was only temporary.

As they traveled north, leaper signs became more and more frequent. At one stop, Runner told Ray, "The leapers are at most a few days ahead of us. We should come upon a herd anytime now."

"Good," said Ray. "I know your food supplies are growing scarce."

"Yes, we must have a successful hunt or face starvation," Runner said. Then, looking at Ray intently, Runner added, "Tell me, Ray, since you say you were trained in your land to study the ways and customs of other peoples, would you want to accompany the hunting party when the time of the great hunt comes?"

Ray looked stunned. The idea had not occurred to him, but scarcely had the words left Runner's lips before the anthropologist in him shivered in anticipation. "I . . . ah, of course," he said finally. "But," he added, "can an outsider join the hunt?"

Runner-with-the-Wind looked at him as if he'd said something outrageous. "An outsider, no," he replied. "But a warrior of The People, a member of the Tribe, yes."

Ray flushed with gratitude. "You are a great and honorable chieftain, Runner," he said. "You have accepted me into the tribe in deed as well in word."

"What else would you have me do? You have slain the *gnur* with your *shar*; you are one of us now and forever."

"Thank you, Runner."

Ray, Mary, Taylor, and Beowulf sat around the fire debating the merits of Ray's participation in the next leaper hunt. Actually, since Ray had made up his mind to participate in whatever way he could, the discussion focused more on *how* he could take part rather than whether he *should* participate.

"What about Sunchaser's suggestion?" asked Mary. "Didn't she say that it might be possible for this warrior called Gnurspirit to carry you on his back?"

Ray agreed that the offer had been made, but he questioned its feasibility. "Gnurspirit is probably the largest of Runner's warriors, I'll grant you, but even so he's no taller than I am," Ray said. "I doubt he'd be able to carry me safely."

"I think Ray's right," Taylor agreed. "Runner's people may have been given the name 'Centaurs,' but they only superficially resemble the half-man, half-horse centaurs of Terran legend. Besides," he added, glancing at Ray, "even though squirt here isn't all that heavy, the Centaurs are relatively small beings themselves—Ray is just too much for even the largest and strongest of them to bear comfortably."

"What about the hover scooter, then, Ray?" Mary asked. "Why can't you use it?"

"I've given some thought to that, of course," Ray replied. "But I can't see using it either. For one thing, I've got to do more than just go along for the ride; as a warrior, I've got to actively participate. That means I must be able to use my *shar* to fell as many of the leapers as I can." He shook his head. "I can't see being able to do that while I try to control the scooter at the same time."

"I agree," said Taylor. "It's too dangerous; if Ray were to fall off . . ." He left the thought unfinished.

"If I fall off," Ray picked up, "then I'm prairie pizza; the leapers will pound my hide right into the ground. You'll be able to slip me under the door of the hover van and—"

"Okay, okay!" said Mary crossly. "We get the picture. The hover scooter is out. What does that leave, if anything?"

"How 'bout me?" asked Beowulf.

"Huh?" said Taylor as everyone turned to stare in the scout dog's direction.

"I said, how 'bout me? I can carry Ray on my back. I done it after Ray done in them hide cats and can do it again."

"Beowulf," Ray said, "I think I may just plant a big wet one on your gorgeous dog face!"

"Okay, Ray," Beowulf said agreeably.

Mama-san, her belly swollen with the puppies that she would soon be giving birth to, cried when she heard the news of the death of one of the Centaur chieftain's wives. Kirinav had died after giving Runner-with-the-Wind a new son.

"You cry," said Sinbad wonderingly. "Why you cry?"

"Why you think, duncehead?" snapped Grendel. "Mama-san pregnant. Going to have puppies—it upsetting and sad for her to learn of mother's death."

Taken aback, Sinbad stammered, "Yes . . . but . . . she Centaur—they killed Anson!"

"And Anson killed some of them," Pandora reminded him. "They dint know 'bout us and we not know 'bout them, that we *all* 'The People.' "

"So you cry for them now," said Sinbad.

"Boy," said Pandora in disgust. "Some dogs—*males*—got 'things' bigger'n their brains!"

Frodo, who'd been listening to all this, now chimed in by explaining to Sinbad, "Mama-san is sad when anyone dies, but she 'specially sad when mother dies in childbirth. It not just the Centaur mother and her child, it *her* birth, too—it Mama-san's birth that is on her mind now as her time approaches."

Grendel and Pandora looked at Frodo with new respect. "Hey, you pretty bright . . . for a male," Grendel said.

"Thanks," said Frodo brightly, ignoring the sarcasm.

Mary looked out the window of the van to see Ray in animated conversation with Beowulf and Ozma. Ray made a shrugging motion and then headed toward the van. Mary dried her hands on her lab apron and waited patiently for Ray to come in.

"For some reason the dogs wish to attend Kirinav's death ceremony," said Ray, shaking his head in disbelief.

"Is there something wrong with that?" asked Mary.

"Wrong?" Ray said. "Hell, no, but the dogs and the Centaurs, they . . . I mean . . ." He stopped, scratched his head, and admitted, "I guess I don't know what I mean."

Mary smiled. "I'm just giving you a hard time. Of course you know what you mean—it surprises you because the dogs and the Centaurs have been slow to warm to each other."

"Yeah, I guess that's it," Ray acknowledged as Beowulf joined them to the extent of sticking his big shaggy head in through the open door to listen to their conversation.

"This might be just the thing to get both groups over their antagonism toward each other," Mary said.

"You may be right," said Ray. Turning toward Beowulf, Ray asked, "Yes?"

"You ask Runner, okay?"

"First chance I get," Ray said. "I'm making no promises, but I don't see why Runner would say no. He might even be touched by your concern."

Mary, aware the dogs didn't always have a sense of humor when it came to Ray, the Man, still looked at Beowulf and took a chance on saying, "Pretty smart for a man, huh, Beowulf?"

Beowulf blinked and then began to laugh—slowly at first, then harder and harder. "What's so funny?" Ray asked.

"What Mary say 'bout you . . ."

"Yeah?"

"Grendel say it 'bout Frodo," Beowulf managed to say before breaking up in giggles again.

Ray looked blankly at Mary. "Dog humor! I guess you had to be there."

Kirinav's face and eyelids were painted with bright earth colors carefully daubed on by the *sharnan* of the tribe. Then her body was stripped and placed on a ceremonial leaper robe. A *shar*, honorably blooded by one of the warriors, was put down by her side so that the spirit warriors in the land of the dead might accept her as one of them. Fine bone jewelry was put around her neck and laid beside her. She was given food—dried leaper meat, roots, and delicacies—that she might not awaken hungry. She was also given *bor* to quench her thirst on the journey.

When all was prepared, the blanket containing Kirinav's body and provisions was grasped at the edges and carried toward the high platform where it would be placed for the *nav* and the elements to wear away the flesh.

Ray, Mary, Taylor, and the dogs waited with the rest of the tribe by the platform that was to receive Kirinav's body. Ray, more than the others, appreciated the rituals people had devised in the face of death. Animals, unaware of their own mortality, do not fear or respect death. People, sentient beings, live each day with the prospect of their eventual death. When death finally comes, the rituals meet two needs: honoring the dead person and allowing those left behind, the living, to deal emotionally and intellectually with the loss of a friend or loved one.

Runner-with-the-Wind watched closely, fearfully, as the *tanakiv* walked around the funeral tower and asked the gods to provide safe conduct for Kirinav's soul. There were many evil spirits which might try to murder her wandering soul before she arrived safely in the land of the dead.

When the ceremony was over, Ray approached Runner and, without saying a word, put his hand on the Centaur's broad back, giving him a reassuring touch. The others did likewise. Soon, however, the tribe drifted slowly away, leaving only Runner-with-the-Wind to stand by the tower as the *nav* blew across the silent prairie and darkness came.

Runner said his final farewells and turned away—back toward the future and the uncertainty that faced the living.

▮▮

Runner-with-the-Wind first heard the approach of the leaper herd while enjoying the late morning sun's warmth. His greenish-yellow skin had been chilled by the persistent wind of the early morning hours. His broad flat nose flared in enjoyment as he realized what the distant rumble his keen hearing had discerned meant for his warriors and for the tribe as a whole.

"Listen, Runner," said Moon-son. "The scouts have surely found a large herd. The noise grows louder by the minute."

"Yes," agreed Runner. "The hunting will be good. The gods have heard our songs. Many a *shar* will taste leaper blood this fine day." Turning to Ray, who was climbing atop Beowulf, Runner asked, "Are you prepared for the hunt, two-legged warrior?"

Patting Beowulf's massive head for reassurance, Ray replied, "As prepared as I'll ever be."

"Good," Runner said. Then: "Try to stay near me, leaper killer," he said, addressing Beowulf.

"I do as best I can," Beowulf said.

"Look!" one of the eager hunters cried. "The dust! The herd cannot yet be seen but the dust gives away its location."

Ray looked and saw that what the warrior said was true. The herd itself was not close enough yet for any of the hunting party to make out any individual leapers or to see it with the naked eye, but a huge cloud of dust raised by thousands of stampeding hooves trailed over the distant herd like a brown thundercloud as the horizontal avalanche that was the leaper herd roared toward them.

As the herd rushed closer, the ground began to vibrate. Some of the younger hunters taking part in their first hunt whispered nervously among themselves and fingered their *shars*. Seeing the same apprehension in Ray's face, Runner smiled, knowing he and the first-time hunters would forget their fear when the waiting was finally over, when they had blooded their *shars*.

"They come," Runner said simply.

As the leapers surged onto the plain where Ray and Runner's hunters waited, Ray noted with satisfaction that Runner's scouts had done their job well. Relays of scouts with bone whistlers and other noisemakers had driven the herd for a great distance at nearly top speed. When they met the hunting party the leapers were already weary, their legs heavy with exhaustion. With the leapers on the edge of collapse, the killing would be easy—or so Runner-with-the-Wind had told a dubious Ray.

"Now!" shouted Runner as he led a rush directly at the center of the oncoming leaper herd. The front runners panicked and turned to the hunting party's left, the rest of the herd following.

Runner's nearly thirty hunters plunged in among the frenzied animals, each hunter choosing an animal and drawing up immediately to one of its heaving flanks. The pursuing hunter would raise his *shar* high and bring it down hard, driving it into the side of a leaper running at full speed. Sometimes more than one thrust was necessary, but if the hunter had chosen his entry point carefully and hit a vital organ, the animal usually fell dead from the first thrust. There was much skill involved in the killing—a hunter had to thrust and then pull his *shar* from the leaper's body before the creature stumbled and fell dead or dying. The danger was that the leaper might pull the hunter down with it when it fell. If this happened the unfortunate hunter was likely to be trampled to death by the following herd. Sometimes two hunters would work as a pair, flanking a leaper on both sides and striking as one.

It was a quick process. Thrust, pull out, and then on to the next victim. The dead were left where they fell, to be skinned and cleaned by the women and children after the killing was over.

After an initial moment of hesitation, Beowulf had plunged in among the leapers just as the Centaur hunters had. Ray, holding on to the "pommel" of the jerry-built saddle that Beowulf wore, soon caught the big dog's running rhythm and relaxed as best he could. He began to choose targets of opportunity. Following the lead of the other hunters, he thrust downward into the back or side of a madly stampeding leaper. The fatally wounded animal would snort and then stumble and fall to the ground. Soon Ray and Beowulf, the dog's ears laid back and his teeth bared, were completely caught up in the heat of the chase.

The dust was thick and stuck to the sweat and blood covering Ray's body, forming a greasy coating. The noise was thunderous and his vision limited to a few feet in either direction because of the swirling dust. Later, Ray would tell Mary and Taylor that he came to appreciate Runner's assertion that to be surrounded on all sides by the madly fleeing leapers as clods of dirt were thrown into the air, and to hear the hunting cries of fellow warriors, was an experience unlike any other. A leaper hunt such as this was one of life's most exhilarating events.

Ray and Beowulf had no way of knowing how much distance they had covered or how many of the herd had been killed; time had no meaning for them. Without turning his head, Beowulf panted, "How many we kill so far, Ray?"

"I dunno, Beowulf," Ray said, himself breathing heavily under the conflicting imperatives of exhaustion and excitement. "We've been in the herd five minutes or five hours—I have no sense of time."

"Jeez!" Beowulf yelped as a Centaur warrior nearly drove into them the leaper he was pursuing.

Ray had the rhythm now: thrust and pull, thrust and pull. Blood. Thrust and pull. Ray and Beowulf were both lost in the frenzied bloodlust of killing, forgetting for a while their civilized veneer and becoming for a few moments two beings acting out a drama that had its roots in the dawn of time.

Enough, a part of Ray finally cried. *Enough!*

"Stop!" Runner-with-the-Wind rasped, his throat choked by dust. "We have killed sufficient leapers for our needs."

"Stop, Beowulf," Ray ordered. The big dog, his chest heaving, slowed to a trot and then stopped completely.

The herd, still running madly, disappeared into the distance, moving off like a passing thunderstorm that has spent its energies long enough in one place. Runner drew his flint *sha* and chose the largest of the dead leapers that had fallen in his vicinity. Quickly, efficiently, he cut open its chest cavity and withdrew the still-warm heart and liver. He cut a small slice from the heart and wolfed it down in one bite.

"Father leaper, I thank you, I salute you by taking your essence into my body." Then he cut out the tongue and laid it with the liver—to be cooked and eaten at a feast prepared by his *sharnan*. The head, Ray learned later, would be cut off and placed atop a high pole so that no predators might violate it before the *nav* could strip the flesh from the bones and ensure that the spirit would be released to drift cleanly and gratefully to the head leaper spirit with the thanks and apologies of the tribe.

★   ★   ★

Secure in the knowledge that the successful leaper hunt would provide his tribe food for many days or even weeks, Runner bathed in a small, meandering stream not far from the scene of the hunt. With him was the two-legged warrior and the massive leaper killer "Beowulf." Runner had to admit to himself that the two of them had acquitted themselves with honor during the hunt. Aloud, he said, "You both did well; it was a good hunt."

Ray's face wrinkled up into that strange configuration which the humans called a "smile"; it meant he was happy. "Thank you, Runner."

The *bor* of the stream was good, Runner thought. It was cool and refreshing after the heat and dirt of the hunt. Runner pulled handfuls of sand and small pebbles from the streambed and used them to remove the crusty sweat and blood which caked most of his body. The Centaur chieftain was not surprised to find blood oozing from numerous small cuts and abrasions; as leathery and tough as his skin was, he had come to accept the many lacerations caused by stones and hooves during the fury and madness of a hunt.

Ray followed Runner's example and also helped Beowulf wash away the dirt and dust of the hunt. Unlike some of the other dogs, especially Frodo, Beowulf loved to bathe. He rolled on his back in the stream, kicking his legs as he "rooched around"—as Ray called it, using one of the old Pennsylvania Dutch expressions from his childhood.

As Runner and Ray bathed, they watched the nearby *sharnan* of the tribe busy skinning the dead leapers which the hunting party had killed. It was *sharnan's* duty and little concerned Runner. As he splashed the refreshing *bor* over his flanks, however, he noticed Ray watching the *sharnan* work.

"Tell me, Runner," Ray said, "how much of the leaper's body do you use?"

"How much?" said Runner blankly. "Why, we use it all—every last bone and sinew." He scratched himself absently and thought for a moment, then continued, "The skin makes good blankets and hut coverings. When it is tanned, the leather can be cut into strips and the strips then used to bind things and to lace up hut flaps. The bones are cracked for their marrow or fashioned into tools."

"Tools?" asked Ray.

"Yes," said Runner. "Many fine tools come from the bones, including needles. The thread comes from the sinews which bind the leapers' bones together."

Ray nodded appreciatively and said, "And then there's the meat, of course." That caused Beowulf, who was now drinking from the fast-running stream, to lift his head and run his tongue around his muzzle hungrily. Beowulf's stomach, responsive to the big dog's wishful thoughts, rumbled and growled.

Ignoring Beowulf's stomach rumblings, Runner said, "Just one leaper provides many fine steaks. Or the meat can be cut into strips and dried for long migrations. The tongue and brain provide delicacies which are enlivened by the wild roots and vegetables the *sharnan* and children gather."

"Centaurs more like dogs than humans," Beowulf offered, surprising Ray by joining the conversation. "You use the whole antelope, not just the meat."

"Yes," agreed Runner. "The intestinal sacs even become *bor*-carriers." Runner looked thoughtfully at Beowulf before saying, "The People still do not fully trust your kind, guardian of the *teve* eaters, but I think they soon shall." He turned to Ray and said, "I must go now."

"I think you impressed Runner today," Ray said to Beowulf. "Now he not only thinks of humans as real 'people,' but dogs as well, I believe."

"Dogs *is* people," said Beowulf as if startled by Ray's words.

" 'Course you are," Ray said, scratching Beowulf behind his right ear.

Looking after the departing Runner, Beowulf said thoughtfully, "Is a bad thing we do here . . . is bad to kill the grass that the antelopes eat." Beowulf looked down, not wishing to look Ray in the eyes while he voiced criticism of Men's policies. "The Centaurs eat the antelopes and the antelopes eat the grass; no grass, no antelopes . . . and no Centaurs."

"You're right, Beowulf," Ray admitted. "That's why Mary and Taylor, and you and I, are in such a pickle."

"Doan talk 'bout food," Beowulf said, his stomach rumbling again.

★   ★   ★

The fire leapt higher and higher. It was fed by a continuously flowing stream of small children carrying dried leaper droppings, twigs, dried *teve*, and whatever else they could find that would burn.

Sitting beside Mary, Ray leaned over to her and told her that one did not simply accept the gift of life spirits without acknowledging that precious gift; Runner and the tribe must thank and properly honor the leaper spirits if they were to continue to favor the tribe with their bounty. As Mary nodded, indicating she understood his explanation of what they were about to observe, Ray prepared to record the ceremony.

Runner occupied the seat of honor and command as the holy one, the *tanakiv*, prepared the dancers for their homage to the leaper spirits. Runner nodded to the *tanakiv* and the shaman gave the order to the drummers.

The drumming began; it was a slow accented two-time. The dancers, imitating leapers in their movements and moving slowly at first, entered in an informal group, moving clockwise around the fire. They stepped heavily on the loud beat of the drum, stamping down hard then bringing a hoof down again on the half beat. Each dancer was mimicking the slow grazing movements of the leapers, head and shoulders moving slowly from side to side. They gathered in a circle around the fire and danced in place. The slow drumming continued and they knelt to face the fire, continuing their dancing rhythm by swaying from side to side.

The drum beat sharply, once. One of the dancers rose and danced in place, his four legs moving in unison. Another sharp drum beat and another dancer struggled to his feet and then another and another. Soon all were up and dancing in place.

The drumming picked up speed and the dancers were given *shars* by those watching by the light of the fire. Four of the better dancers seemed to charge the watchers but pulled up suddenly. Another four pretended to fight each other as leaper bulls do in the spring.

The drumming grew louder still and several of the dancers were handed bells made from hooves. They shook them vigorously and the other dancers leapt into the air joyously. The drumming subsided, returning to the original beat, and the dancers regrouped and exited.

Runner stood. "The spirits of the air and land have smiled upon us and given much *teve* for the leapers. The father leaper has heard our pleas and given us many leapers that their bodies might sustain us. The leapers fulfill the duty nature has given them—as we must do by glorifying the unity of all things as part of the godhead of nature."

Runner paused, then broke into a wide smile. "The spirit has done as it must, now let the flesh rejoice also. I would make a song of the hunt!"

"Ho, Runner, sing then," a voice cried out from the darkness.

"Yes," insisted another, "give us a song of the hunt."

Runner paused, then began to sing:

> Thunder, thunder across the prairie
>   rumbled,
>
> Clouds of dust swirled and tumbled.
>
> Hooves uncounted smote and beat,
> O hear the sound of striking feet!
>
> Warriors with tails alashing,
>   awaited the herd leaping and flashing.
>
> I, Runner-with-the-Wind, *shar* blooded and steady,
>   held my warriors eager and ready.
>
> Quick—chase and pursue,
>   thrust and thrust anew.
>
> Blood, bodies falling in death,
>   thrusting right, thrusting left.
>
> The *teve* first virgin and green
>   then trampled and red.
> Everywhere leapers fall dead!
>
> Ho, all hail Runner's tribe,
> Let mighty hunters prosper and thrive!

"I, too, would make a song!" shouted a warrior when Runner had finished to appreciative murmurs.

"And I!" shouted another.

Checking his holocorder to be sure all was well, Ray said to Mary, "It's going to be a long night."

III

Although Beowulf's experiences had softened his attitude toward the Centaurs, Littlejohn and the others were still less than comfortable in their presence. But after the leaper hunt, Beowulf and Sunchaser acted as mediators and brought the two sides together. Most importantly, it was to be a meeting of the "foot soldiers"—neither Ray nor Runner-with-the-Wind were to be present; if peace were to be made between the antagonists, they would make it themselves. Ray had helped to the extent of teaching the dogs as much of the Centaur tongue as he thought they could quickly master.

Now, while songs were being sung around the tribal fire, the two groups had gathered out on the empty plain to see what common ground they could find that might draw them together as equals. After much hemming and hawing, and much nervous shuffling about, Leaperstalker broke the ice by saying brusquely, "Well, companions of the two-legged warrior WWhey, we have brought skins of *vez.*" He shuffled nervously and continued, "It is a special drink, to be downed in friendship."

"Thank you, Leaperstalker," Beowulf said, thereby startling the Centaur warrior who did not anticipate Beowulf's knowing either his name or so much of their language. "As token of our good will, we have brought special foods and other treats."

Stiff as wooden Indians, the two groups arranged themselves in a large circle and began to pass the food and skins. At Sunchaser's suggestion, the Centaurs had brought with them leather bowls for the dogs to drink from. As Beowulf's huge tongue lapped up the strange-smelling brew, Littlejohn watched carefully and asked, "What you call this drink again?"

"*Vez,*" replied Moon-son as he accepted one of the dried peaches the dogs had brought with them. Mary had certified the acceptability of all the food for Centaur consumption.

"Hey, this stuff pretty good," Beowulf commented, lifting his dripping muzzle from the bowl of *vez.*

The Centaurs, too, after seeing the look of delight on

Moon-son's face, were now eagerly sampling the dried fruits the dogs had brought.

Whereas Ozma had at first stood back from the circle of Centaurs and dogs, fearing to approach, she now shoved her way in between Grendel and Sinbad to try this wonderful new drink that everyone else was slurping down in huge quantities. "Please," she whined, "I need bowl." One of the Centaurs cheerfully complied, passing down one of the leather bowls.

The Centaurs did their best to keep up with the thirsty dogs, draining whole skins of *vez* directly into their mouths. Whatever walls of suspicion separated the two sides initially, they came tumbling down before an onslaught of alcoholic glee and good fellowship. When Gnurkiller patted Littlejohn on his massive head, the big dog just swiped his tongue across the Centaur's greenish-yellow rump. "Hey, you got pimples there," Littlejohn commented when he sensed the tattoo ridges.

"He got lots in common with Taylor, then," Frodo said in English so the Centaurs would not understand. "Taylor gets zits on his ass, too."

At that, the dogs broke out in gales of hysterical laughter. "Oh, Frodo," wheezed Beowulf as he rolled on the ground in a near fit, "you such a funnybones!"

The dogs and the Centaurs soon fell into exchanging raucous dirty stories, swapping tall tales and exaggerated personal narratives, and generally cementing interplanetary relationships. When the supply of *vez* was threatened, Moon-son simply sent someone back for more.

It was a *good* night.

★   ★   ★

"This way," said Frodo. Ray followed the scout dog through the gloom of the dark night to the hut that Runner had provided for the birth of Mama-san's puppies. Even before he parted the rawhide curtain that served both as a door and a guarantor of privacy, he could hear Mama-san's intermittent yelps as the pain came in waves.

"How is she?" he asked of those inside as he joined them.

Littlejohn looked up with concern on his face. "Don't know, Ray. Seems to be taking much time."

As Ray stepped forward the circle of dogs broke to allow

him to bend down beside Mama-san's rude bed of leaperskin blankets. Her flanks were heaving and a stab of concern pierced Ray. "Don't worry, Mama-san, everything's going to be all right." Mama-san tried to show her teeth in a smile but the pain made her wince instead.

Ray looked at the anxious dog faces staring at him through the musky gloom of the hut's interior. "Don't be so damned long-faced; she's not in any danger as far as I can see. Hell, I've delivered dozens of puppies in my time," Ray lied. "You don't think you mutts are the first scout dogs I've ever seen, do you? Before I got my own team I trained with some of the best handlers in the Bureau—birthing a pup is the easiest thing in the world. We just have to wait and be patient; time will bring the babies." He squinted at the darkness in the hut. "Frodo, go and fetch one of our electric torches from the hover van; Taylor knows where they're kept. Then get yourself back here as quickly as possible."

"Right, Ray," rumbled Frodo, pleased to have something more to do than sit around moping.

In time-honored tradition, Ray had some water boiled and prepared Mama-san as best he could. He explained to her what she would feel—it was her first birth—and what to do when she felt certain pains or sensations. Then he settled back to wait.

"Aren't you gonna do anythin' else for Mama-san?" asked a worried Sinbad.

"I've made her as comfortable as possible. That's all I or anyone can do until the pups decide they want to come out; now we must wait for their arrival."

Frodo returned with the electric torch and Ray set it aside for when it would be needed. He saw no reason to waste the energy cells when there was no special need for more light. The present sources of illumination were leaper fat candles, and they sputtered and hissed, dripping wax as they burned. The amount of light they threw was rather limited but sufficient for the time being.

As the night crept by it was impossible for the other dogs to maintain their level of excitement and, one by one, they dozed off. Ray, though sleep called to him to lie down and close his eyes for just a moment, managed to stay awake by occasionally feeling Mama-san's swollen belly and whispering words of reassurance into her ear.

Finally, in the dregs of the long night, Mama-san twitched and then twitched again. As Ray bent over her, she cried, "They're coming, they're coming!"

Instant pandemonium. Ray shushed everyone down and took up his position as head midwife.

"It be okay, Mama-san," soothed Grendel.

"Yah, we with you," agreed Littlejohn.

"We all love you," crooned Ozma.

Mama-san smiled gratefully, then whined as the contractions grew stronger. Ray told her to help the contractions along, to press down with all of her might when the waves came. She murmured that she would try.

Ray, with his hand on her swollen belly, also felt for the strong birth contractions. "That's it, press down hard." Mama-san obeyed and soon a tiny head popped into view.

"Jeez, look at—" one of the dogs began.

"Shut up!" Ray snapped, instantly regretting his outburst but aware that he needed no distractions at this particular moment.

Letting Mama-san's instincts do most of the work, Ray did no more than carefully guide the little body out. When the first puppy had exited its mother's womb and entered into a whole new world, Ray placed it near Mama-san's head so she could both see it and lick it dry of the birth lubrication.

There was a bit of a wait before the second and third ones came, but soon their heads, too, made their initial appearances in the world and Ray guided them both out as he had the first puppy. Numbers four and five came along in rapid succession, little bundles of life from an assembly line.

The sixth—and last—puppy did not want to give up the womb quite so easily.

"It will not come," Mama-san whined, "it—"

"Damn!" Ray swore in frustration. He pulled on a sterile latex glove, lubricated it, then groped around for a moment until his fingers told him the story: The sixth baby wasn't in the correct position to be expelled from the womb. Working by feeling, Ray turned the tiny body in an attempt to free it.

"I think I've got it," he said to Mama-san. "Press down again." Almost immediately puppy number six backed into life—leaving its mother's womb rump first.

There was a sigh of relief from the assembled dogs anxiously watching the whole drama. Ray pulled off the glove and again placed the newborn puppy near its mother's head for its post-birth licking.

Ray stretched, then massaged the muscles at the back of his neck. "I think that's it, but we'll have to wait some time to be sure," he said, "and there's the placenta yet to come." He picked up the yelping little balls one at a time and peered at their nether parts. "Hm-m-m, looks like we've got three little girls and three little boys here. Well done, Mama-san."

"Thanks, Ray," said Mama-san as the placenta came out. Ray knew she would eat it, as dogs always do, and he looked away. The other dogs, meanwhile, broke into cheers and joined Ray in congratulating the proud but exhausted Mama-san. The puppies were praised and admired as perfect, as too beautiful for words. Actually, Ray thought they looked more like drowned rats than tiny dogs, but then Ray mused to himself that every newborn baby is beautiful to its family.

"I've had enough excitement for one day," said Ray. "I'm hitting the sack—and see to it that Mama-san is allowed to do the same shortly."

"G'night, Ray," said Grendel, "and thanks."

"Sure. Good night."

PART THREE
Ringgren

9

Ray walked to where the dogs were camped and put down the several bags containing their suppers. "What're we having tonight, Ray?" asked Sinbad.

"Oh, let's see," Ray said, digging in the bags. He pulled several plastic containers out of a bag and popped the lid off one, peering inside. "Well, it looks like ground leaper meat here." He popped the lid off another container and announced, "Various veggies in this one and some of the others have some grains mixed together."

"Jeez, Ray," said Littlejohn, "we've been eatin' lots of leaper meat lately."

"Yeah, well, we all have," Ray said. He put the food into the dogs' bowls and jumped back out of the way as they surged toward their suppers. "Say, you guys wouldn't want a little *vez* to wash that down with, would you?" he asked maliciously. When Beowulf raised his muzzle and gave him a look, Ray said, "No, I guess not."

"Beowulf's head not stop throbbing for two days," said Pandora. "It be while before he or Littlejohn want do that again."

Ray walked back to the van for his own supper. "What're we having tonight?" he asked Mary.

"Leaper casserole."

"Again?" he asked incredulously.

"Don't say anything," cautioned Taylor good-naturedly. "She's still looking for a way to liquefy it; we've had it in every other possible form."

"Well," said Ray, trying to make the best of the situation, "we'll be having vegetables with it, of course. . . ." His voice trailed away as he noticed Mary shaking her head.

"No vegetables tonight, Ray. Taylor forgot to go looking for edible plants with the women and the children today," Mary explained as Taylor looked sheepish.

"It's just as well, I guess," Ray said, again looking on the bright side. "I'm supposed to go to the sweat lodge for my vision tonight, and Runner *did* say I shouldn't eat for a few hours before. I'll just skip supper to be on the safe side."

"About this 'vision' ceremony," began Taylor. "I'm not sure if it's such a good idea. I mean, I realize you have to go native sometimes to be privy to the innermost secrets of the people and culture you're studying, but isn't this getting to be ridiculous?"

"Taylor's right," agreed Mary. "You killed a hide cat—three, actually—and you and Beowulf even went on that insanely dangerous antelope hunt. All that should prove your worth. You've been through a lot in the past couple of weeks; can't Runner see that?"

"Really," insisted Ray, "it's not that big a deal. I just have to fast a little and then go sit in a sweat lodge for a night. Sometime during the night I'll have a 'vision' of an animal or an inanimate object and from that I'll take my tribal name. Every Centaur youth goes through it after winning his *shar*." *Besides,* Ray thought, *it's been a long time since I've tried a weird experience like this—I'm actually looking forward to it!*

Unaware that Ray had made up his mind to do it regardless of what she had to say, Mary continued. "Yes, but *you're* not every Centaur youth—you're a mule-headed human being. This strange stuff you have to drink to experience the vision—this *kiv*—who knows how it might affect a human being?"

Exactly! thrilled Ray to himself, *exactly, my dear*. Aloud, he just said, "That's it, don't you see? It'll probably have no effect on me at all. I'll just fake a vision, get my name, and all will be well again." He laughed, "No sweat."

The hut had been built on the top of a small plateau approximately five kilometers outside the camp. It huddled among boulders nearly twice its size, a small oasis of warmth and comfort among the cold, angular rocks jutting from the ground like misshapen teeth.

The six rocks hissed and threw off copious clouds of steam when Ray poured water over them. The air was steamy and thick enough to cut with a knife. The air outside was cold and, where the mud covering had been insufficiently applied to the exterior of the hut, it managed to get in. The boulders shielded the hut from the main force of the wind but still the chill air swept over it like a river, the cold air penetrating the cracks in the dried mud and dribbling down the walls to the dirt floor to flow across it in tiny rivulets until it touched his hot, sweaty skin.

Ray shivered when caressed by the icy fingers of the cold air and waited patiently for his vision. According to Runner, his soul would leave his body behind and travel for one night, encountering many animals and strange creatures. When he awoke from his drugged sleep, one animal or creature would be uppermost in his mind. From that vision would come his warrior's name, the name that would bind him to the tribe and vice versa.

To launch Ray on his night of soul-traveling, Runner had the *tanakiv* prepare a foul-tasting concoction which Ray was supposed to drink. Lifting it to his lips, Ray said, "Couldn't I just kill another *gnur* instead?" When Runner said nothing, Ray held his nose and drank as much as he could in one gulp. "Ugh," he choked, "what's in this stuff?"

"Just *bor* and the *kiv* itself," Runner replied as he prepared to leave Ray to his night of soul-travel.

Alternately sweaty-sticky and chilled, feeling miserable and sorry for himself, Ray sat in the little hut and awaited his vision. *This is going to be great,* he thought. *Well, either great or a great waste of time—I hope this experience doesn't turn out to be a dud. On the other hand,* he realized nervously, *I could go far, far away and never come back—I could end up a basket case!*

After sitting patiently for what seemed like forever, Ray began to doubt anything was going to happen. Disgusted, he started to chide himself for the position in which he found himself when a wave of nausea overtook him. He closed his eyes and felt himself falling into a death-black void.

Ray's senses told him his body was being consumed by the furious heat of voices given shape and form; he forgot all about the steamy heat of the sweat lodge as he was swept up in sensations he'd never before believed possible. His ears were assaulted by the bombastic, shrill keening of the colors of the spectrum: A wretched red buzzed fiercely at him, yellow ycleped, and brown gurgled like an excrement-smeared baby.

"Jesusgodmary . . ." Flashing images reared up at him like hydraheaded monsters on a field of writhing bloodworms, the very texture of their shapes dissolving into sweet-tasting, sour-smelling bile that burned with the corrosive edge of acid.

Ray felt himself melting, his skin splitting to allow his mucus-slick innards to ooze out while his parents watched and applauded, singing, "For he's a jolly good fellow . . . which nobody can deny!" He collapsed into a mass of protoplasm that bubbled furiously before it flowed outward, dividing into three equal sections. Each puddle coalesced into a carbon copy of his original body. Ravens, with enormous female breasts and long, flaming penises, took hold of each Ray and nailed the three of them to crosses of painful self-awareness. Ray willingly confessed to every sin he'd ever committed and some he hadn't.

His three bodies evaporated in the glare of a nova-exploding sun and merged once again as a heavy rain carried them into the cracks of the dry soil.

Tendrils reached out from his mind and caressed the limpid softness that was the flaccid underbelly of an understanding beyond the capability of the conscious mind. Taking root, the tendrils drew him to that wholeness (holeness?) with nature usually reserved for the unfertilized egg and the freshly dead corpse.

Ray slowly became aware of his surroundings. The occasional hiss or pop from the fire held a new fascination for him, and he could feel the heat of the stones on his sweaty skin. Aware of each cell, almost, in his body, he did indeed feel his soul or mind lusting to break free of the bonds that held it to his corporate self. Suddenly, he gasped and collapsed backwards, falling flat on his back. Simultaneously, he was outside of himself, watching as his own body went limp on the floor of the sweat lodge.

Feeling freer than ever before, his disembodied self ventured gingerly beyond the confines of the hut. The stars burned brightly in the cloudless sky, a million candles flickering amid the folds of a black velvet ceiling. He sensed a kinship with them, secure in the knowledge that he was among friends, among eternal companions. "Ray," they called to him, "we've been waiting for you. There's a place for you here among us deep and alone in the corners of this mad universe. Join us, friend, and your burning soul will light the heavens forever as ours do."

"Ah, no, sorry," a part of Ray responded. "I'd like to, but—"

. . . Then he heard *It*. It seemed a million kilometers away at first; then he could tell it was coming closer. He wanted to run but a futile attempt convinced him that some force rooted him to the spot.

The heavy tread of its footsteps came closer and closer and soon he could hear its breath rasping in and out of its throat. Boulders began to roll toward him, bounding across the rough-surfaced ground like poorly thrown bowling balls. He shrieked in terror and threw up his arms, trying to shield himself from what he supposed was imminent doom.

When nothing happened, he opened his eyes. The boulders had been shorn in half and had missed him by meters. Somehow, he had summoned the power to save himself. But now the elemental force that was stalking him was at hand.

It came over the top of a small rise and halted, staring greedily at him. It seemed to possess no permanent shape, now assuming the outlines of a giant Kodiak bear, now flowing into the outlines of a killer ape, now into the shape of some long-tentacled horror from the deep. *Whatever* it really was, Ray knew it had come for him: "I want your soul, two-legged one," it seemed to be saying directly in his mind. "I will devour you and you will exist no more." Assuming the configuration of an upright lion with the head of an eagle, the beast began to stride toward him.

Terrified, Ray turned to run. Too late. The eagle-headed

monster caught him from behind, sinking its claws into his
back. As he screamed in pain and fear, the eagle's beak slashed
and tore at him, opening gaping wounds in his neck and
shoulders. Suddenly, without actually seeing it happen, he
knew the thing had metamorphosed again. Fearing that what
savaged him now was something too horrifying to even
contemplate, he rejected trying to see what the shape-changer
had become. Instead, he reached out his arms and dug into the
loose soil with his fingers, trying to pull himself forward.

As he scrambled and crawled, the thing roared hideously and
began to tear great hunks of flesh from the backs of his legs.
"No-no-no-no!" he shrieked as he tried to pull away. With a
sudden lurch, he lunged forward. His joy at "escaping,"
however briefly, soon subsided when he realized his freedom
had come at the cost of his legs—which the beast had pulled off
as easily as a small boy would pull the wings off a fly: *I cannot
die*, Ray told himself. *This is only a vision, a dream—even so,
I MUST defeat this apparition!*

Suddenly, Ray felt a great rage building in him; a rage so
immense it drove whatever thoughts of death and defeat he
might have from his mind. He looked to the stars and said, "If
you are my friends, then give me your energy, your fire!" He
thrust his right hand high into the night sky and molded a
fireball from the air. Pulling the starfire down from the
heavens, he turned over and, ignoring the pitiful remains of his
legs, he cocked his arm and hurled the flaming mass at the
still-advancing monster. The fireball missed as the thing
stepped aside stiffly. Again Ray molded a fireball from the
nuclear furnaces of the sky, and this time the fireball hit the
monster squarely in its chest. Immediately the beast was
covered from head to foot in a raiment of fire. He heard the
stricken apparition bellow, a roar that made the very earth
tremble.

It turned to run away but it was obvious to Ray that the thing
was doomed. The fire crept up its body like a quickly moving
disease, covering the thing and clinging to it. It writhed within
the flames and stumbled to its knees, its shape changing
futilely from moment to moment. As Ray watched, its form
blurred as it melted into the ground. Great clouds of steam
vented into the cold night air as it dissolved, twisting and

funneling as they went. Suddenly the creature was no longer there.

Looking down slowly, fearful of what he might see, Ray now observed that his legs were still attached to his body. *It's all in the mind,* he reminded himself. Then he got up and walked over to the still-sizzling ground and stared at the smoking remains of the beast and smiled. With his new awareness he could hear . . . feel . . . bits of thought from the sleeping dogs five kilometers away. He laughed and began to run.

Ray's disembodied self dashed from the small plateau and ran down its slopes to the floor of the plains. A will-o-the-wisp, he darted among the grazing leaper herds, leap-frogging over individual leapers' backs. It was such a marvelous feeling; they weren't even aware of him. He was a ghost, a shade impossible to see in the darkness of the night. Suddenly, he knew this was how Runner-with-the-Wind got his warrior's name.

He felt his body reaching, growing, toward the beckoning stars. He picked several out of the inky blackness of space and toyed with them as if they were a child's marbles.

"Yes, yes, YES!" he shouted to the night.

Ray felt his shoulders being shaken vigorously. He awoke to see Runner-with-the-Wind, accompanied by Mary and Taylor, peering down at him with concern.

"He's coming out of it now," he heard Mary say.

"Good morning, Ray," Runner addressed him. "How are you feeling?"

"Like I've been beaten with clubs. That brew really packs a wallop."

"You had a vision, then?" Runner inquired.

"I did indeed," Ray answered, putting a hand to his aching head. He sat up, instantly regretting it. "I suppose you'd like to hear about it?"

"That would be useful if you are to receive your warrior's name," Runner said genially.

"Okay, here goes." Mary and Taylor could only look on as Ray related his vision of the previous night to Runner, trying not to leave anything out and pausing only to gulp for breath. Mary laughed once—a sort of hiccup that she looked properly abashed for allowing to escape—and Taylor seemed to have difficulty keeping a straight face at Ray's recitation of his "adventure."

"Hm-m-m," mused Runner. "I would talk to the *tanakiv* so that he might identify your name. It would seem, however, that a name such as 'Monster-destroyer' would be appropriate."

At that, Ray grinned. In Federation-standard English, he said, "Monster-destroyer? Well, whatever."

When Runner had left, Taylor and Mary looked at Ray and both blurted out at the same time, "Monster-destroyer!"

"Now, don't be jealous of my terrific new name," Ray cautioned.

"It does have a ring," agreed a laughing Mary, "but I can't see myself saying, 'Monster-destroyer, dear, please take care of the garbage!'"

In spite of himself, Ray laughed too.

With the active assistance of Mary and Taylor, Ray continued working long and hard to put together a comprehensive assessment of the Centaurs' intelligence. Untrained as anthropologists, Mary and Taylor were still doing quite creditable jobs of cataloging the Centaurs' customs and rituals.

Mary, to the delight of the *tanakiv,* was interviewing the old shaman about his duties, including the special visionary powers he used to aid the tribe in hunting, in raiding, in the curing of illness, and in other such life activities.

Though his hands were no longer as steady as they once were, the *tanakiv* showed Mary his considerable skill in tattooing—both decorative and religious patterns. Mary watched as he used his bone needle to implant various hues under the skin of a young male Centaur who'd just been made a warrior of the tribe.

"You are so beautiful—for a two-legged one," the *tanakiv* said to Mary. "Why do you not bear any scars or tattoos? Do your people lack the skills or are you not religious?"

Mary tried to think of the appropriate response. "We have many religions where I come from," she began. "Some require such self-decoration but many do not."

"I see," said the *tanakiv*—who clearly did not.

"But it is not true that I bear no tattoos of my own," confided Mary as the young warrior left the hut. "Come see."

When the old Centaur approached her, Mary eased her coveralls down her hips and showed him the small butterfly she had tattooed on one buttock.

"Ho," laughed the *tanakiv*, "you two-legged ones surprise me more each day; perhaps you *are* a strange form of The People!"

The puppies made tiny squealing sounds and snuggled closer to Mama-san's swollen teats. Their eyes were due to open soon, but they had had long practice at finding their meals without sight.

"They're getting cuter every day," Mary noted. "Have you decided what you're going to name them yet, Ray?"

"Yes," Taylor agreed. "You've had plenty of time to make up your mind."

"I know. The dogs and I have decided."

"It's about time," sniffed Mary.

"Well, I'm going to name two of the males Tajil and Maximilian—Taddy and Max, for short—and the other one Gawain. The three little females are to be called Clementine, Emma, and Telzey."

"Tajil?" questioned Mary. "Why Tajil?"

Ray looked at the ground, a hint of sadness in his eyes. "Oh, let's just say that's the name of a dog I once knew a long time ago; a long time ago."

Seeing the sorrow in his eyes, Taylor said, "And Telzey?"

"Telzey," Ray explained, "is a name the dogs and I like for our own private reasons. Let's just say I like the sound of it." He smiled. "And the other names are ones that go with the names of the team—Maximilian, Gawain, Emma, and Clementine. Is that okay?"

"Sure, Ray," said Mary.

"*I* like the names, Ray," said a voice from near the ground. It was the feeding Mama-san.

"Thank you, Mama-san."

"I guess we'd better get back to work," suggested Taylor, taking Mary's arm and walking away.

Ray smiled and watched them go. "Tajil, Telzey, Maximilian, Gawain, Clementine, and Emma?" he faintly heard Mary saying to Taylor as they disappeared around the corner of the van.

★   ★   ★

Even though Taylor had long since repaired the communications antennae, he was careful not to transmit messages to the other groups by means of the stationary communications satellites hovering overhead in geosynchronous orbits. Instead, he raised the highly directional dish atop the van to its highest position and transmitted directly to Vaslow Khorsegai's group. As he explained to Mary and Ray, he had begun to share their paranoia and had decided to take no chances that any transmission might be monitored by agents of the Triumvirate.

At Ray's urging, Taylor suggested to Vaslev that a multigroup hookup be arranged between as many of the groups as possible, at least among those on the northern continent.

"I'm all for it," responded Vaslev, "and I think I can not only convince the other group leaders to agree to the linkage but also arrange the hookup in less than a week."

"That's great."

"There's just one thing, Taylor," cautioned Vaslev, his face in the tiny screen betraying his concern.

"Oh, what's that?"

"There's no way to accommodate such a complicated linkup without going through the satellites." When Taylor did not respond, Vaslev said, "Taylor . . . did you copy my last transmission?"

"Affirmative," said Taylor finally.

"Well . . . ?"

"Well, what?" Taylor shot back. "What do you want me to say? I know what the dangers are without you reminding me."

"Yes," said Vaslev, drawing his finger across his throat in an unmistakable gesture.

The multigroup hookup was going better than Ray had a right to expect. After a great deal of initial grumbling and self-serving, if understandable, moaning about the chances of losing their investments and/or going to a Federation prison planet, most of the terraformers bowed to Ray's and Mary's arguments about the legal and moral aspects of the situation and agreed it was not right that the Centaurs' intelligence be allowed to go unreported to the Judge Advocate's Programmers.

Juan Morales, the spokesperson for his group, was typical in his reluctant acquiescence to the situation. "First time in my friggin' life that I have the chance to get in on the ground floor of a good deal and me and my group has got to pull the plug on it!" he fumed.

"Hey, nobody said it was going to be easy," Ray said. "We might lose our shirts, too."

"As the instigators of this whole 'revolt,'" said someone else, "you might lose more than that."

Suddenly, Ray thought that it might *not* be such a great honor to be the discoverer of the Centaurs' sentience. He recalled that J. I. Guillotin, the French physician who invented the execution device that bore his name, was one of the victims beheaded by it.

As if to confirm Ray's worst fears, someone signed on with news that cast a pall over the proceedings. "Hello, everyone, this is Sohael Rashid. We're having a bit of a storm where we are and have been unable to transmit for the past hour or so. I hate to be the bearer of bad tidings, but I must speak up concerning something which one of us observed this morning."

"Yes . . . ?" said Ray slowly, dreading hearing Rashid's next words.

"Sasheen, my wife, thought she saw a bright light just to the east of our position; either a light or something shiny. She says the 'light' rose into the sky." He paused to take a drink out of a blue cup before continuing. "Having an idea what she could have seen, but discounting it as crazy, I got out my telescope and pointed it in the general direction of the area she reported seeing the flash. Nothing. Then, on a whim, I set up the tripod and looked to the sky. That's when I saw it."

"Saw what?" a voice asked quietly.

"In addition to the communications satellites, there's a small space station above this continent."

■

Each morning, Dr. Ake Ringgren cleaned his instruments. Not that they needed it—the young and not-so-young men of the Cadre were exceedingly healthy specimens. In the months the Cadre camp had been on Chiron, Ringgren had treated a handful of patients—and then it was for things like simple everyday accidents or sunburn. There was little for a doctor to do here, so Ringgren spent most of his free time either reading medical journals or wandering about the camp.

Any suspicions his casual but thorough examinations of the camp's defenses might have aroused were allayed by his innocent blue eyes and the look of bemused confusion he habitually wore on his face. His skinny body with its corpse-flesh complexion still drew an occasional remark from the guards, but they soon grew used to seeing him wander about the encampment, staring intently at everything about him.

"Morning, Doc," the guards would call out as he passed.

"Morning," he would acknowledge as he slowly ambled about aimlessly. Ake Ringgren, as ominous in his appearance as a stick-limbed scarecrow, was something considerably more than the false front he presented to the outside world.

Today, as Ake Ringgren walked around the camp, he had something very disturbing on his mind. Last evening, dawdling near the communication room, he'd overheard a conversation between Captain Bloom, the commandant of the small Cadre force, and his second-in-command, Hassib Amastan.

"Impossible!" Captain Bloom had said. "You mean to tell me they've been communicating about the Centaurs for over a week now and you've just picked up a transmission?"

"True, Captain," Amastan had replied, "but let me explain. Until yesterday they kept all communications between themselves short-range—a message would be passed from one group to the next group down the line, rather than being beamed to all the other groups simultaneously by means of the satellites. It is analogous to a line of workers handing a bucket of water to the next in line: Each takes a sip and passes the bucket on. It was impossible for us to intercept those transmissions and be aware of the fact that they concerned the Centaurs. The transmission signals were extremely directional. It was only when this Vaslev Khorsegai linked up all the groups for a 'town meeting' type of discussion about the Hollister-Brennan-Larkin group's findings that we became aware of what was going on."

"Goddamn civilians!" Bloom snarled. "They can't follow simple, unambiguous orders and keep their goddamn noses out of things that don't concern them! Well," he said with grim satisfaction, "curiosity killed the cat."

"You think extreme action is warranted, then, sir?" Amastan asked.

"What I think is unimportant; soldiers aren't paid to think. I have my orders, however, and there's only one thing I can do," Captain Bloom said. Then, scratching his nose thoughtfully, he added, "Just to cover our asses, I think tomorrow I'd better have you take the shuttle up to the *General Vann* and report back to Terra via the subspace communicator. If we've drawn the dubious distinction of eliminating some nosy terraformers, I'd like to have the authorization come down from on top."

Amastan grinned an oily smile. "I think, sir, that if you pull this off, there'll be a promotion in it for you."

Returning his second-in-command's smile with a broad one of his own, Bloom said, "And for several of my officers, too, eh?"

Ringgren had listened for a few more minutes and then slipped away.

"Yes, what is it, Doctor Ringgren?" Captain Bloom said without looking up from the maps he was examining.

"I understand Lieutenant Amastan will be taking the shuttle to the space station this morning."

His forehead creased by the narrowing of his eyes, Bloom looked up suspiciously. "Yes, that's right, Doctor." He paused, looking the civilian doctor over with the critical and disapproving eye of a lifetime military man. "How did you know about that?"

Ringgren just shrugged helplessly. "One hears things, I suppose."

"This is supposed to be a military outpost," Bloom snorted. "There's too damn much loose talk." Having said that, he added, "Why do you wish to go to the *General Vann*, doctor?"

"I need to pick up a few supplies and to run a test or two."

"How the hell can you need any supplies?" Bloom asked rhetorically. "Nobody's gotten sick yet."

"True, Captain," agreed Ringgren. He fidgeted as if reluctant to say something. "This is embarrassing to have to admit, but several of my live virus serums were accidentally thawed and I have to bring down replacement vials." That was at least partially true, Ringgren told himself. Several vials *had* thawed out—after he deliberately took them from the freezer and left them out overnight.

Bloom just sighed and shook his head. "Civilians—save me from goddamn civilians," he said, more to himself than to Ringgren. "Permission granted," he said without enthusiasm. "Go tell Lieutenant Amastan to expect a passenger."

Ake Ringgren almost preferred the inside-out feeling of a hyperspace jump to the "falling elevator" sensation of riding a Daae-Fujiwara negative gravity surface-to-space shuttle. Looking across the small cabin at Ringgren's pale and sweaty face, Lieutenant Amastan could not resist commenting, "What's the matter, Doc, is your stomach in your socks?"

Refusing to give Amastan the satisfaction of a curt reply, Ringgren simply said, "Yes, I suppose so."

Dejected that he was unable to get a rise from Ringgren, Amastan just grunted and stared at a viewscreen showing the world rapidly falling away from them.

Following Amastan's lead, Ringgren also looked at a viewscreen. Unlike the lieutenant, however, Ringgren chose to stare at the one which was focused upward, looking at the giant Lego construction hanging above the planet—the space station. Ringgren gulped; while it was better to look up than down, he nevertheless had the uneasy feeling that the shuttle was going to continue its rapid upward journey until it smashed into the space station.

"Ah, there we go," said Lieutenant Amastan as the shuttle craft began to slow its precipitous ascent into the heavens. *Thank God!* thought a relieved Ringgren.

Moving much slower now, the shuttle craft made its way unerringly to one of the docking bays and eased into the waiting receptacle like a bullet going into a revolver's chamber. A series of metallic sounds informed both men that their journey was over. Ringgren wasted no time in opening the door and stepping out into the *General Vann's* airlock. "Take it easy, Doc," laughed Amastan. "You made it."

A Lieutenant Srinavas was there to greet them. After a few perfunctory words of welcome, he and Amastan went off together and left Ringgren to carry out his own duties. Ringgren looked around and saw that the few others aboard the

General Vann were ignoring him for now. Apart from Srinavas, Ringgren knew, there were three others on the small station. Automation and robotic devices made possible the small number of human caretakers on board.

Serving as a backup base and communications center, the station contained medical and surgical facilities occupying a whole deck, including a dozen hospital beds; a security level; a recreation containing a substantial library of entertainment chips; a holobar where a lonely soldier could wet his whistle while enjoying the company of a lovely young woman (really just a three-dimensional projection of the station's computers, but so realistic that many an amorous patron believed she was real . . . until he put his hands through her); and other recreational facilities unavailable on the planet's surface. *Any* planet's surface, since the *General Vann* followed and supported the Cadre regulars wherever they went. All this Ringgren knew from his incessant and unauthorized forays into the camp's computer's memory.

Wandering about the station until he believed he had a good mental fix on the positions of the three crewmen, Ringgren nonchalantly but efficiently made his way toward the *General Vann*'s communications deck. Suddenly remembering something, he stopped halfway down a hallway and got down on one knee as if to tie his shoe. When he was sure no one was in the area, he swiftly transferred the needle gun he had strapped to his calf to his wrist, rolling down his sleeve so that the weapon was hidden from sight.

Taking a lift tube to the upper levels of the multideck station, Ringgren approached the main communications center. As he got closer, he could hear voices: Amastan and Srinavas.

"And this will give me all the power I need to transmit a message to Terra on one of the secure subspace channels?" Ringgren heard Amastan ask.

"Yes," Srinavas's voice replied. "I've shut down all non-essential functions of the station and activated another forty energy cores to provide you with the brute power you need to reach Terra." His back to a wall just outside the room, Ringgren heard Srinavas take a breath before saying, "I wish Captain Bloom himself were here—demobilizing the station to give you the power you need is not normal procedure." When

Amastan answered with a short, barking laugh, Srinavas asked, "Did I say something amusing, Lieutenant?"

"It's just that everyone's looking to cover his ass, Srinavas," Amastan explained, "our beloved commander-in-chief included. The reason I'm going through this whole business is because Captain Bloom wants to get the word, officially, from the bigwigs himself before proceeding."

"I see," said Srinavas dubiously.

"Good," said Amastan. "Now, if you've shown me everything I need to know, I'd appreciate it if you go find something to occupy your time while I transmit."

"Are you sure—"

"Take a hike!" snapped Amastan.

Ringgren barely had time to run down the passageway and find an open hatchway to duck into as Srinavas strode angrily from the communications room. "That was close . . . too close," Ringgren whispered to himself.

Ringgren quickly made his way back to the communications center and, upon hearing a tremendous hum, peered around the hatchway and into the center of the room. Amastan, his back to the hatchway, was leaning over a complicated-looking control console. As Ringgren watched, fascinated, a wall of readouts which indicated the power consumption began to light up like a Christmas tree. *Jesus*! Ringgren thought. *He's using enough power to blast a small moon out of orbit*! Just as starships "jumped" between normal space A and normal space B, so too did subspace messages; otherwise, to communicate between Terra and outposts many light-years distant would take years, Ringgren realized.

A barely audible chiming sound, incongruous amidst the impression of unimaginable power being harnessed by the superconductive instruments in this room, indicated that the connection had been made with Terra. Slipping into the back of the room and taking refuge behind a desk, Ringgren watched as Amastan quickly and efficiently fed the computer the secret recognition codes that would direct his signals to the top echelons of the Federation—to someone within the offices of the Triumvirate itself.

Within minutes, a second, deeper, chiming sound announced a presence at the other end of the linkage. As Ringgren watched, craning around the desk and pointing a tiny holocorder at what was before him, a figure coalesced in the center of the holo projection area. Ringgren almost gasped audibly; with no need to keep silent, Amastan *did* gasp upon seeing the figure. Although Ringgren had never seen the General, there was little doubt in his mind as to the identity of the tall man dressed in a gray Ganymede uniform devoid of insignia.

Amastan snapped to attention so quickly and completely Ringgren wondered why he didn't throw out a spinal disc. "Sir, I—" began Amastan, stopping when the General put his finger to his lips.

"Do not say my name or rank," the General cautioned. "Even a Federation triple-prime security transmission may be intercepted by hostile eyes and ears."

"Yes, sir, I understand."

"Do you accept that I am who I appear to be?" the figure questioned.

"Why, yes . . . yes, sir," said Amastan as he stared at the General's shimmering holo projection.

Just under two meters tall, with burnished gray eyes, dark blonde hair closely cropped, and a classic Roman nose, General Andrei Carras was not easy to mistake for anyone else. Ringgren noted that he bore the almost obligatory dueling scar, but on his right cheek—where it was put by a left-handed opponent.

"Good," said the General. "Then you will understand why I am doing this." At that, the General reached toward Amastan until his hand disappeared out of the picture. Suddenly, the picture dissolved into a shower of colored specks.

"Sir?" said Amastan questioningly.

"Not to worry, Lieutenant," reassured the General. "I simply wanted to establish my bona fides before going to voice transmission only. You understand my caution?"

"Yes, of course," said Amastan. *Even members of the Triumvirate protect their asses!* he told himself wonderingly.

"Now then, what is the status of your camp on planet X and why has your commander gone to the extreme of utilizing this emergency frequency?" the General asked.

Ringgren listened with interest—his holocorder getting it all down—as Amastan summed up what had happened on "planet

X" to warrant his commander's plea for clarification of his orders.

When Amastan was done, the General was silent for a minute or so, the nothingness transmitted by the projector exaggerating the length of his nonresponse. Finally he said, "Tell your commander that he has official backing for any extreme measures he feels compelled to take."

"Thank you, Gen—ah . . . *sir*," a nervous Amastan began, "but, with all respect, I think my commander is looking for something more concrete."

"Oh, he is, is he?" roared the General. "And what exactly would he like—a signed order authorizing the execution of these troublemakers?"

Relieved that he could not see the General's eyes, Amastan conceded, "No, of course not, but—"

"Listen, Lieutenant," the General said, "obviously, I *cannot* put any of this in writing because of the danger of it reaching our electronic watchdog and its guardians. I *can,* however, tell your commander that I have *never* gone back on my word to a fellow officer. If the fecal matter hits the ventilation system, his ass will be protected. More than that, I cannot promise."

"Yes, sir," said a chastened Amastan.

"Tell your commander I want the exterminatory action initiated as soon as possible." The General paused, then added, "He has his orders; he shouldn't need any handholding from me or anyone else. And tell him I don't want this channel used again unless it is a genuine emergency. That is all." After a few seconds had passed, the General asked, "Is there anything else . . . *Captain*?"

"No, sir," Amastan said. Then his jaw dropped and he said, "Thank you, sir."

Ignoring Amastan's gratitude, the General said, "I suggest that this conference is at an end."

"Yes, sir," said Amastan with more than a little bit of relief showing in his voice.

It took both Ringgren and Amastan a moment to realize that the connection had been broken. When the doctor understood that the General was no longer in contact with the station, he withdrew the holocorder and slid down behind the desk that hid him from Amastan's view. He had much to think about. But first, he had to slip out of the communications room undetected.

As he got to his feet, albeit still crouched over to avoid being seen by Amastan, Ringgren glanced up . . . and into the surprised face of Lieutenant Srinavas. "Hey, you . . . what're you doing here?" he shouted, fumbling for his side-arm.

"Oh, shit!" Ringgren said, raising his arm and shooting Srinavas in the throat with the needle gun. Standing up, he turned and fired at Amastan, the needle hitting him in the eye and making a rather disgusting *plopping* sound. Amastan fell dead without a word.

Trembling, Ringgren's gaze alternated between the two bodies. In all his years of service, he'd never had to kill so much as a fly before. Looking at the two bodies, he realized anew the high-stakes game he'd found himself involved in.

10

With both his needle gun and Amastan's energy pistol in his hands, Ringgren had no trouble persuading the three surviving crewmen to do as he wished. First, he forced them to take the two bodies and carry them to the cryogenic laboratory, then put them into individual lockers and activate the "freezing" function.

"Jesus," said one of the men, "why're we freezing them? They're dead, aren't they?"

"I rather imagine that they have families back on Terra," said Ringgren not unsympathetically. "When you're released, you can see to it that their bodies get home—if the Cadre bothers with details like that."

"When we're released?" asked one of the crewmen.

"I've got some unfinished business back on Chiron," explained Ringgren. "It wouldn't do to have you alerting the Neanderthal Captain Bloom about my activities up here the past hour, so you're going to take a short vacation, all expenses paid by the Cadre."

Ringgren then had them gather up about a week's worth of provisions and carry everything to the security deck. Once there, he locked them into one large holding area that possessed drinking and sanitary facilities in addition to a half-dozen cots. It may have appeared to be more rec room than prison, but Ringgren made sure it was a secure lockup.

"Why are you doing this?" one of the crewmen asked.

"I'm a psychopath," Ringgren said mildly as he went about his business. Then, closing the main cell door and making sure it was locked, he said, "You have enough food and other provisions to last you about a week—longer if you grow understandably conservative about your consumption levels as the days pass. Before you run out of anything, I should be back to see that you're released—either me or someone sent by me."

"Yeah, and what if something happens to you?" challenged one of the three men.

"That's why I want you men to say your prayers every night and ask the good Lord to keep me safe," Ringgren told them. "Ever see anyone die of starvation? Nasty sight, very nasty."

"Hey, wait!"

Ringgren turned and put his finger to his lips. "Now, now, children, there's no one to hear you. You just do as I say and I'll be back in a week or less. You've got a lot of holochips; here's your chance to see a whole year's worth of *Captain Trimble—Space Ranger* at once. Ta, ta."

Walking briskly back to the communications deck, Ringgren hoped that Amastan hadn't depowered the system and that the subspace carrier signal was still functioning. As he looked over the board, a smattering of dried bloodstains standing out vividly against the white surface, he hoped his training of so many years ago hadn't been made obsolete by new equipment. Fortunately, it all came back to him as he ran his fingers lightly over the control panel. He'd never seen a board quite like this one. Still, he told himself, *A board is a board is a board*.

His fingers danced, activating panels and causing small colored squares and rectangles to light up. Finally, everything was ready and the tremendous hum he'd heard earlier returned. "Thank you, Captain Bloom, for giving me this opportunity," Ringgren said out loud. "I would never have been able to contact Terra on my own."

Punching in his own set of secret recognition codes, Ringgren soon heard the faint chiming sound that indicated he had achieved linkage with his Terran superiors. Just as the image of the General had filled the room earlier, another figure was painted electronically in the center of the holo projection area.

"What is the meaning of this? Who has summoned me so?" demanded Thane Wyda, the Judge Advocate's Prime Programmer in NorAm and, hence, one of the most powerful people in the Federation. "You!" she cried, surprised to find Ringgren standing before her.

"Hello, Prime Programmer Wyda," Ake Ringgren said amiably, "meeting" the woman who'd sent him on this secret mission for only the second time in his life—both within the past four months. As was her wont, Thane Wyda followed the General's example in that she wore a simple black suit of rather severe cut. Her high standing permitted her the luxury—*if luxury is the right word,* Ringgren thought—of shaving her head completely with the sole exception of a single half-credit-piece-sized growth of hair directly on the crown of her head. Lesser members of the Order of Programmers were not so easily identified. Like Ringgren himself, this enabled them to lose themselves in the general populace when necessary.

"Your mission is intended to be top secret," she reminded him, adding crossly, "I daresay it's too late to remind you that you're also not supposed to break your cover."

"I'm sorry if I seem to have taken things into my own hands," apologized Ringgren, "but events are moving quickly here, too quickly for me to follow my original orders."

Then, as if realizing for the first time that such a transmission took an enormous amount of power—and access to one of only a handful of subspace communicators—Wyda asked, "Where *are* you, Programmer Ringgren?"

"I'm on board the *General Vann*, the Cadre space station in orbit above Chiron, " he explained. Glancing down at the floor guiltily and then quickly back up, he said, "I've not only broken my cover," he confessed, "I've done so in a major, major way: I've been forced to kill Federation personnel." A pained look crossed his face. "It was self-defense, to be sure, and they were Cadre regulars engaged in illegal and immoral activities, but—"

"We'll sort all that out later," interrupted Wyda. "For now, just tell me what's going on there."

Ringgren took a deep breath and quickly and efficiently explained to Wyda what Captain Bloom and Lieutenant Amastan had learned from the terraformers' ill-advised town meeting. Then he pointed to his holocorder and said, "Why don't I show you a recording I made as well? When you've seen it, I think you'll understand more readily the gravity of the situation as it is developing here on Chiron." He made the necessary adjustments to play the recorded chip through the station's equipment.

Wyda's face scrunched up in a way that suggested that whatever Ringgren showed her, it had better be damned important. Then, as the holo ran, her expression changed. Slowly, her features softened as a look of great sadness crept across her face. When the recording ended, she was silent for twenty or thirty seconds, lost in contemplation.

"Programmer Wyda?" said Ringgren tentatively.

Her holographic image—just a meter away from Ringgren, near enough for him to reach out and touch her, if he could have done so—straightened and looked him squarely in the eyes. "You have done well, Programmer Ringgren," she said in a firm, clear voice.

"I have done *right*," corrected Ringgren. "Fearing what this will do to our political system, to the Triumvirate and to the Cadre, I hesitate to call my actions an accomplishment."

"Yes, I understand," said Wyda so softly that Ringgren was beginning to wonder if this sympathetic woman was really the fearsome Prime Programmer of legend who supposedly ate junior Programmers for lunch, swallowing them whole. He needn't have worried.

"Great Caesar's balls!" she suddenly exploded. "I'll have Andrei Carras's head on a platter for this!"

Ringgren swallowed. The Judge Advocate, the ubiquitous world computer that both he and Wyda were sworn to serve and protect, was the "judicial branch" of the Federation, the watchdog which monitored and enforced the decisions reached by the executive branch, the Triumvirate. While the Order of Programmers had a small security force, it was nothing to rival either the regular armed forces or the Cadre, the special military arm of the Triumvirate. The Judge Advocate and its Programmers held the balance of power in the government, however. As the central nervous system of Terra and the entire Federation, the Judge Advocate could paralyze the Federation to enforce its judgments. Payrolls for the troops and the bureaucracy would not be met, food would not be distributed, and water mains and electric power would be cut off. Everything would grind to a halt and the Cadre and other armed forces themselves would force the three Consuls who made up the Triumvirate to resign their offices.

"Tell me, Prime Programmer," Ringgren asked, "why would the General risk a negative judgment by the Judge Advocate simply to deny the intelligence of an alien species on a planet so far from the rest of the Federation? I understand about the gee-wave stations, but can they be *that* important?"

Prime Programmer Wyda weighed her response for a long time. Finally she said, "Several weeks ago I did something almost unheard of these days: I spoke with the Judge Advocate 'in person' by means of one of the individual voice booths deep within the NorAm center. We had received more than sufficient data pointing to the Centaurs' probable intelligence and I wished to ask the Judge Advocate, which as you know can neither lie nor avoid its prime directives, why the Chiron project was being allowed to proceed." Wyda reached "off screen" to pick up a glass of water.

After taking a sip, she continued, "As so many of us have suspected, the Judge Advocate was content to allow the project to go forward because the Centaurs had not yet been *officially* labeled as a sentient species." Wyda raised a hand to ward off Ringgren's objection and continued. "I pointed out to the Judge Advocate that this seemed a rather callous judicially nit-picking attitude—one that met the legal obligations of the Code but which failed to meet the spirit of the law."

"Indeed," agreed Ringgren.

"Let me quote to you the Judge Advocate's response," said Wyda. "'Less than a year ago the signals we were receiving from so far away increased in number. Then, a sun in that vicinity went nova and the signals decreased in number. Quite possibly this was a natural occurrence, but a strong possibility exists that a star was blown up as an act of war. It is for this reason that we've deemed the gee-wave program on Chiron to be of the utmost importance.'"

Ringgren's mouth worked as he tried to assimilate this new information. The implications . . . *A race that blows up suns*! his mind screamed. "Jesus and Mohammed!"

"You can see why the General was allowed to corrupt the system so far," Wyda said. "But now, with this new evidence, with your recordings and the findings of this terraformers' group, things must be halted. We can play no more games."

"Tell me what I must do, Prime Programmer Wyda," Ringgren said.

"First you must prevent or, if necessary, defeat any attack on those courageous if foolhardy terraformers your Captain Bloom is planning to exterminate." Her image looked at him thoughtfully. "If we cannot secure the evidence of this anthropologist before it is destroyed by the Cadre regulars, your tape alone will not be enough to convince the Judge Advocate that there has been wrongdoing. No matter how guilty he appears, the General's precautions were wise: He can argue that the figure in the recording is a look-alike impostor and that the voice is not his either. The poor quality of the original transmission and the subsequent recording of it mitigate against your evidence being anything but circumstantial."

"You're right," conceded Ringgren.

"We must do something while it is still possible to contain the damage," said Wyda.

After a moment's pause, Ringgren brightened, saying, "I think I have a plan."

Following his transmission to Terra, Ringgren rerouted most of the station's power back to its normal functions and deactivated the subspace communicator. *Now for the most important part*, he told himself as he violated the inner workings of the communicator to detach and remove one of the key parts. It wasn't very big; it easily fit into the hiding place in the hollowed-out heel of his boot, but without it the communicator was just an expensive piece of junk.

Similarly, Ringgren sabotaged three of the *General Vann*'s four shuttle craft. Now, if Captain Bloom sent a signal to the station to send one of the shuttles down on automatic pilot, there would be no response. Ringgren would have the only operational shuttle on Chiron.

Climbing into the shuttle for his return flight to Chiron, Ringgren thought, *Well, I've pretty much bollixed things up as much as possible here—now let's see if I can find these damned terraformers who're causing so much trouble by insisting on doing the right thing!*

After administering himself a motion sickness nasal spray—and experiencing a moment of doubt—*I feel as if I'm forgetting to do something . . . but what?*—Ringgren punched in a series of commands that caused the shuttle to drop away from the space station. This time Ringgren's sensation of falling was even stronger than before because the shuttle really *was* falling.

As Chiron rushed up to meet him, Ringgren muttered, "Well, here goes nothing!"

ll

Runner-with-the-Wind moved cautiously, keeping downwind of the leaper herd. "They haven't spotted us yet, have they?" Ray asked, seated atop Beowulf's broad back.

"No, they'd have panicked if they had seen us or smelled our scent," Runner replied in a low voice.

"Think it's big enough herd?" Beowulf inquired.

"It will suffice." Runner laid a hand on Ray's shoulder. "Come, the scouts were right—the leapers have only just begun to graze this area. We will begin preparing for the hunt; they will still be here tomorrow."

"Fine, I—" Ray stopped in mid-sentence. The leaper herd had begun running away, bounding high in the air with those incredible leaping gaits that gave them their name.

"They could not know we were here," Beowulf said, hoping against hope that they had not smelled his own occasionally pungent body scent.

"Perhaps there are some *gnur* nearby," Runner said.

"No, Runner, look!" Ray exclaimed, pointing at the sky with his outstretched arm. "Something is descending." He shielded his eyes with his hand. "It looks like a shuttle craft."

A shuttle craft it proved to be, and it was growing larger by the second as it came closer, dropping toward the prairie in a blur of high speed. Still, even as it grew in size, Ray could tell that it would touch down anywhere from twenty to forty kilometers distant from them. *Well*, Ray thought, *now we know what the "light" Sasheen Rashid saw rising into the sky was*!

"You say this is a 'shuttle craft'?" said Runner. "You know of such wonders, then?"

"Yes, Runner," Ray said.

"This monstrous thing . . . is it from the heavens—from the gods?" Runner asked.

"It *is* from the sky," Ray admitted, "but not from the gods or the heavens; it comes from another land, a land far off and above the sky."

"Above the sky . . . ?" said Runner dubiously.

"It is where Beowulf and I come from, Runner," said Ray.

"Then it brings more two-legged ones like yourself?"

"Yes."

"Are they friendly or hostile?"

"I don't know, Runner," Ray confessed. "I just don't know."

"Come, then," Runner said. "Let us find this wonder and confront the new two-legged ones it brings."

After an hour or so of walking, the three of them stopped to refresh themselves by a fast-running stream. "It not be far from us now," Beowulf said. "We must be gettin' close."

"I don't know," Ray said. "On the plains, distances can be so deceiving."

Runner sipped a handful of the cool *bor*. "I agree with Beowulf," he said. "We must be getting close to where this marvel fell to the ground. Perhaps if we—" He stopped, cocking his ears questioningly.

When Beowulf joined Runner in rotating his ears toward a point on the horizon, Ray asked, "What is it?"

"Listen," said Runner. "Can you not hear it?"

"I think it's a hover scooter, Ray," said Beowulf.

"A hover scooter?" Even as the words left Ray's lips, he heard the high-pitched whine of a hover scooter engine not far off. Turning to Runner, Ray said, "I don't know if he's friend or foe, so here goes nothing." Ray asked Beowulf to allow him to stand on the scout dog's strong back. Steadying himself by placing a hand on Runner, Ray scanned the prairie for the source of the sound.

"Here! Here!" he waved his arms madly when he saw the hover scooter hurtling across the plains and ready to whizz right by their location without catching sight of them.

Ray was successful in attracting the driver's attention and the scooter turned toward them in one smooth and broad arc, sacrificing little of its speed. The high grass whipped viciously at the scooter's driver; he seemed oblivious to its effects as he skillfully guided the scooter directly toward the spot where Ray, Beowulf, and Runner were standing.

The scooter began to shed its speed finally and it stopped less than two meters from where the three bemused observers stood waiting in anticipation. Ray cradled his energy rifle in the crook of his arm and unobtrusively clicked off the safety.

"I'm glad to see you—all three of you," the scooter driver said as he dismounted stiffly and stared openly at Runner. "I was afraid I was hopelessly lost."

Ray looked at the skinny, red-haired man who couldn't have amazed him more if he'd materialized out of thin air. The man beat at the dust clinging to him and deposited on the ground the two energy rifles he'd had slung across his back. Somewhat mollified, Ray fingered his own weapon's safety and grudgingly clicked it back on.

He can't be more than twenty-nine or thirty, Ray told himself. *And whoever he is, he shouldn't be out in the sun with that complexion.* Already the young man's skin had started to redden; by nightfall it would be fiery red and burn like the devil.

Ray figured he'd better make the first move. "Well, this is my scout dog leader Beowulf," he said following the newcomer's lead and speaking Federation English. Beowulf, panting in the heat, just nodded. "My name's Ray Larkin and this—" he gestured toward Runner—"is Runner-with-the-Wind, my friend and chieftain. And unless you're looking for me or my group, you're lost all right." He paused for a moment, then continued, "I really think you'd better put something on quick to shield yourself from the sun—you're getting a great burn."

The young red-haired man looked at his bare arms and said, "I'm afraid you're right about that. It couldn't be helped, though; I was in too much of a hurry to reach you to take the time to think about things like dressing properly."

"To reach *me*?" Ray asked, not quite sure he could believe his ears.

"Absolutely. You *are* the young anthropologist who was bullheaded enough to ignore the PCB orders and demonstrate that these fellas here are intelligent beings, aren't you?" Ringgren said, pointing at Runner.

"See, Ray, you famous already," said Beowulf proudly.

"Yeah, like Custer," Ray said dryly. "To answer your question—yes," he said to the red-haired and red-skinned young visitor from the sky. "Now may I know who you are and what you want?"

"My name is Ake Ringgren. I'm supposed to be a civilian contract doctor assigned to the military outpost here on Chiron."

Ray did his best impression of a double take. "*What* military outpost? And what do you mean, you're *supposed* to be a doctor?"

"I guess it's a bit of a surprise"—*there's an understatement*! Ringgren thought—"but the General himself ordered the landing of a small force of Cadre regulars on Chiron less than a month after you and the other contract terraformers were put down. You aren't supposed to know about that, of course." Ringgren smiled disarmingly. "As for me, I *am* a doctor by training but my real job is serving the Judge Advocate by keeping my ears and eyes open for just this sort of illegal operation." As Ray's eyes widened, he added, almost as an afterthought, "I'm a Programmer."

"You're a Programmer? A spy for the Judge Advocate?"

Ringgren shrugged. "I prefer to say I'm a member of the Judge Advocate's intelligence-gathering branch."

With Runner looking on in polite puzzlement, Ray sat on the ground and crossed his legs. "I'm . . . I mean, I don't know what to make of all this; it's a lot to suddenly have to assimilate." He shook his head in wonderment. "A Cadre base here on Chiron . . . the Judge Advocate."

"Yes, I'm afraid I've given you a great deal to think about, but the truth is we haven't much time. They'll be missing the shuttle's return soon and not long after that Captain Bloom will discover that he can't contact the space station or call down another shuttle. So, if you'll just take me to your camp . . ."

"Runner," said a thoroughly bemused Ray, "it looks as if we're about to have company."

Ray, Taylor, and Mary sat directly across from Ake Ringgren in the living room area of the van as he explained more fully why he had sought them out.

"Let me get this straight," Taylor was saying. "You weren't sent here to determine whether or not the Centaurs are intelligent under the Bureau's accepted definitions, but simply to observe the Cadre force the General ordered here after we were landed."

"That is correct," Ringgren replied. "When we learned such a force was being sent, the decision was made to penetrate it in hopes of preventing any illegality, if such was planned."

As Mary and Taylor exchanged puzzled looks, Ray exploded, "If such was planned! Why the hell else would the General or the whole Triumvirate send a Cadre force to Chiron if not for some gross violation of the Code?"

Ringgren took a sip from the water glass in front of him and replied, "I was wondering when someone would raise just such a question. Can none of you guess why this Cadre force was put in position here?" he asked patiently.

"Surely not to protect us from the Centaurs," said Mary, "or else there would have been no reason for the shroud of secrecy they draped over everything."

"That much is obvious," agreed Taylor.

"You mentioned they were monitoring all satellite intergroup communications," Ray said. "Could it be that they're to prevent any of us—any group—from sending back information to Terra which might force the Judge Advocate to step in and halt the terraforming of Chiron—such as reports establishing the Centaurs as Code-protected beings?" Ray smiled grimly and added, "We didn't just arrive at that conclusion; it's something we've been discussing for a long time now."

Ringgren also smiled grimly. "You are absolutely correct, Ray. I recently learned that your reports to the other groups have—" He stopped suddenly and said, "Rather than explaining all this, perhaps I'd better let you see and hear it for yourselves."

With Taylor's assistance, Ringgren connected his holocorder to their system and started the recording he'd made on board the space station. The three terraformers watched and listened to the General in stunned silence, their only reaction an increasing hardness in their expressions.

"You heard Consul Carras give the order himself," Ringgren said when the recording was over. "Captain Bloom is presumably preparing an attack on your group this very minute."

Taylor blurted out, "They wouldn't dare!" Then, more softly, "Would they?"

"Oh, no?" demanded Ringgren. "Nothing to it, actually. All Captain Bloom has to do is blast you off the face of the planet and then make a report to Terra that you were killed by the wild animals of the planet—the quote unintelligent unquote Centaurs. He and his men will arrive too late to save you but *will* succeed in exterminating this particular band of killer Centaurs. Ties everything up neatly, eh?"

"Too neatly," insisted Mary. "There are bound to be questions, an inquiry. That recording itself is proof."

Ringgren looked at their shocked faces and felt sorry for them, for their blind faith in Federation "justice." He just shook his head and explained to them what Prime Programmer Wyda had said concerning the recording's worth as evidence. Then he added, "The Federation needs those gee-wave stations too much to allow the death of a few contract-team members to slow down their construction. No, there'll be very few questions asked . . . *if* the Cadre succeeds."

"So," asked Ray, "where does that put us?"

"On the offense, of course," stated Ringgren. "It's obvious, isn't it? The only subspace communicator within light-years is on the space station. I've already sabotaged it, but that's not enough—we've got to get them before they get us."

"Us?"

Ringgren looked pained. "I'm a Programmer for the Judge Advocate; I can't sit idly by and allow a crime to be committed—no matter what the reasoning behind it may be."

"Oh, really?" said Ray dubiously. "It seems to me that the Judge Advocate's office has been a little too knowing in all this—why hasn't anything been done before? Why wasn't this Cadre expedition stopped before it started?"

Ringgren looked at their faces, searching his mind for an answer. What Wyda had told him was, presumably, top secret. If word of a warlike alien race or races possessing hyperdrive *and* the ability to blow up suns were to become public, the resulting panic could be devastating. Still, these terraformers' lives were in danger and they had surely *earned* the right to know.

"What I am about to tell you must never, I repeat NEVER, leave this room," Ringgren said.

Ray looked at Mary and Taylor, shrugged, and said, "We agree, of course."

"Well, then . . ." Ringgren told them what Wyda had learned from the Judge Advocate itself, all the while trying to downplay the Judge Advocate's part in it. He was not entirely successful.

"All this hair-splitting about the Centaurs being formally and *officially* recognized as intelligent!" scoffed Ray. "Legal bullshit!"

Mary then surprised Ringgren by saying, "I always thought of the Judge Advocate as being nothing more than an electronic *brain*; it sounds to me like it is starting to develop a *mind* of its own—and a peculiarly Machiavellian one at that."

"I must believe that the Judge Advocate was willing to permit things to progress only so far—and then no farther," said Ringgren. "To the brink of illegality, perhaps, but not over."

"You're sure about that 'not over,' are you?" Mary pressed.

Ringgren's eyes flashed angrily. "The Judge Advocate is incapable of allowing Federation law to be broken under *any* circumstances or for whatever reason. *That* is why I was ordered along to observe—to see that no overt action which would result in an illegal act being committed should go unreported or unpunished."

"Hey, just a minute," interjected Taylor, his mouth dropping open as he realized the implications of what he was saying. "We've got a shuttle."

"What?" asked Ray.

"The shuttle—we've got the goddamned shuttle he came down in!" Taylor shouted gleefully. "We don't have to attack the Cadre troops, or even defend ourselves from them . . . we have the shuttle."

"That's right," Mary agreed. "If we take the holos and other records we've gathered up to the space station, we can use the subspace communicator to transmit everything back to Terra. There would be no point in their trying to eradicate us after we've done that."

Ray was the first to notice the rather pained look on Ringgren's face. "What is it?"

"The shuttle's energy cells are depleted," Ringgren explained sheepishly. "I forgot to repower the cells while the ship was at the space station, and the only other generator capable of doing so is in the camp."

"The van . . . ?" offered Mary hopefully.

"All the power you have in reserve might get us ten kilometers off the surface of Chiron before being exhausted," Ringgren explained.

Taylor laughed mirthlessly. "Well, for a moment there, it was Christmas morning, wasn't it?"

"Sorry," Ringgren said.

"Let's get started planning the attack, then," said Ray, as if nothing had happened. "I guess we'd better begin by talking things over with Runner."

Runner paced the council meeting hut, looking over Ray's shoulder at the newcomer. "Are you sure what this new one tells you is true?"

"I think so. Anyway, we have no choice but to accept as the truth what he tells us, Runner," Ray said.

"Hm-m-m. If what he says *is* true, what will happen?"

"The soldiers will come to kill us and the dogs."

"And my tribe?"

"Yes—but not if you can be far away from here before they come. I rather imagine they'd have no way of telling your tribe from any other."

"And then what?" Runner questioned.

"And then others will come to live here and to serve the gee-wave station I have told you about," Ray responded. "They may or may not harm you, but they will treat you as animals."

"More *teve* eaters will come?"

"Eventually, yes."

"And what if you kill the warriors first as this stranger would have you do?"

"Then we can call Terra on the subspace communicator, report what has happened, and present the evidence I've collected. If we can do that, no more humans or *teve* eaters will come. Most of those already here will leave."

"And you—will you leave?" Runner asked.

"I'll stay—if you'll have me—and study your people so that wise men where I come from will know your traditions and learn The People's *menteba*, your tribe's way of life."

Suddenly Runner smiled and grasped Ray's arm. "Then we must form a *sharn* and kill these two-legged warriors before they can do you harm."

Ray was touched; he blinked, as if to clear his eyes. "Thank you, Runner."

Ray turned to Ringgren to explain but the Programmer just

nodded his head knowingly. "Yes, I know—even I can translate Runner's gesture."

"Let's start making our plans," said Ray, clapping Ringgren on his still-reddening arm.

"Ouch!!"

"Oops, sorry about that," Ray apologized.

★　　★　　★

"To Prime Programmer Wyda," Ringgren spoke into his holocorder, beginning his report. "I am about to undertake an extraordinary mission with the Brennan-Hollister-Larkin terraforming group. We are preparing to attack the Cadre base here on Chiron. I think my plan is a good one, but the odds still favor the Cadre. This Runner-with-the-Wind has sent scouts to bring back the warriors of several more tribes, but even though the Centaurs are most likely formidable fighters, I fear they are no match for automatic weapons." He paused, aware that he was speaking for a doubtful posterity—no one, even Wyda, would see or hear this report if the Cadre repelled the attack and killed or captured him before it could be transmitted.

"By the time you receive this report—if indeed you do receive it—the outcome will be known. I can only hope and pray in the name of the Judge Advocate that our plans meet with success.

"I have activated the explosive device implanted in my rib. If our attack fails and I am captured alive, it will detonate within forty-eight hours; the resulting explosion should take out an area approaching five square kilometers. If I can, I will attempt to beam this recording and the evidence Ray and the others have collected up to one of the communications satellites if I get the opportunity. There's a chance I can do so undetected by the Cadre base.

"Ake Ringgren signing off. In the name of the Federation and the Judge Advocate I pledge allegiance."

III

As the sun slowly fell toward the horizon, its light extinguished for another day, Ray and the dogs walked slowly across the prairie. A light wind was blowing, ruffling the dogs' fur as they ambled along, noses to the ground. Only Pandora and

Ozma seemed to sense Ray's melancholy mood. The others searched for antelope or hide cat scent.

The six puppies, too roly-poly and uncoordinated to walk very well yet, rode in a basket draped across their mother's back, their little faces peering out at the great, wide world which would soon be theirs to explore at will. "Stop that!" cautioned Mama-san as Tajil, already a grade-one trouble-maker, nipped at his sisters. Tajil made a gurgling sound that sounded nonsense to Ray but which Mama-san interpreted as acquiescence to her parental authority.

"I guess this is as good a spot as any to stop and talk," said Ray when they reached a bowl-shaped depression, a natural amphitheater with a low, flat rock he could sit on.

Sinbad asked, "What's up, Ray?" as the other dogs made themselves comfortable, circling around several times in that peculiar canine way before settling down.

"I just thought we might spend some time alone together tonight," Ray said.

Beowulf looked across at Littlejohn and then Frodo, who was in the midst of a mighty dog yawn. "We not do this for long time," Beowulf asked. "Why now?"

"Yeah," added Grendel, "why tonight?"

Ray sighed. "Because by this time tomorrow, I may be dead; so may several of you." There was shocked silence. The dogs knew about the Cadre base since Ray had told them as soon as he could, but they had not stopped to consider what it might mean.

"The hell with this!" Ray said as he got up from the rock he was sitting on and got down on the ground among the dogs.

Clasping his arms around his knees, Ray began to speak, looking not at any of the dogs but at the last rays of the dying sun. "Remember that day at the crèches?" He smiled at the memory. "I'll never forget it; it was the day I met you all for the first time, the day I got more than a team—the day I found nine new friends." He glanced around at the silent and unmoving dogs. "Whatever happens tomorrow, I want you all to know how much you've meant to me and how much I love you."

"We love you, too, Ray," said Beowulf softly.

Ray smiled and said, "I miss Anson so much. He would be joking about tomorrow and even looking forward to it. You know, I'll never forget the time Anson, still only half grown, tried to climb a tree." Ray laughed and said, "He always insisted he could do anything a 'damned scout cat' could do."

Frodo chuckled. "Anson got his big behind stuck halfway up tree and when you started up after him . . ."

". . . he fell out of tree and landed on your head!" finished Ozma.

Everyone laughed. Then the laughter died away and they grew silent as their lost comrade lived again in their thoughts. To break the silence, Beowulf told an Anson story of his own. Then Sinbad and, one by one, the other dogs added their remembrances.

Finally, Ray said, "Guys, I don't know what the future might hold, but it's been great knowin' you."

"For us, too," said Beowulf, coming over to lick Ray's face with his huge tongue. Ray clasped his arms around him and buried his face in the fur of his neck. Pulling back, Ray rubbed Beowulf's head and then welcomed Pandora. One at a time the dogs approached Ray for their hugs.

11

As Ray looked down at the Cadre encampment, Beowulf and Littlejohn joining him and Ringgren, he again marveled that it was so closely guarded. The camp's defensive setup was excellent. About four or five hundred meters to the right of the camp was a line of sheer-faced bluffs. This was where Ray and the other three were now—atop the bluffs and scanning the camp with high-power field glasses.

Natural defense number two was the river running directly behind the camp and about seventy or eighty meters from the defensive perimeter. The river flowed toward the bluffs and through them in a natural watergate cut by thousands of years of water action on the soft rock. The flow was by far too swift for anything to move upstream. With two such formidable natural defenses to build upon, the Cadre commander had a good start.

Yes, thought Ray in begrudging admiration, *this Captain Bloom has chosen his campsite well*.

Ray turned to Ringgren. "I think we'd better use the time until Runner and Taylor arrive with the war party to think this thing through as carefully as we can." He squinted at the sun glaring down harshly. "We have at least three hours until nightfall, and Runner's *sharn* can't possibly be here any sooner than five or six hours from now."

"You're right," conceded Ringgren. He eased over on his

side and looked at Ray. "I'm just an intelligence agent and not a soldier, so I'm leaving it to you and your Centaur chieftain to smooth out any of the rough edges in the battle plan I suggested to you."

Ray put the field glasses to his eyes once again. "Okay, please go over the defenses one more time."

"A dozen times if it'll help," said Ringgren. "All right, the defensive perimeter is a giant square with sixty-meter sides; at the apex of these sides are five-meter-high guard posts. There are four guard posts in all, of course—one for each apex or corner. In each guard post there is a single sentry on watch, armed with an energy rifle.

"Between the guard posts is a force field set to a level sufficient to stun—if not kill outright—an average-sized man. The important thing to remember is that if the guard posts are destroyed, you can cause the force field to fall. The power source to the force field is inside the camp itself, but the guard post towers house small generators to maintain the amplification of the field." He looked at Ray and asked, "You got this all so far?"

"I'm with you, keep going," Ray said impatiently.

"Just checking. To continue, there are two semiautomatic slug-throwing rifle positions near the front of the square which can lay down a deadly crossfire," Ringgren said. "Their firepower is concentrated, from what I can gather, at a point just outside the front of the perimeter." He frowned in concentration. "I don't completely understand the principle, but I've been told that the slugs have been treated in some way to allow them to pass through the force field unimpeded—perhaps they carry a special charge or polarity. All I'm sure of is that if the force field can be breached, the effectiveness of those positions can be substantially decreased.

"Just behind the barracks building by about five or ten meters is the main building." Ringgren looked seriously at Ray's watching face. "The main building is where the power generator is located. This is a fairly spacious prefab plascrete building divided into four separate rooms: the communications room, the central room used as the mess and for briefings, the commander's quarters, and the generator room. Directly on top of this building, Captain Bloom has placed a fully automatic slug-throwing weapon—a machine gun is the old accepted term, I believe."

"Yeah," growled Beowulf. "Machine gun."

"They're neither very reliable nor accurate," Ringgren said slowly, "but I recall one of the sergeants telling me that in a fight they demoralize the enemy—they make a lot of racket and tear people up pretty good."

"Jesus and Mohammed!" exclaimed Ray, thinking of the killing power they were up against.

"Yes . . . well," said Ringgren, aware of Ray's sudden doubts about the wisdom of attacking a fully armed Cadre encampment, "that pretty much wraps up the defenses. The position atop the command building is manned by three men—no more than four at the most. That's what we're up against."

Pushing the machine gun from his mind, Ray looked at Ringgren in admiration. "You certainly know the camp's defenses, all right; how'd they let you get away with it?"

Ringgren just smiled without saying anything, paused, and then assumed the standard look of bland innocence he'd affected in the camp.

"I see," Ray grinned. Then he asked Ringgren how many men were usually on watch at any one time.

"Oh, I'd say seven—four in the outposts and the three on top of the main building. The two forward semiautomatic rifle positions are not manned unless there's a drill."

"A drill?"

"They have one every day," Ringgren explained, "and as a result they're *good*."

"*That* is what we'll be finding out tonight—one way or the other, Ake."

★　　★　　★

"Lookit!" Frodo whispered excitedly to Ozma and Pandora. "Them antelopes—ever see so many?"

"Never," replied Ozma. "They surely be 'nuff, donja think?"

"Yah," agreed Pandora as Sinbad joined them, crawling on his belly up to their position overlooking the massive herd.

"Holy mackerel!" exclaimed Sinbad. "There must be a million of them antelopes!"

Ozma, whose grasp of numbers was the best of all the dogs, dryly said, "Or mebbe even five or six thousand."

Frodo lifted his head and checked the position of the sun. "That way," he said, gesturing with a shake of his head. "We gots to drive them in that direction."

Frodo began shouting orders in his deep, gravelly voice: "Ozma, you go get Grendel and take up a position on the far left—over there by those coupla scrubby bushes." Looking around for the others, Frodo said, "Pandora, you and Sinbad take your place on the right flank. I'm gonna go get Moon-son and the Centaurs with the whistlers and other noisemakers. When you hear us start, you join in, too. Everyone got that?"

"Got ya, Frodo," Sinbad said as the others nodded agreement.

"Good. If'n we do this right, we might just save some lives—'specially Ray's."

The others nodded seriously. Frodo could not have chosen a better way to motivate them do their best. With swishes of their tails, they trotted off to assume their positions.

Ray, Frodo thought, *I hope we get there on time!*

By nightfall, Ray and Ringgren were patiently waiting for the others a kilometer or two up the valley from the camp. Taylor arrived with Runner, who had assembled a huge *sharn* by merging the fighting men of his own tribe with the warriors of several other tribes. Ray heard their approach first: the thumping of hooves striking the resonant ground as they drew near; the harsh, rapid breathing that whistled in their flared nostrils; and, to Ray's complete astonishment, the thin, piercing keen of the hover van.

When it drew up and Mary had scrambled out the door, Ray took her by the arm and said, "Mary, I didn't know you planned to bring the van."

"I didn't at first, but then I just thought that it has so much we need in the way of medicine, first-aid instruments, and drugs." She shrugged, throwing back her long hair. This action seemed to cause her to have second thoughts and she carefully ran her fingers through her hair, gathering it into a ponytail and dextrously tying it up.

Looking at her lined face, Ray put words to his thoughts,

saying, "You look tired. The drive must have been exhausting."

"Of course it was—and I'd do it again in a moment if need be." Her eyes flashed angrily. "And who are you? Captain Trimble, hero of the holos?"

"Sorry, hon. I don't mean to underestimate you," he said, wincing at the thought that he had inadvertently patronized her. "I'm . . . well, I'm just concerned about your welfare, that's all."

"That's all, huh?" Mary said. "What about you? The Cadre can't kill you, eh? *I* shouldn't worry about *you*?" She then gave Ray a look he couldn't quite figure out, and added softly, "Shouldn't you be with the dogs now?"

"Huh?"

"What's going on here?" asked Taylor as he saw the two of them together when he pulled up on a scooter.

Giving Ray one last look, Mary turned toward Taylor and said matter-of-factly, "Nothing. We were just waiting for you so that Ray could tell us the plan."

Taylor didn't seem prepared to accept that explanation but neither did he press the point when Ray began to speak. "It's nothing much—the plan, I mean. Part of it you both know," Ray continued as Taylor climbed off his scooter and joined them.

"What's that, the part about the leapers?" Taylor asked.

"Yes, did Moon-son or Frodo have any difficulties with that aspect of things?"

"I don't know," Taylor admitted. "I don't think so."

Shivering slightly, Ray looked at his watch. The wind still blew strongly at night and the air was crisp and cool in a way the hot, humid day could not have possibly forecast. "Well," he said, "they still have some time to get here." Looking at Mary, he asked, "Is there any coffee in the van?"

"No, but I can make some."

"Hey, I'm not a cripple," Ray said, starting toward the van. "I'll do it—I'd like to keep busy anyway."

Littlejohn watched Ray leave, then nudged Beowulf. "What 'bout them antelopes?"

"Don't worry, Frodo and the Centaurs not let us down."

"I hope not."

II

The force field was not something you could see with the naked eye. Rather you *sensed* it with your skin as you approached it closely, or *felt* just the slightest twinge of pain in your ears if you had especially acute hearing. Strangely, it was more evident at night than in the daylight—something to do with the rather large number of nocturnal creatures which blundered into it.

There were the flying insects placidly droning into the force field and going *pffmp*, becoming instant fireflies as they sparked into tiny incandescent specks. Then there were the large airborne creatures—birds and kiting mammals. They were too large to burst into flame; instead, they were suddenly mashed as if by a giant fist and hurled, bloody little balls of flesh or feathers, onto the ground. Larger and more deliberate animals sensed the oddness of the singing air and ventured no closer than a meter or two, wisely deciding to leave well enough alone.

The camp's sentries lazed, the droning monotony of the field's single note an irresistible siren call to sleep. Energy rifle muzzles tilted at odd angles were straightened by the sentries, then tilted again.

The night was dark, and far off a dull roar of thunder warned that lightning might yet light up the sky and turn night into day as electricity flowed between sky and ground. The distant rumble grew as the storm moved closer. Here and there someone shifted his weight uneasily, his mind dimly aware that something violent was coming his way across the imperceptible rise and fall of the prairie.

The thunder grew louder, growing and redoubling. Heads began to straighten, eyes to focus. The roar grew louder yet, no longer a distant storm but an approaching tidal wave, a tsunami of doom. Lights were turned on in the camp, voices murmured in puzzlement, an oath echoed off the distant walls of the cliffs.

Into sight of the camp they came, their hooves simultaneously tearing up and pounding down the sea of grass. They were a bobbing, leaping river of brown and sun-burnished gold that followed the natural contours of the land that pointed them like a dagger at the heart of the camp.

Berserk with fear, running with their hearts in their throats, the leapers hit the force field head-on. They hit a force field that was set for an assault by perhaps five or six men; a force field at its next-to-lowest setting, the power correspondingly weak.

The force field's protest screamed into the clear night air like the sound of a fingernail being rasped slowly across a chalkboard amplified a thousand times. No one who heard it would ever forget that terrible electronic scream. The force field's power rose in response to the demands being put upon it.

The first wave of leapers to hit the force field smashed partway through—as if into some giant net—and were immediately thrown back; then their bodies were forced forward again by the unrelenting forward progress of the mass of leapers behind them. As bodies piled up against the force field they began to smoke and then to burn. And still the leapers came.

The vast juggernaut that was the stampede finally forced the overburdened force field to implode. The bodies of dead and dying leapers, horribly mangled, were pushed, spurted, squeezed, and thrown into the camp.

The leapers were an irresistible force and the force field— not an immovable object—fell, dropping away from the outposts and exposing the men inside to a hail of *shars*. Each of the four guards tumbled from his post filled with the short spears, a human porcupine.

As a series of flares exploded into searing miniature suns that illuminated the scene with their eerie blue-white light, the camp's energy rifles and automatic weapons opened up, raking the still-oncoming leapers and blowing many of them into bits. But it was like trying to stop an avalanche by shooting the individual flakes of snow—no one death could halt the stampeding mass of leapers in their maddened state.

Soldiers of the Cadre scattered and ran for some place to hide as the leapers smashed headlong into the three plascrete barracks buildings. Shrill animal screams were mixed among the sounds of bones breaking and plastic finally splitting and rending in response to unrelenting pressure. Leapers climbed the bodies of the dead and hurled themselves onto the tops of the three barracks buildings, causing them to collapse completely. The horrible shrieks of dying men trapped in the wreckage, their bodies being crushed by the increasing weight of the leapers overrunning the structures, were all but lost amid the confused cacophony of the attack.

The smell of blood and scorched flesh and the loud chattering concussions from the machine gun and the energy rifles finally turned the leapers. The surviving soldiers, the lucky ones who escaped from the shattered barracks buildings in time, now milled about among the leapers inside the compound, looking for someone, anyone, to fight back against.

"Now!" Runner's men dashed in from the camp's sides while the machine gun atop the main building continued to cough hoarsely and spit small pieces of metal which tumbled while in the air to better rend on impact the warm, living flesh they were aimed at. To Runner-with-the-Wind's right and left, warriors fell—gaping holes torn through their arms and legs. Runner wept for his men and for the men of the other tribes.

It was not one-sided by any means—there were energy rifles to answer back the machine gun. Ray, Taylor, and Ringgren, firing as they went, followed the Centaur warriors into the Cadre camp's heart and tried to work their way toward the main building while all around them Centaurs were fighting and dying.

A bald man took aim at Ray with his energy rifle but fell before he could squeeze the firing stud, a *shar* driven through his back to protrude from his chest. Ray saw the man fall and felt as if he were in some strange nightmare, walking in slow motion through a shooting gallery while strangers tried to kill him.

The first semiautomatic rifle position to fall did so under a concerted attack by dogs and Centaurs. Beowulf and Littlejohn leaped into the sandbagged position from the side and knocked over the men firing and feeding the weapon. Before the two hapless soldiers could regain their feet, the dogs had torn out their throats.

On the other side of the camp, Runner and a band of his warriors carried a charge directly into the maw of the semiautomatic gun position there. The slugs hit home, doing hideous damage, but the Centaurs refused to be turned aside and the men inside the sandbagged position went down with a host of *shars* driven through their bodies. Runner, his body covered with his own warriors' blood, was one of only three who survived that terrible charge.

But it was the weapon on top of the main building which was doing the most damage, and Ray could see no way of taking it without an all-out assault which would make the losses already sustained by their force seem paltry by comparison. Yet it was as costly to wait as attack: The gun coughed and sputtered and warriors fell limbless or headless or rent across the chest by ugly gaping wounds.

Ray crawled to where Taylor lay supine in the grass, bullets and energy bolts kicking up clods of dirt as they impacted all around the two of them. "Taylor!" Ray yelled. When Taylor turned his head toward him, Ray said, "The main building—that's got to be our target." When Taylor nodded, Ray added, "Let's concentrate our combined firepower on it. Maybe we can keep those bastards with the machine gun flat on their stomachs."

"I dunno," Taylor replied. "My charge is getting low. I can help hold 'em down for a while, but we gotta silence that weapon permanently."

After a rapid burst of gunfire raked the grass in front of them, Taylor yelled, "I'm moving away—no point in us both being in the same place."

"Good idea."

Ray felt a tap on his shoulder. He turned his head and saw an agitated Ringgren. "What is it?"

"The gun, the machine gun—you've got to knock it out!" Ringgren shouted above the din of battle.

"I know, for Chrissakes!" Ray shouted back. "But how?"

Before Ringgren could answer, something small and round came flying down from the top of the building. "Grenade!" Ray shouted, and both men tried to flatten out against the ground as much as possible. The grenade landed a few meters away and bounced toward a soldier and a Centaur warrior struggling over possession of an energy rifle. The soldier saw death rolling toward them and his mouth opened in a soundless scream of horror. The grenade blew both of them apart.

"You gotta get that gun!" Ringgren reiterated. Another burst of fire in their direction made both hug the ground again and almost caused Ray to miss Mary's audacious assault.

Looking back toward the front of the camp, the night made as bright as midday by the automatically launched flares, Ray saw the hover van swing around the mass of leaper bodies piled there and come roaring into camp as Mary applied full power. Individual battles were still going on and, in Mary's mad rush toward the main building, the hover van hit and tossed living bodies aside like rag dolls. Not all were soldiers, Ray realized in horror.

The van bucked and lurched madly but continued to pick up speed as it hurtled toward the building. Even with his stomach churning with fear for Mary's safety, Ray could not help but recall an old sinny image: an unrealistically monstrous white whale bearing down on a nineteenth-century sailing ship. Ray gulped—like the white whale, Mary was prepared to sacrifice herself to guarantee the destruction of her foe.

Traveling at perhaps one hundred or one hundred and twenty kilometers per hour, the van hit the headquarters building directly in its center, the huge vehicle's mass and momentum punching through the tough plascrete shell of the structure. The building split like a dropped watermelon and the men on top of the roof were sent whirling through the air like toy soldiers. The rear of the van flew high off the ground as the building absorbed the vehicle's inertial forces; then it slammed down hard with a sickening thud.

It was deathly silent for a few brief heartbeats. Then Ray could hear the cries of the wounded—the pain-filled cries of the Centaur wounded; it seemed entirely possible at that moment that not a single Cadre soldier had survived the bitter firefight. Whether the soldiers were all dead or not, the Cadre's automatically launched flares kept coming, keeping the scene garishly lit.

Ray felt dizzy, sick. Bitter stomach acid rose in his throat but he forced it down. His legs felt rubbery and he let go of his rifle. *MARY.* Her name was all he could concentrate on; all he could find to keep his benumbed brain attuned amid the horror of the situation around him. He wanted to shut out the world outside his head, to lock away the screaming and the moaning and the blood and the smell and the way a man looks when his face is peaceful and relaxed yet he has no chest.

"Mary! Mary! Mary, where are you?" He remembered what they'd come for—the power generator. It could be smashed into a million pieces for all it mattered if anything had happened to Mary.

Ray followed the twisted plasteel sides of the van toward the hole it had punched into the wrecked headquarters building, his hand sliding along the outside absentmindedly as if he were stroking one of the cholos. He saw a severed human foot, part of the calf still attached to it, lying on the ground in front of him and he casually stepped over it. He marveled at how quickly one could accept as normal horrors ordinarily beyond the ability of the average human being to imagine.

"Help me, please help me." Ray glanced down and saw a Cadre soldier half obscured by the bulk of the van. Blood trickled from the man's mouth and Ray saw a half-meter or so of his intestines protruding from his ripped tunic.

"You need more help than I can give you," said Ray. "I'll get Dr. Ringgren."

Looking down at his ruined body, the young man said, "Never mind, no doctor can help me now."

"You don't mean that," Ray began. "It looks bad, but—"

"Bad?" the soldier laughed bitterly. "I'm fuckin' dead." Then he opened his hand to reveal a grenade with the pin already pulled. "You're coming with me," the soldier said, adding, "No pain, no pain when you're dead."

"Christ Almighty!" yelled Ray, turning to fling himself out of harm's way. A reddish-brown streak interposed itself between Ray and the grenade rolling from the man's hand.

It was Pandora.

Even though Pandora had leapt between Ray and the blast, the shock wave of the blast still caught him as he turned away. Hot furnace air passed by him, lifting him up and sending him flying. Stretching out his arms, more in reflex than in conscious contemplation of the best course of action, he hit the dirt face first, his chin scraping against the ground and his forehead hitting a good-sized rock. For a moment, he saw stars. *And I'm not even drinking* kiv, he told himself. Then he thought: *If I can make a joke, I guess I'm not dead yet.*

Then he remembered why he was still alive and all thought of jokes was forgotten. "Pandora!" he screamed.

Almost immediately, Beowulf and Ringgren were at his side. Ray felt something reassuringly cool and moist touch the side of his neck: Beowulf's nose. "He's alive," he heard Beowulf's gravelly voice inform the others. When he heard the dog say nothing about Pandora, Ray knew she was dead.

"Gently, gently," Ringgren cautioned himself as they turned him over gingerly.

"Mary," Ray croaked at Ringgren. "Go find out if Mary's alive."

Ringgren just nodded. "I think Taylor's gone to see how your wife is," the red-haired doctor told him. "I'll join him as soon as I'm done here."

Watching the doctor work quickly, Beowulf asked, "How you feel, Ray?"

Out of the corner of his eye, Ray could see a patch of reddish brown and white; it wasn't moving. "I'm alive—alive because of Pandora," he said through his pain.

Ringgren efficiently and professionally ran his fingers over Ray's body. "You're right—she seems to have saved you from serious injury."

"Ray be okay?"

Ringgren looked into the dog's blue eyes. "Yes." His eyes involuntarily darted toward the unmoving clump of brown and white fur. "Because of his dog . . . ah—"

"Pandora."

"Because of Pandora's quick thinking and fast action, most of the shrapnel seems to have missed hitting him." Ringgren rocked back on his heels. "Oh, he's taken a nasty bump on the head, but most of the damage was done by the grenade's concussion. He won't be able to listen to Mozart or Propp for a few days—no high notes—but he'll be okay soon enough."

"Then get the hell out of here, and see how Mary is," Ray said testily.

"Yes, you're right," said Ringgren, getting up.

The inside of the smashed building was, Ringgren saw, less gruesome than the outside; there had been relatively few defenders inside the headquarters. The Programmer found Taylor trying futilely to force his way inside one of the sliding doors near the van's ruined front. Buckled by the impact and inert with the power off, the door refused to budge. Frustrated, Taylor pounded on the crushed door's side and shouted, "Goddamn it!"

"Here," said Ringgren, pointing at one of the windows a little farther back along the van's side. "If we smash this, we can climb in back here."

"Good idea," agreed Taylor.

When a chair failed to do more than just bounce harmlessly off the window's surface, Ringgren picked up an energy rifle and said, "Stand back." He fired once, blowing in the window. Taylor was inside in seconds, and Ringgren scrambled in after him almost as quickly.

Mary was semiconscious when they reached her, still strapped tightly in the driver's seat by the safety restraints. "Mary . . . Mary, can you hear me?" Taylor asked tentatively.

She sighed and lifted her head to look into his eyes. "Oh, there you are," she said. "I've been waiting for you."

"Now that that's out of the way," said Ringgren, gently but firmly pushing Taylor aside, "I'll have a look." Ringgren's expert hands moved up and down her body, alighting here and there to feel for broken bones or any signs of internal injuries.

"Hey, are you *sure* you're a doctor?" Mary slurred. Ringgren just smiled, pleased that, like Ray, she had spunk enough to joke with him despite her injuries.

"Well?" asked an anxious Taylor.

Looking at Mary and speaking to her as if she had asked the question, Ringgren said, "You're a very lucky young lady. You've got a broken arm and you have a number of broken ribs—I'm not sure of the number yet—and you might have some broken bones in your feet. At first glance I'd say you've certainly got a lot of minor injuries, and you may be more shaken up inside than it looks to me now, but you're not seriously hurt."

"That means my life is not in danger?" Mary asked.

"That's correct."

"Good," she said, letting her head fall back against the headrest. "I know Ray'll want to kill me himself for what I just did." Ringgren smiled but said nothing.

Mary took his silence as something more ominous. "Hey, where is Ray?" She looked at their faces. "He's . . . he's not . . ."

"Dead?" Taylor finished for her. "Hardly. It would take more than a Cadre grenade to kill that little turkey."

"Grenade?"

"Yes, grenade," said Ringgren, readying an injection gun. He placed the gun against her shoulder but before activating the gas charge, he said, "He's been wounded, but his injuries are less serious than yours . . . okay?"

"Okay." Ringgren shot the painkiller into her shoulder and she sighed gratefully. Then, alarmed, she said, "The power generator . . . everything's okay there, too?"

"Things are fine," Ringgren reassured her.

As Mary's eyelids started to droop, she said lazily, "I'm so relieved about the generator; I was hoping the van didn't damage it."

"Oh," waved Ringgren, "to the contrary. You smashed it up pretty damned good."

"But, you said—" Mary protested before the blackness swept over her like a blanket being drawn up over her head.

III

Taylor guffawed as if in reaction to a joke Ray was missing. "The communications officer—who's still alive, by the way— told us he was trying to raise the base on Freehold, the nearest Cadre-occupied planet, when Mary came smashing through the center of the building with the van. It seems the commander wanted to call for reinforcements and then destroy the power generator and the spare parts for it."

"Taylor's correct," added Ringgren. "What Mary accomplished by arriving when she did," he said, glancing at the peacefully sleeping Mary, "was to destroy—or at least render inoperative—the generator *before* they could contact the outpost on Freehold. Captain Bloom probably suspected they were doomed but he wanted to guarantee that our victory would be short-lived. And without the generator we couldn't get up to the space station to send our message, and the reinforcements could have mopped us up at their leisure."

"Am I missing something?" Ray asked. "If the power generator is badly damaged—"

"Sure it's damaged," explained Ringgren, "but they didn't have time to destroy the spare parts, thanks to Mary; it can be rebuilt in a matter of days."

Ray's shoulders sagged, weary from the load he'd been carrying for the past several weeks. "You mean we've finally won?"

"Just about," Ringgren assured him. "We're safe—or will be as soon as we contact Terra again with your findings."

"Yeah—safe," said Ray, thinking of Pandora's sacrifice. "Safe," he repeated dully, massaging the back of his neck as he stared out across the hellish scene of dead bodies. "Over thirty Cadre regulars," he murmured. "And how many of Runner's warriors?" He laughed harshly and shook his head. "Safe."

"Here comes Runner," said Beowulf, and they all looked up.

★   ★   ★

"You know," Ringgren was saying, "if we don't get the generator repaired soon, three fellows on the space station are going to starve to death."

"That's not true," Taylor said, grinning wickedly. "They'll die of terminal boredom from watching the holos you left them long before they starve to death."

Mary, hobbling about on makeshift crutches, made a face and said, "I hope that means that you're joking about a possible horrible fate because you've repaired the power generator."

Taylor nudged Ringgren. "Impossible to put anything over on Mary, eh, Doc?"

"Just show us some results!" challenged Mary.

After a modest cough, Ray explained, "I think you're going to find that our by-the-seat-of-our-pants repairs will allow the unit to function just as efficiently as when it was new—with two fewer parts, too."

"Oh, I see," said Mary. "Not only do you two fix 'em, you *improve* them too. Well, let's see the results of your labors."

A cocky Taylor pressed an enabling panel and the unit began to hum with a sudden surge of power. But before anyone could congratulate the two Mr. Fixits, an internal speaker began to issue ominous warnings: "Danger! There is a power overload in circuit Able-Niner. Beware of powwwwwwww—" A flash of blue light leapt from one of the vents on the generator's side, followed immediately by a cloud of dense and acrid black smoke.

Taylor quickly depowered the unit and looked at Ray as chagrin replaced pride on his face. Glancing over at Ringgren—who didn't know whether to be amused or horrified—Taylor said, "Ah, well, we're not quite there yet. Maybe another day."

"Yes," agreed Ray quickly. "We know what the problem is now; we'll get back to you in a day or so."

"Sure, guys."

While Taylor and Ray struggled to restore the generator to operating condition, Mary and Ringgren helped Runner-with-the-Wind do what could be done for those wounded in the attack on the Cadre camp. But first, of course, Ringgren had to heal Mary. Using the camp's Akito bone machine, Ringgren was able to mend Mary's broken arm and ribs in a matter of twenty-four hours. The bones in her feet were another matter, however.

"But *why* can't you use the machine?" Mary asked.

"It works *too* well," Ringgren explained. "Admittedly, I *can* run the current through your feet for a few minutes a day, but to do more than that risks fusing some of the smaller bones into a single mass. Feet are delicate machines," he told her. "Each one contains twenty-six individual bones and the ligaments and muscles necessary to make it work. Believe me, the last thing you want to do is screw up such a complex arrangement."

"You're the doctor," Mary conceded grudgingly.

Unfortunately, since the Centaurs were a nonhuman race, the Akito bone machine had no effect upon them and Mary and Ringgren were reduced to putting many of their broken limbs into casts. The warriors were not always gracious patients.

"Runner," complained one injured warrior, "must we submit to these indignities? It is bad enough to have oneself bound up like a babe against the winds of winter, but to have such binding done by a *sharna* is intolerable!"

"You forget that this *sharna* herself was injured in the battle against the bad two-legged ones and that it was she who risked her life in destroying their hut of death." Using his voice of authority, Runner added, "A warrior must know when to submit himself to the healing arts so that the tribe does not lose his *shar*! Too many of us died in the attack; rejoice that you live to complain."

Runner did even more to mollify his warriors, however. Like Ray before her, Mary had a chance to observe Runner's shrewdness as a leader. Instead of merely ordering his men to undergo treatment, Runner had the *tanakiv* cast some of his shaman's spells to hurry along the healing. Thus, the skeptical warriors submitted more readily to Mary and Ringgren's ministrations, content to believe that the power of magic was what was really mending their bones and healing their wounds.

"Runner," said Mary to the Centaur chieftain one day as she went about her duties, "we're sorry for what we've done to your tribe. It's not supposed to happen like this when we encounter another form of 'The People.' "

Runner put a slender hand on her shoulder. "You acted with honor once you understood our ways; you fought your own people to make right a great wrong." He stared into her eyes with understanding and forgiveness. "Moon-son, Gnurfleet, Pandora, and the others died fighting for the future of The People; they died for my children's heritage."

"That's true," Mary agreed. "Now we must do all we can to ensure that their sacrifices were not in vain."

"Your great chiefs must learn the truth."

"Yes."

Just then Ray, himself still shaking off his injuries, hobbled up, his face filled with excitement.

"Mary, we—"

"Fixed the power generator finally," she finished for him.

"Yes, how did you know?"

"Just a lucky guess."

"Well, come on," he told her. "We're going to start charging up the portable power cells to transport back to the shuttle."

"The portable units?"

"Yeah," Ray explained. "While they haven't sufficient reserves for a trip up to the station, they do have enough energy to fly the shuttle to the camp for a complete recharging here."

"Then it's over."

Ray frowned and "knocked wood" against the side of his skull. "Hey, don't say that, kid. It ain't over till it's over."

Mary sighed. "You're right. Let's go."

Even though the hover scooter's anti-grav engine enabled it to ride atop a cushion of air and not bounce across the surface of the plains, Ray decided that he'd had taken more comfortable journeys in his life. The scooter still reacted to the rise and fall of the ground, and Ringgren and his scooter set a rapid pace. "Ouch, ouch . . . Jeez!" Ray bit off as the jostling jarred his tender ribs.

Ray didn't think Ake could hear him, but the red-headed Programmer's scooter began to slow and finally came to a stop. Ray pulled up beside him and settled gently to the ground. "I'm sorry, Ray," Ringgren said, pulling out his canteen for a much needed drink. "I guess my hurry to get to the shuttle isn't doing a thing for your injuries."

"I'll live," said Ray, with a grin. Then he added, "But the shuttle's still gonna be there whether we get there at noon or a quarter after."

Ringgren took a long pull from the canteen and then handed it over to Ray. "You're right, of course," he admitted. "I'll try to restrain myself."

Ray drained the last of the water from the canteen and gave Ringgren a funny look. "What?" asked the Programmer.

Ray threw the empty canteen toward Ringgren and started his hover scooter up before the Programmer had grabbed it out of the air. "Last one there is a skinned hide cat!" he shouted before streaking off at full power.

"Why, you sneaky . . . !"

12

"I don't understand it," Mary was saying. "*I* can't go with you, but you're taking Runner. Is that it?"

"It's not that you *can't* go with us," Ray explained, "it's just that we're also taking up one of the dogs and the Cadre officer who survived. There's just so much room in the shuttle."

"That's bullcrap and you know it!" Mary blazed. "The truth is you think there's a chance, however small, that these guys could have figured a way to escape from their cell. That's it, isn't it?"

"Of course not, Mary, I—"

"I'll stay."

"Huh?" said both Ray and Mary simultaneously, turning to look at Taylor.

"I said I'll stay. Going up to the space station is no big deal, so if you want to go, Mary, it's fine by me."

Now Mary did something that always bugged the hell out of Ray: She suddenly did an about-face on the issue. "Well, sure I want to go, but only if you really don't want to."

"Mary, he *made* the offer, so just take him up on it," Ray said.

"Sure, but I don't want him not to go if he really wants to go, and—"

"Just get in the fucking shuttle and shut up!" Taylor roared and stomped away, almost knocking over Ringgren, who was coming over to see what the holdup was all about.

Damn! Ray thought. *What's happening to us? The pressure's off, we've won and we're not going to die . . . why are we biting each other's heads off all of a sudden?* Ray looked at Mary to find her staring at him with a strange look on her face.

With everyone strapped in, the shuttle slowly lifted off, its destination the space station that hung overhead, so near and yet so far away. Ray glanced at Runner-with-the-Wind and said, "Just relax, Runner, the flight won't take long." Runner just grunted and looked around nervously.

Ray sighed. Beside him sat Mary, mute and unmoving as a stone. Next to her was Ringgren. Oddly enough, to Ray's mind at least, Ringgren seemed almost as uneasy as Runner. Even as Ray glanced at him, Ringgren, his small holocorder nestled in his lap, patted his face with a handkerchief, sopping up the sweat that poured from him. Beside Ringgren, his hands manacled, was their prisoner, on his way to join the three men imprisoned in the holding area aboard the space station. On their captive's other side sat an impassive Beowulf. Although the scout dog's role was to keep an eye on the communications officer, the prisoner made it clear from the way he shied away from Beowulf, leaning into Ringgren, that he intended doing nothing to rouse the big dog's ire.

"Are we all comfy?" Ray asked, wanting to break the silence.

"Humph," Mary grunted.

"Sure," said Ringgren, wiping his brow.

Runner, watching the plains fall away in the viewscreen, said nothing. The prisoner, his eyes on Beowulf and not knowing the Centaur tongue which Ray used around Runner, remained silent as well.

"I like to ride the shuttle, Ray," growled Beowulf happily. "I comfy."

"Good, I'm glad someone's having a good time," Ray said.

With that, the conversation, what little of it there was, died out again. *Gonna be the longest short hop I was ever on*, Ray thought, looking at the space station starting to grow larger and larger in the "up" viewscreen. He glanced at Runner, the Centaur chieftain's face an unnatural color, and said, "You're very brave, Runner. To fly in a shuttle for the first time takes a great deal of courage."

Runner finally spoke. "Almost as much courage as it takes for a two-legged one to face a *gnur* with only a *shar*."

Ray shook his head in admiration; Runner had again demonstrated to him why he was a great chieftain. "Thank you, Saminav," Ray said formally.

When the linkage with the space station was complete, the hatch hissed open and everyone scrambled out in so much haste that Ray mumbled, "Women and children first," under his breath.

"Mary, why don't you take Runner to the observation deck while the rest of us head down to the detention level?"

"Fine," said Mary. "Suits me." Again she gave Ray that peculiar look that he could not interpret.

"Hello, gentlemen," Ringgren said as he approached the lockup that held his three prisoners.

"Christ Almighty!" said one of them. "I've never been so glad to see anyone in my whole life!"

"I've missed you, too," Ringgren replied.

"Cut the crap and let us out of here," said one of the other two men.

"Yeah," agreed his companions.

"*Au contraire*," Ringgren said, gesturing toward the entry hatch to the security area. "I have a new playmate for you." The manacled communications officer entered, followed immediately by Ray and Beowulf.

"Ah, Jesus!" one of the prisoners moaned.

"Now you have a fourth for bridge," deadpanned Ringgren. After unlocking first his prisoner's manacles and then the cell door, Ringgren prodded the new arrival in the middle of his back, indicating that he was to join the others in the large cell.

"What now?" asked Ray.

"You and Beowulf stay and fill our friends in on recent events, explaining just why they have to remain here for a while yet, and I'll go down to the food lockers and bring up more supplies."

"Okay, Doc."

As Ringgren hurried off, Ray found a place to sit and said to the communications officer, "Why don't *you* tell your buddies what's been happening down on Chiron?"

Runner-with-the-Wind was in the main observation lounge with Mary, preparing himself for the shock of what he was about to experience. "I . . . I will see our whole world from up here?" he asked, still not certain of this new concept of a "planet."

"Yes, Runner."

Runner swallowed hard. "I am ready. Go ahead."

Mary passed her hand in front of a small, focused beam of light and the far wall slowly went from being opaque to transparent. Runner gasped. There, like a blue-green ball, hung the most achingly beautiful thing he had ever seen. "That . . . that is my home?"

"Yes, that is where you live, Runner," Mary said. "To your people it is 'The World.' My people call it . . ." She fumbled for a Centaur equivalent to the word "Chiron." Finding none, she said simply, "We call it Chiron."

"Kkai-run," Runner said softly. "Kkai-run."

★　　★　　★

"Okay," said Ringgren, "I think our guests are fully resupplied now, don't you?"

"Sure," agreed Ray.

"Then let's do what we came here to do."

"Lead on, McDuff," Ray said, making an "after you" gesture toward the hatch.

As they walked briskly down the corridor, Beowulf at his side, Ray suddenly realized something. "Ah, say, Ake, are there full-size drop tubes on board this station?"

"Full-size?"

"Yeah, you know—ones meant for equipment and such." Ray looked at Beowulf's anxious face and added, "The dogs don't really like to use the smaller drop tubes; they make them feel a bit claustrophobic."

"Beowulf likes the shuttle, but the drop tubes make him claustrophobic, eh?" said Ringgren, shaking his head. "Oh, well, come on down this way. There's a cargo lift/drop tube near the station's hub." Once they found the cargo drop tube, an immense cylinder capable of moving large machinery or massive amounts of stores, they went up to the command and communications level.

With Ringgren leading the way, they entered the communications room. Looking around with moderate interest, Ray's eyes swept the room. Everything appeared normal. Then Ray felt Beowulf nudge his arm with his cool, moist nose. With a twist of his neck, the scout dog pointed out the bloodstains on the white surface of the communications console. When Beowulf grinned a canine grin, Ray just raised his eyebrows and said softly, "Never underestimate Ake."

"What's that?" Ringgren asked.

"I said, 'Nice decor for an official room.'"

Ringgren blinked at that but said nothing. Clearly, he knew, Ray had said something to Beowulf about him that the anthropologist wasn't about to repeat for his sake. With more important matters to concern him, Ringgren bent to his task of restoring the communicator to working condition. He slipped off his boot and removed the tiny but vital piece of the communicator's innards he'd hidden in the hollowed-out heel.

Beowulf watched all this in amazement. Ray just laughed and said, "I've read about things like this, but I never thought spies *really* did such things." When Ringgren, half jokingly and half seriously, shot him daggers with his eyes, Ray coughed and amended, "I mean, I never thought that 'intelligence gatherers' actually did such things."

"You're impossible," laughed Ringgren, unable to keep up his stern demeanor. "You know that, don't you?"

"He know it," said Beowulf.

Ringgren carefully replaced the small part that made the subspace communicator whole again, straining as he reached down deep into the frame of the machine. "There, that should do it," he told his two interested observers.

"I guess this is the moment of truth, then," Ray said. "Go ahead if you're ready."

Ringgren's fingers danced over the console and, as the communicator called up the tremendous power it required to punch a hole in the fabric of space, the deep hum of pure energy massing for its effort that he'd heard before returned. "That noise—what is it?" asked Ray.

"That's the sound of enough power to light up Boswash for a month," Ringgren said as his fingers continued their educated dance across the pressure controls of the console. "Or, more impressively, it's enough power to hurl our words and images across space." Ray gulped as bank after bank of readouts on the wall lit up. Beowulf, his fur rising in ragged clumps, growled involuntarily as his canine senses reacted to the gathering power in the room.

"Here goes," said Ringgren, activating the transmission enabler. Within a few minutes, the chimes sounded, indicating that the connection was complete. "And now my recognition codes," Ringgren explained, keying in the sequence of numbers that would link him to Prime Programmer Wyda's own communications console. The chimes sounded again and there, standing in the center of the communications room, was Wyda herself.

"Ah, I was hoping it was you, Programmer Ringgren," Wyda said, relief plain on her face. "Am I to assume that this very transmission is proof of your success?"

"Your assumption is correct," Ringgren confirmed. "With the help of Ray and his team, I was able to neutralize Captain Bloom's regulars."

"Neutralize? Neutralize, my Aunt Effie!" exclaimed Ray. "We kicked their effing butts."

A slight look of disapproval crossed the Prime Programmer's face. "And this . . . adventurer . . . I take to be Mr. Larkin?"

Somewhat abashed by his impolitic outburst, Ray said, "Uh, yeah, that's right, I'm Ray Larkin." He pointed at Beowulf and said, "And this is Beowulf, my head dog."

" 'Lo," Beowulf said, his tail wagging.

Ringgren just put his hand over his face and sighed.

"I've never been introduced to a dog before," said Wyda dryly. "How quaint."

More than a bit annoyed at Wyda's overall tone and attitude, Ray opened his mouth to say something (*After all*, he reasoned, *we saved this lady's bacon as well as our own!*) but Ringgren spoke up first. "If it weren't for Ray and his dogs, I doubt very much my mission would have been a success, Prime Programmer Wyda. In addition, he's the anthropologist who gathered the proof of the Centaurs' intelligence."

"I see," she said, impressed by her junior's defense of the impulsive Mr. Larkin. Catching sight of the holocorder clipped to his belt, she asked Ringgren, "And that, I take it, contains Mr. Larkin's proof, the evidence which I will be presenting to the Judge Advocate?"

"Yes, Prime Programmer."

"Very well." She turned and spoke to someone "off screen," using a tongue Ray didn't recognize. *That's interesting*, Ray thought. *I've heard that the Programmers have a secret language which they use among themselves; I've never heard it spoken before.*

"We are ready here," Wyda said. "You may transmit the chip's contents now." Ringgren did and the equivalent of hundreds of pages of Ray's notes, findings, evaluations, and other basic research streamed out across space as pure energy to be reconstituted on Terra. As the process continued, Ray felt a tenseness leave his shoulders. *NOW it's over, Mary.*

While Ringgren wrapped up things with Wyda and his Terran masters, Ray and Beowulf made their way down to the observation deck where Mary and Runner waited. Looking at Runner, who was staring intently at the panorama beneath him, Ray said, "It's beautiful, isn't it?"

"Yes," agreed Runner, his eyes shining.

"Well?" Mary asked. "Did everything go okay?"

Ray nodded. "Prime Programmer Wyda is probably informing the Judge Advocate of our findings at this very moment. It's over at last. The fat lady finally sang," he said, using a slang term Mary had never heard before. Ray laughed to himself, trying to reconcile the lean and intense Wyda with his mental picture of a Wagnerian Valkyrie in a steel helmet and pigtails.

"You're in a good mood," Mary commented.

"Yeah, shit, why not?" said Ray as he swept her into his arms. "We've won. We've won it all." He gave Mary what started out to be a long, hard kiss. Unfortunately, it didn't last very long at all.

"What's wrong?" he asked, pulling away.

"Wrong?"

"Usually, you kiss back."

Glancing at Runner, still entranced by the novelty of seeing his own world, Mary replied using Terran-standard

English, "Oh, Ray, my poor, dear Ray—you have no idea, do you?"

"No idea?"

"Ray, dear, I think it's over."

"I know, that's what I've been say—"

"I mean between us," Mary interrupted. "It may be over between the two of us."

Holding her shoulders and looking into her face in disbelief, Ray said, "What? How can you say that? What are you talking about?"

"You've got someone else."

"That's crazy!" he protested. "I haven't got anyone else—how could I?"

"Actually," Mary said, "there's a whole bunch of someone elses: It started with nine of them, then there were eight, now there are thirteen of them."

Slowly the light of comprehension crept into Ray's eyes and he turned to stare in Beowulf's direction. Not sure what was happening, but not liking it, Beowulf stared back balefully. "The dogs? You're speaking about the dogs?"

Mary put her hand to the side of his face and caressed it lovingly if somehow distantly. "Of course it's the dogs; it's always been the dogs. I just recently came to see the truth."

Ray sputtered. "But . . . well, of *course* I love the dogs—I couldn't lead a team if I didn't—but, Mary, I *love* you, too."

"You like me a lot, I think," Mary agreed, "but your first and last loyalty will always be to the dogs."

"Mary, this is insane, I—"

She put her hand to his lips. "Hush, dear. We'll talk about this some more, with Taylor, too, at some point. But for now, let's agree to let the matter rest for a few hours." She looked at him with concern. "You have a lot to think about—and to accept, I believe."

■

"What is it you want to show me?" Ray asked, sticking his head into the communications room.

"Just come in and have a seat," Ake told him. After Ray did

as he was told, Ake said, "Prime Programmer Wyda sent me a special transmission. I want you to see it."

"What is it?"

"It appears that when the General knew the game was up, he made sure all the recording devices in his office were activated. This holorecording is the result."

"Do I want to see this?" Ray asked nervously.

"I think you need to," Ake replied. "Now shut up and watch." He keyed a control panel and the interior of the General's office leapt into life in front of them.

"Come in," the General said to Thane Wyda as the door hissed open to reveal her standing there with a needle gun in her hand. "I expected someone, but I didn't know it would be you, Thane."

"How long have I known you, Andrei—ten, fifteen years?" The General shrugged. "Something like that."

"You must see then that I *owe* it to you, Andrei. I couldn't allow another to do my job; a man shouldn't have to die at the hands of a stranger."

"A noble sentiment."

Wyda shrugged.

"But what about my subordinates?" the General asked.

"They will be disciplined."

"Nothing more? They were only following my orders, you know."

"The Judge Advocate is aware of that," replied Wyda. Her eyes fell on the open book in front of the General. "The Bible? I never knew you to be a particularly religious man, Andrei. Are you seeking solace?"

"No."

"Then, why . . . ?"

"Let me read you the passage I've been studying," the General said.

"If you wish."

"And the Lord spake unto Moses that selfsame day, saying, 'Get thee up into this mountain, Abarim, unto Mount Nebo, which is in the land of Moab, that is over against Jericho; and behold the land of Canaan, which I give unto the children of Israel for a possession:

And die in the mount whither thou goest up, and be gathered unto thy people; as Aaron thy brother died in Mount Hor, and was gathered unto his people:

Because ye trespassed against me among the children of Israel at the waters of Meribah Kadesh, in the wilderness of Zin; because ye sanctified me not in the midst of the children of Israel.

Yet thou shalt see the land before thee; but thou shalt not go thither unto the land which I give the children of Israel.'"

The General closed the book slowly. "It was *my* project; *I* fought for it; *I* made the gee-wave stations a reality. And now, like Moses, I'll never be a part of what I caused to come into being."

"Please explain something to me, Andrei."

"I'll try."

"Why, Andrei?"

"Why what?"

"Why did you ignore the reports concerning the Centaurs?" Wyda asked. "There are other worlds capable of hosting the gee-wave stations, aren't there?"

"Yes," he admitted. "One's even been designated already by my fellow Consuls, the original second choice."

"Then why, Andrei?"

"I couldn't wait," he said. "Chiron wasn't just the first choice, it was the *best* choice—it tested a full eighty-three percent positive."

"I see," said Wyda, who didn't, not really.

The General sighed. "This anthropologist who went against the directives—this Ray Larkin—what's he like?"

"A lot like you were twenty-five years ago, I think. Under different circumstances, you might have become friends."

"*Very* different circumstances, I should imagine," the General said. He took a ring from his finger—the only jewelry he wore—and placed it on his desk in front of him. "See that he gets this," he told Wyda.

"Of course."

"Goodbye, Thane." He slowly swung his chair around

until he stared out the window, his back to the Prime Programmer.

Quickly, mercifully, Wyda raised the gun.

At that point, the recording faded to nothingness.

"Jesus," said Ray softly.

"It looks like you've got something coming to you on the next shuttle," Ake said.

"His ring. But why me?" Ray asked.

"Think about it," Ake counseled him. "You'll figure it out."

III

Runner-with-the-Wind walked slowly up to where Sunchaser stood, peering anxiously at the large hut where Ray, Mary, and Taylor were discussing their future at this very moment. "Come, little one," Runner said. "It is not right to gawk at the misfortunes of others."

"I know, Saminav," Sunchaser replied with great sorrow in her voice. "I know."

Runner stroked her long neck with his hand and she moved closer to him. "I do not understand these 'hue-monns' at all," she said. "Why now, after all that has happened, does the *sharna* of Ray's hut decide that they must no longer be together?"

"Even though Ray and the others are not of The People," Runner said patiently, "we must never forget that they are from another world. Their ways are not our ways and that is why Ray will stay with us for a while longer—to learn more about us."

"Perhaps we can learn more about them, too!"

"Perhaps," Runner agreed. "Perhaps." He took his young wife by the hand. "Come on, we must not stare at their hut in this unseemly manner any longer."

"Look," Taylor was saying, "if anyone was going to break this triple up, I thought it was going to be me, Mary. I just don't understand what's come over you all of a sudden."

"It wasn't 'all of a sudden,'" Mary insisted. "It was a slow awakening to the facts."

"And just what *are* the facts?"

"Ray loves us both," Mary said, looking at Ray's troubled face. "He loves us and would die for us if we asked him. But, as much as he loves us, his first and only *true* love is for his team, for his dogs."

"Ray, what do you have to say to that?" Taylor asked.

Rubbing his eyes as if he hadn't slept for days, Ray said, "There's a lot of truth in what Mary says, a lot of truth. But how am I to separate the love I feel for you two and the love I feel for my dogs? Am I to somehow weigh them to see which is the truer, deeper, more sincere love? Goddamn it, I *do* love you all. Is that a crime?"

"No," said Mary softly. "It's not."

"Mary," said Taylor earnestly, "I won't pretend there weren't times when I wanted you to myself—wanted Ray out of the picture—but, damn it, I don't feel that way anymore."

"How *do* you feel?"

"You want the truth? You want an honest answer?"

"That's what we're here for, isn't it?"

"Okay," Taylor began slowly. He looked at both Mary and Ray and then down at the floor, avoiding their eyes. "I love you both . . . but only as a package, I think."

"A package?" Ray asked, puzzled.

Still not looking at either of them, Taylor said, "I think our arrangement, our triple, has a cohesiveness that no ordinary marriage contract could match—not for the people involved, not for us." Finally meeting their eyes, Taylor said, "I think with us it's a triple or nothing."

Ray stuck a finger in his mouth, sucking on it contemplatively as he ruminated about what Taylor had just said. Removing his finger, he said to Taylor, "You know, you long drink of water, I think you might be right."

"What are you two talking about?" Mary all but shouted. Turning on Taylor, she said, "You mean you think that it has to be all three of us or none of us? Is that it?"

Taylor nodded. "That's it."

"That's the craziest thing I ever heard," Mary said.

"Is it?" asked Ray. "Think about what Taylor's saying for a minute, Mary, and then think back to when we all first got together."

"One for all and all for one," said Taylor wistfully.

"That's right, the Three Musketeers," Ray acknowledged.

"At first it was Taylor and me, and then Taylor and you, and finally it was me and you. And it wasn't bad, but it was never as good as when it was the three of us, was it?"

"Jesus, I don't believe this!" Mary said. Sighing, she reached out and picked up a cup filled with *vez*, the Centaurs' potent brew.

"Hey, you're really gonna drink that?" asked Taylor.

"What do you think?" Then Mary softened and said, "The Three Musketeers . . . damn."

"Or maybe three lone wolves," Ray said.

"You really think it would come to that?" Mary asked.

"*I* do," said Taylor. "I think that the three of us—together— have a unique chemistry that is lacking when any two of us get together."

"Oh, yeah?" challenged Mary. "What about you two guys? You seemed to have something special when you were bosom buddies, didn't you?"

Ray, pursing his lips, turned his head and playfully gave Taylor what the two of them had jokingly dubbed "the look." Despite herself, Mary smiled. "I didn't say the two of you were sods, but you know what I mean."

Getting serious again, Taylor agreed. "Yeah, we know what you mean, Mary, but I doubt our relationship would have lasted much past the University. Since we're *not* sods, we would have gone our separate ways eventually. You were the unifying element, you drew us together—all three of us."

Mary sipped the *vez* thoughtfully. "So if Ray goes it all goes, is that it?"

"I wouldn't put that way exactly," said Taylor, "but, yes, that's one way of looking at it."

Mary was silent for a long time, staring into the cup as if she would find an answer there. When she finally spoke, she said, "And you don't feel that Ray is cheating us by putting his relationship with his dogs ahead of his relationship with the two of us?"

"Mary, Ray doesn't have only so much love to give—he doesn't have to ration it or decide who gets a slightly bigger or smaller slice," Taylor said earnestly. "Ray is *always* going to put the dogs first—that's Ray. And if that's the price of having Ray's love and affection, I for one think it's worth it. We're all selfish lovers, hon, but that doesn't mean we have to throw out the baby with the bath water."

"You guys and your archaic expressions," Mary said, shaking her head. Ray smiled and looked at her, aware that something had changed. *Taylor's made her reconsider*, he thought. *I can see it in her body language.*

"What now?" Ray asked.

"What Taylor's been saying makes a lot of sense," Mary conceded. "But we're not past this problem just yet."

"What would you have us do?" asked Taylor.

"First," Mary said, "we get a couple more skins of *vez*. Then we bar the door, and we don't leave this hut until we've settled this thing for good."

"Sounds like an excellent plan to me," Taylor beamed.

Ray pushed aside the rawhide curtain that hung over the entrance and gestured at Beowulf. "Yes, Ray?"

Sporting a festive air and accent, Ray said, "Be a good fellow and see about getting us several skins of *vez*, would you? That's a good chap."

"Yes, Ray," said Beowulf, his tail wagging, as he got to his feet. *Ray happy*! Beowulf exulted. *Ray happy again*!

★   ★   ★

Runner-with-the-Wind was taking his friend Ray on the same journey of discovery his father had taken him on many years ago: He was taking Ray to one of the camps of the Tribeless Ones. "Tell me, Runner, why didn't anyone ever tell me about these camps when I sought to understand your *menteba*?"

"They are deemed to live without honor. One does not sing songs nor spread tales of those who live by means no man of honor would accept."

"Yes, of course," Ray said as if the word left a bad taste in his mouth, "honor."

Later, under the harsh glare of the sun, Ray looked up at the low mountains they were steadily advancing toward. "What are these mountains called?" he asked.

"The are known as 'the steps to the sky,' " Runner told his friend. Soon the prairie began to slope upward and here and there Chiron's skin was pierced by great rocks thrust out from the nether regions below. The trail became harder to negotiate and Ray followed Runner's lead as he picked his way through the outcroppings of rocks strewn about as if by a careless giant.

As they climbed the low mountain's side in pursuit of a cleft above them, Ray reflected that he'd relied far too much on the hover scooter to transport him in the past; his legs were hardly in the shape they should be to carry him up such a vertical slope. Ray was hot and sweaty by the time Runner led him through a narrow opening between two walls of rock barely wide enough for a single man or Centaur to squeeze through. Once through the opening in the rocks, Ray was momentarily surprised to find himself in what was apparently a high mountain valley.

"Now we go down again," Runner stated. And they did. The rocks on this side of the pass soon thinned out and then disappeared altogether as they merged rapidly into open spaces that were more meadows than great unbroken stretches of prairie.

"Look." Runner pointed to figures on the horizon. "The sentries. No one can enter this valley unobserved. We have been watched since we first set foot on the slopes of the mountain."

"I must surely appear as a two-legged monster to them," Ray decided. "Are you sure they won't—"

"No, Ray," Runner laughed. "I would guess you're quite safe as long as you're with me. You must remember, they will probably only be curious; the first time my tribe saw you was after we'd seen what the great *teve* eaters could do. We had ample reason to fear and even loathe you. Here," Runner nodded ahead, "there are people with only one arm or perhaps three legs; what can they find so monstrous about a being with but two legs?"

Plenty! Ray thought, but said nothing.

Soon they were approaching a herd of leapers. Ray walked carefully, trying to see how close he and Runner could approach before the herd sensed them and bounded away. *That's odd.* . . . It suddenly dawned on Ray as they walked closer and closer to the herd that they were *not* going to run away. He could not imagine what wonders he might see which would amaze him more than the sight of a small herd of leapers placidly grazing on sweet mountain *teve* while he and Runner passed by not more than a few strides away. "Runner," he began, "the leapers . . ."

"Yes," said Runner, enjoying Ray's bafflement and clearly unwilling to do anything to ease it.

"See there?" said Runner pointing. Besides the fields and fields of wild flowers, Ray saw something he did not think existed on windblown Chiron: short, stubby trees. Soon Ray smelled cooking fires. That meant that they were not far from the camp Runner had brought him to see.

Ray's first glimpse at the still-distant huts puzzled him. He was still more an outsider than he liked to admit, but in the past few weeks he had seen enough other camps to know that this one was very different—although he could not immediately discern just what it was about this camp that made it so different. Unless . . . Yes, that was it—the huts. The huts were similar yet as unlike as children born of the same father but of different mothers. The explanation was immediate and simple: A hut is a hut, of course, and one tribe's huts were much as another—except that the tribes of the north liked to decorate their huts with *gnur* skulls and the like, Ray had learned, while the tribes of the south, of the west, of the mountains, of the lowlands, and elsewhere all chose designs peculiar to their own ways of life.

The huts all had to be different, Ray knew, because the Tribeless Ones were all from different tribes. When put out from their tribes when there were not enough females of marriageable age to warrant a raid, the individuals involved did not suddenly forget the ways of their tribe; they kept them as their own.

Ray also had never seen so many old people in a Centaur camp before. The laws of the tribes concerning old people were seemingly harsh, but life itself was harsh and there was no one to hunt for an old one or a cripple. Yet here there were old ones in abundance. Another wonder.

When at last they entered the camp, trailed by excited youngsters and openly curious old people, Ray suspected that what he might see in this strange place might have far-reaching consequences for the future of not only Runner's ravaged tribe, but for all the Centaurs, for all The People.

"Ho, Runner-with-the-Wind," someone called out.

"Ah, my friend!" Ray heard Runner exclaim. Ray looked at the one approaching who Runner had addressed as friend. He, too, was old; his tail was almost completely white and he moved slowly and painfully. Ray was astonished to see that this old and frail Centaur wore a rawhide patch over one eye.

Ray saw a look of pleasure cross Runner's broad face. "Ho, old one. You cannot know the joy it gives me to see you again. I feared you would not be here when I returned; it has been a very long time."

"And I was ancient when you first met me, eh?" the old one laughed. "Don't you know death and I are blood enemies? If he wishes to take me he must come for me at my hut armed with many weapons—I will not go willingly!"

Then the old one glanced at Ray with wonder and curiosity showing on his wizened features. "And what strange apparition is this you bring with you, Runner-with-the-Wind? Your father brought his sons to see us; what do you bring to us, then, a half-warrior?"

Is this old guy in for a shock, Ray thought gleefully before he spoke. "Do not be so quick to judge my worth, old one. Not only am I a full warrior of The People, but I both understand and speak your tongue as well as any warrior with four legs."

At that, the old one fell back amazed and the crowd that had gathered about the trio murmured uneasily. "Ai-i-i, Runner, I see it now—for having once shown you wonders, I am repaid by you with an even greater wonder!"

Runner laughed, fully enjoying the old one's amazement as much as Ray. "He speaks the truth. Although he has come from a far distant land, this two-legged one, also known as Ray, is indeed a member of my tribe. He duly passed his test of manhood, blooding his *shar* honorably, and he now bears the warrior's name of 'Monster-destroyer.' "

The old one had seen many strange sights in his life and he recovered quickly. "Ah, Runner-with-the-Wind is no different from the prideful boy he once was, I see; he still speaks to me of honor. Has he not learned yet that honor resides only in life and not in death?"

Runner had yet another surprise for the old one. He nodded and answered, "I *am* much changed since you last saw me as a mere boy. I have often pondered the wonders I saw here, and their import was something I sought to understand. Recent events, I believe, have finally made my father's unknowing lesson clear to me. If he were here today perhaps he would counsel me that we of the open plains must learn some of the ways of the Tribeless Ones."

The old one's one good eye brimmed with tears and he turned to Ray. "O strange-formed being who speaks as one of The People, if it was you who brought Runner-with-the-Wind to this new understanding, may all The People sing your praises! It is a new day, a day I feared I would never live to see."

Embarrassed, Ray had no answer to the old man's emotional thanks.

"Come now, old one," Runner said gruffly, "you just boasted that death would never be permitted to enter your hut. I prefer your bold talk to this nonsense."

"Listen," said Ray after clearing his throat loudly, "why don't you two show me these marvels I've been promised by Runner?"

"Marvels, eh?" said the old one. "Come, I will show you."

Runner and Ray followed the old one through the camp. It was a short but eventful journey. More old Centaurs than he could imagine seeing in one place came out of their huts or looked up from their work to stare at them as they passed. "They have seen much in their lives," the old one said to Runner, "but nothing to match the two-legged warrior of The People, I'll wager."

Not that the camp was full of old people only. As Runner had told Ray on their way here, there were young warriors who'd probably been deemed misfits, and *sharnas* and even youngsters laughing and playing their games of tag and follow-the-leader.

Ray was glad when the short journey was over and the old one led him out the other side of the camp. "Here we are," the old one said.

What have I been brought to see? Ray wondered. There was nothing here but . . .

"Good," the old one said when he saw Ray's eyes widen. "You have seen the secret of the Tribeless Ones for yourself."

Plants. Row upon row of plants consciously cultivated by the Tribeless Ones. "See there," the old one pointed, "in that place are all tubers and roots; over there are sweet and leafy vegetables; and those tall plants are grains."

Next, the old one showed them a pen holding leapers grown

fat on the sweet mountain grasses, never having known either the freedom of the open plains or the fear of attack by roving prides of *gnur*. Born and bred in captivity, they had begun the process of accepting domestication as the natural order of things.

"So, you do not hunt leapers at all, then?" Ray asked the old one.

"How are we to hunt leapers? You have seen us—we are the ones to whom nature or fate has been unkind. Or, worst of all, we were sentenced to death for merely growing old. There are not enough young misfits among us that we can hunt leapers, but we *can* catch them and keep them inside bramble bush barriers, breed them, and then kill them when we need meat."

"But that way has no honor!" Runner could not help blurting out, good intentions or not.

Looking at Ray as if sharing his disappointment at Runner's outburst with him, the old male replied, "We are already outcasts—can one without honor further dishonor himself? I think not. Besides, do the dead have honor? I do not know; I know only that we are alive. The price of honor is not something everyone can afford."

"The old one is right," said Ray to Runner. "And you have already accepted the wisdom of his words or you would not have brought me here today to see these things."

Runner glanced around the bustling encampment—almost fearfully, Ray thought—and said, "All this is good, I suppose, but what does it mean for those of who live on the plains? What will happen to a way of life as old as the hills?"

"I can't answer that, Runner," Ray said. "I don't think anyone can."

13

Several senior-level Programmers were with the regular Federation armed forces which arrived several weeks after the defeat of the Cadre camp and the exposing of the General's illegal actions. Transferring from the F.S.S. *Gorbachev*, which stayed well out from Chiron, they made the *General Vann* their headquarters. Since no one was allowed down to the planet's surface except by direct permission of the Prime Programmer in charge, a matronly appearing woman called Mirani Youanmi, Ringgren and Ray reprised their earlier journey to the space station.

After receiving them pleasantly, if a tad too correctly for Ray's taste, Programmer Youanmi got straight to business. "I understand the other terraforming teams and their cholos are rendezvousing at four central points in anticipation of their withdrawal from Chiron," she said to Ringgren, her words more statement than question.

"That is correct, Prime Programmer," Ringgren said. "The *Gorbachev*'s shuttles will transport everyone and everything up from the planet's surface."

"You realize that *nothing* brought to Chiron by a human being is to be left behind."

"Yes, Prime Programmer."

"Oh," she waved, "please call me Mirani."

After his experiences with the ascetic Thane Wyda, Ringgren was not sure he was able to call any Prime Programmer by his or her first name. "Ah . . . Mirani . . . I would much prefer calling you Programmer Youanmi, if you don't mind."

She smiled understandingly. "As you wish, *Programmer* Ringgren." Ringgren just reddened and nodded.

"What about us and our equipment?" Ray asked. "*We're* going to be left behind."

"Of course," conceded Youanmi. "You may continue to use anything the Centaurs may have seen you using prior to the embargo on the transfer of advanced technological knowledge."

"They've seen our van, our weapons, and our medical capabilities," Ray noted. "And Runner-with-the-Wind even saw Chiron from space when he flew in one of the *General Vann*'s shuttles."

"That was unfortunate," said Youanmi. "However, no other Centaur will ever fly unless it is in a machine of their own invention. In time, long after you leave, this Runner-with-the-Wind's flight will be a heroic tale of 'The People' no more accepted as a true story than is our own legend of Jason and the Fleece."

"We could help them so much," mused Ringgren. "The state of their medicine is appalling and—"

"They must learn to help themselves," interjected Youanmi. "Any path they take must be of their own choosing."

"I hope they choose to remain just as they are," Ray said. "Their way of life is hard and full of uncertainties, but it is a good way of life." He shook his head at the memory of the camp of the Tribeless Ones and its implied taming of nature and the beginnings of agriculture. "Already they may be moving toward a 'higher' level of development, one that threatens their present state."

"Is that necessarily bad?" Ringgren asked.

"No," Ray admitted, "but it isn't necessarily good, either. I think they're better off the way they are now, the way we found them—nomads, children of the wind without cares and responsibilities beyond having enough food to eat and huts over their heads."

"Children of the wind?" repeated Youanmi. Then she smiled grimly and said, "Children have to grow up sometime."

Ray scratched his head thoughtfully. "Do they?"

* * *

"I wish you weren't going," Ake said to Taylor, who'd shuttled up to the *General Vann* to visit him. "I've been a Cadre doctor so long it's hard for me to fit in with my own kind again, if you understand what I mean."

"Yeah, I can identify with that," Taylor acknowledged. "But does anyone ever know who his 'own kind' are or ought to be?"

"What do you mean?"

"Look at me," Taylor said, pointing toward himself with his thumb. "I sure as hell don't know who my own kind are." He sighed so deeply that Ringgren looked at him gravely. "A terraformer. I always thought I wanted to be a terraformer and see the galaxy. Take a rough, new planet and make it fit for human beings."

"Yes . . . ?"

Taylor laughed. "I've discovered I prefer comfort and routine. My idea of an exciting night is a couple of drinks and watching a show *about* a band of brave terraformers. I'm no terraformer, no adventurer. And," he added, swiveling his head to stare thoughtfully into Ringgren's puzzled face, "neither is Mary."

"What about Ray?"

"Hell, yes, man! Isn't it obvious? That little peckerhead is the best goddamn natural scout team leader and daredevil around—he was made for this sort of thing." Taylor put his hand to his chin and rubbed it thoughtfully. "He runs the dogs so well they're like an extension of himself, and he speaks the Centaurs' language like a native. When he was captured, he adapted so quickly and so well that I think, if we hadn't found him, they'd have made him king of the Centaurs!" He smiled: "I exaggerate slightly—but you get my point."

"Maybe yes, maybe no," said Ake cryptically.

"Huh?"

"What are you driving at, Taylor?"

Instead of responding immediately, Taylor looked away, staring in the direction of the shuttle. Then he returned his gaze to Ringgren and said, "Come on down with me, Ake. Come down to Chiron with me."

"I'm needed here."

"Bullshit," Taylor exclaimed. "These folks don't need a doctor on call every minute of the day any more than your old Cadre company did."

"That's true," Ringgren admitted. "They're reeking with good health, aren't they?"

"So come on down with me," Taylor insisted. "I know you're allowed, since you've already been down and the Centaurs have been exposed to you."

Ringgren's brow furrowed and then he seemed to win an argument with himself. "All right," he agreed. "Wait here, I have to get permission from Programmer Youanmi."

"You mean 'Mirani'?" teased Taylor, aware of Ringgren's reluctance to use his superior's first name.

"Yes . . . Mirani."

It's good to feel Chiron's wind in my face again, Ringgren told himself. The same wind that blew over him from the direction of Chiron's massive yellow-white sun rustled the knee-high grass.

"You look awfully serious standing there staring into the dying sun," said Ray, joining Ringgren by his side.

"I'm just thinking about a conversation I had with Taylor on the station and in the shuttle on the way down."

"Oh, was it about me?" said Ray brightly.

Still looking into the sun, Ringgren replied, "As a matter of fact, it was."

"Well, you've got my attention," said Ray. "Don't stop now."

"Taylor thinks you're going to leave when all this gets to be routine."

"Jeezus!" Ray ejaculated. "Not you too!" He shook his head. "What do I have to do, open a vein and sign a contract with my own blood?"

"That would be a start," replied Ringgren mildly.

Ray shook his head. "Taylor's been talking to you? I don't understand—he's the one who helped convince Mary not to break us up."

Ringgren waved a hand. "Oh, he still feels that way; it's just that he's starting to see things in himself that he refused to acknowledge before."

"Such as?"

"He knows you're a wanderer, Ray, and—"

"I thought we were discussing things he saw in himself."

"—And he's come to the realization that he's not. When it looked like the terraformation of this planet was a given, and the terraformers were in line for healthy chunks of land and responsibility for adding it to the list of Federation planets, Taylor was content to eventually sit back and reap the rewards of his youthful initiative."

"Yeah?"

Ringgren looked into Ray's questioning blue eyes and continued, "So when this Centaur business upset that apple cart, Taylor realized that the three of you would have to start over, on a new planet."

"Well, of course," said Ray. "And—"

"Ray," said Ringgren patiently.

"What?"

"Not everyone's so enamored of such an unsettled lifestyle."

"Meaning?"

"Meaning everyone but you seems to feel that sooner or later you're going to 'make a break for it,'" Ringgren explained.

"What do *you* think?"

"I think Taylor's right."

"I see," said Ray slowly.

"I also think," began Ringgren slowly, "that even though you consider yourself a loner, you're going to need a partner, a second pair of hands to help you with your expanding team."

Ray's eyes widened. "You?"

"That is the individual I had in mind," Ringgren said modestly. "What do you say?"

"Let me sleep on it."

"Oh, you have lots of time," agreed Ringgren. "It'll probably be a year or two until you start to feel the wanderlust."

"Now cut that out!"

■

Ray jogged down the slight slope of the prairie, not running full out but not ambling along slowly, either. Ahead of him ranged Tajil, Emma, Maximilian, Gawain, Clementine, and Telzey. "Puppies," he muttered.

"Puppies?" said Beowulf, trotting easily by his side. "Puppies? They gettin' awfully big to be called puppies."

"I know, I know," Ray acknowledged, "but they'll always be the puppies to me."

"Yeah, I knows what you mean," said Beowulf.

"Know," said Ray absently.

"KNOW," repeated Beowulf.

"Hey," said Ray, glancing over at the big dog beside him. "You were the one to suggest that we set a good example so that the little furballs learn to speak better than you guys, not me."

"*Me* know," laughed Beowulf.

As they ran through the low grass, the stalks whipping at Ray's knees, they were joined by Littlejohn. "'Lo, Ray. 'Lo, Beowulf."

"Hiya, Littlejohn," Ray replied. "Is everything okay?"

"Yah, I just comed over to join you."

Beowulf snickered, recalling his dialogue with Ray about teaching the youngsters to speak better than their "uncles and aunts." "Somethin' funny?" asked Littlejohn.

"Just rememberin' joke Ray told me," Beowulf said.

"Okay," said Littlejohn dubiously. Then he brightened and asked, "Is it okay for us'ns to chase antelopes, Ray?"

"Yes and no," Ray replied. "You can *chase* them, yes, but Runner's people prefer that you not kill them for sport—it displeases the animal's spirit."

"Okay, I tell the others," Littlejohn said and trotted off.

Ray looked at Beowulf out of the corner of his eye. "Aren't you going to join them?"

"Not this time," Beowulf replied. "I have question."

"Yes?"

"We bin on planet more than a year and a half now, right?" Beowulf asked rhetorically.

"Uh-huh."

"When we goin'?"

Ray stopped and turned to stare full into Beowulf's large face. "Aren't you happy here, Beowulf?" Ray asked. Without waiting for a reply, he continued, "There's me and you guys, Taylor and Mary, and Ake. We're part of Runner's tribe and still learning their ways—we could stay here another five or six years."

"Yeah," agreed Beowulf, before insisting on repeating his question: "When we goin'?"

"You guys feel that way, too? You want to leave?" Ray asked.

"Yes," Beowulf said. "We ready for a new challenge."

Ray looked up at the sky, imagining all the unseen worlds that existed beyond the envelope of air that sustained them—all the worlds waiting for a man and his team of scout dogs. Turning his gaze back to Beowulf, he said, "Soon—I must talk to Mary and Taylor first."

"Good," said Beowulf. "They go with us?"

"Maybe," said Ray, remembering his talk with Ake, "but probably not; I don't know for sure."

"Ake?" queried Beowulf.

"Yeah."

Watching the big dog trot away to rejoin the others, Ray pulled a stalk of grass—*teve*, as he thought of it now—from the soil and stuck it into his mouth. "One for all and all for one," he said softly.

Then, whistling, he looked back at the beckoning sky and said, "Look out, universe—here we come!"

WILDERNESS

FRONTIER STRIKE
David Thompson

LEISURE BOOKS **NEW YORK CITY**

To Judy, Joshua, and Shane

A LEISURE BOOK®

June 1996

Published by

Dorchester Publishing Co., Inc.
276 Fifth Avenue
New York, NY 10001

Printed in the United States of America.